Dead

FORBES BRAMBLE

HAMISH HAMILTON
London

First published in Great Britain 1985
by Hamish Hamilton Ltd
Garden House 57–59 Long Acre London WC2E 9JZ

Copyright © 1985 by Forbes Bramble

British Library Cataloguing in Publication Data

Bramble, Forbes
  Dead of winter.
  I. Title
  823′.914[F]   PR6052.R2687
  ISBN 0-241-11686-4

Typeset by Sunrise Setting, Torquay
Printed in Great Britain by
St Edmundsbury Press Ltd, Bury St Edmunds, Suffolk

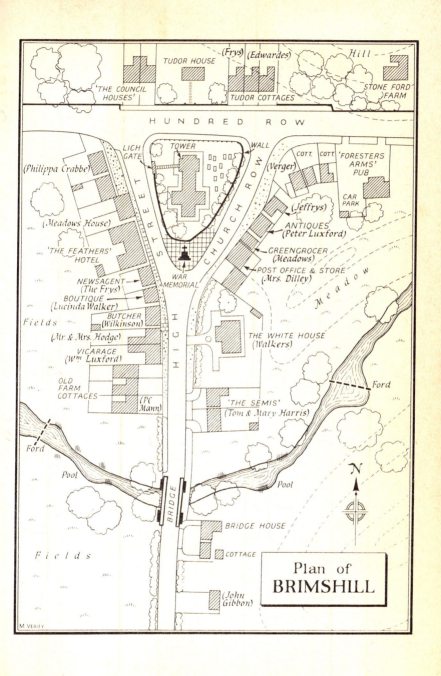

Chapter One

In the moonlight, the snow glittered with a thin rind of ice. The feet of the running man crunched through this topping and the compressing snow made small squeaks. His breath misted and fell behind him, heavy in the cold.

There had been a pale sun of particular beauty and no warmth that afternoon, that had caused the slight melt. The man kept his eyes directed downwards, watching his feet, avoiding knuckles of ice, diverting round drifts. A small scattering of particles snaked across the surface from behind him as a sifting wind followed him. The half moon gave a clear light for his adjusted eyes.

The man wore a track suit and black and white training shoes. He was rather overweight, and his running was far from easy. Round his neck he wore a red tartan scarf to keep out the cold. Every so often he wiped the end of his nose quickly with his left hand. He was much happier now that his footfalls were making a regular rhythm with his breathing. Second wind. The cold burned his throat from his mouth to somewhere in the bottom of his chest, where his ribs ended, a searing pipe.

This must be doing me good, he said to himself. At least I can think of nothing except my own physical pain. I am mesmerised by my feet. I will them forward in front of each other and my legs groan and obey. I see and hear all manner of small things. The drifting crystals that rattle in a beech hedge are a tiny fusillade. Beech keeps its brown leaf until nature wears it away. Shrews or mice leap up through the drifts as though fired from a catapult, scamper over the surface in alarm – or as a game – then disappear into some other black eye in a drift. The hunting owl is there. On that post or in that old broken tree. He hurtles past, feathering noisily. Sometimes there are small screams, a quick flurry of noise, to show he is deadly.

Far away, on a major road, there is an occasional glare from the headlamps of vehicles. They shine like a lighthouse, sweeping in an arc across gleaming fields cut with thin black hedges, then disappear. There will be no cars down this road, thinks the running man. It is blocked by drifts in several places, and a tree has fallen. The Council men may get round to it on Christmas Day. More likely they will not.

1

People can pass on foot. If they want to drive, they can come round by the longer route.

He was approaching the village now, and the verge on which he had been running gave way to pavings. They had remained warmer than the earth, and he could feel the solid base of them under the snow. Compacted snow that had partly thawed and re-frozen. He placed his feet with care, feeling a slight slip at each stride. Ahead in the centre of the village he could see the multi-coloured lights of the Christmas tree. There had been a lot of argument about whether they should be left on all night, and who would pay the bill, as they were plugged in to a point in the Church vestry.

They were to be left on all night.

It had not been decided who would pay the bill.

The running man felt his feet skid suddenly, and had to throw up his arms to keep his balance. That was all he needed, to break his ankle on Christmas Eve. He had passed the first houses, the old farm cottages set back from the road. They all three had paths onto the pavement, and the paths had been cleared, leaving the merest trace of snow dust to melt and set as ice. The pavement became gravel briefly, in the way of English villages, and suddenly he was trying to run on cobbles. He moved sideways onto the road. These were round, orange sized pebbles, river washed and far too dangerous. The butcher had flung down sawdust, and that seemed to have done some good. His shop window was alight, but empty. Any last unsold turkey was back in the cold room. His marble slab was decorated with plastic parsley. A large garish notice with a jovial Father Christmas and holly leaves said 'A Merry Xmas to All My Customers.'

What did he wish the others? thought the running man. My Christmas may depend upon it. A frozen turkey, a nice bit of Stilton, and enough wine to stay drunk for a month. Not a conventional family affair, but appropriate to a man in my position. Christmas alone, trying to keep fit, trying to forget.

There were no lights on over the butcher's shop, and none over the knitwear boutique. In its window were the usual balls of wool, and the party dresses bought in specially for the season. The newsagent was next and had concentrated on paper chains and stars. A lot of books had been arranged under a spotlight, and packets of small cigars, crystallized fruits and boxes of chocolates. They were at home. From the upper windows a television picture flickered. There seemed to be no one else about. Everyone must be in the Church.

He ran past 'The Feathers', with its coaching entrance firmly shut behind faded grey doors. All the snow had been desecrated here. Pink rock-salt had been flung down, exposing the paving stones for the full length of the building. The bars were shut now, and only the two Victorian street lamps glowed. Tomorrow would be a busy day;

their Christmas lunches and dinners were considered good. A Christmas tree winked at an upper window. Fairy lights had been strung round the Georgian portico. It was a handsome building of mellow yellow stone, with fine lime joints. A wisteria as old as time was wired to the walls. It formed a trellis of snow ledges over the bare stone face. From somewhere behind, he heard music and voices. Someone was having a party. It was a night when everything was amplified, all sounds were precise in the clear dry air, all outlines crisp. A thin rattle of snow sifted down, and the running man looked up to see if it had blown off a roof. It was beginning to snow again, with flakes as fine as sawdust. They hissed in the evergreens in the churchyard and behind the war memorial and rattled through the branches of the village Christmas tree. They blew in swirls around the corners of buildings and stung his cheeks. If he wanted to punish himself, the man thought, he had found the perfect way of doing it. He held his right hand up in front of his mouth, deflecting the particles, sucking in the warmth of his own exhaled breath. It helped the searing in his throat, but he could not keep his hand there and run. He plodded on with grim enjoyment.

Mrs Fry was congratulating herself on the decorations. It had been a bad year for holly and the field-fares had descended in hundreds to gulp down whatever berries they saw. She had had to scour the countryside for a decent tree. Of course there had been one in the village all right, that wretched yellow thing in the Tudor House garden. Even the birds didn't eat that. Not surprisingly. Wild horses wouldn't have forced Mrs Fry to use it.

Yes, they looked very good indeed, and very traditional, despite the distinct and very ungracious pressure from that pushy young Mrs Walker from the knitwear boutique. She had told Mrs Fry that she used to be a window-dresser, and was quite expert in such things, and wouldn't it be nice to do something a bit more 'Out of the way,' as she put it. Mrs Fry sniffed, and drew in a deep breath that had nothing to do with the carol they were all singing. It was not as if Mrs Walker had been in the village more than a year, and besides, she wasn't even white.

Her husband was booming away tunelessly beside her. She was pleased she had got him there, *and* looking half decent as well. He smelled offensively of drink, having spent the evening up to eleven in the Foresters Arms, but then so did a lot of them. She had made him clean his teeth and suck peppermints, but it was no good. He was a burden, there was no doubt about it, but then as a good Christian, she would bear it.

Yes, it had been quite an excitement getting the holly. She had made her husband drive the car, because he had flatly refused to crawl through the hedge. He had made a terrible fuss about it being theft to take it from someone's garden, but she had told him that was

3

all nonsense, and crawled through herself, armed with secateurs.

George Fry had sat there like a getaway driver, heart thumping, wondering how she had the nerve and what he would do if she had to run for it. He toyed with the idea of driving off and leaving her. He could do that anyway, let her carry the damned stuff home in full view of the village. They would all want to know where she had got it from.

He had sighed, and decided it wasn't worth the upheaval. They would pretend it was from the tree in their back garden again, not stolen from Stone Ford Farm.

He was ashamed when, next day, he saw what she had done to the tree.

'The holly and the ivy!' Cynthia Fry fairly shrieked.

'When they are both full grown!'

Mrs Walker looked up at that moment. They were both in the front row, but of course on opposite sides. Their eyes met briefly. Mrs Cynthia Fry thought she had never collided with such a cold look before. She might have those big black eyes, she thought, and all that pink lipstick and shameless curves, but her eyes were as beady as a snake. Fancy coming to church in that tight yellow thing, and with an off-the-shoulder fur stole and that neckline!

Then the look was gone. Mrs Lucinda Walker smiled charmingly. What a pretty young thing, the vicar thought, who should have had his mind on the next lesson.

Smashing, thought the fourteen year old choir boy.

Too bad she's happily married, thought George Fry, who had shared the full blast of her charm. What I could do with that! Just what I need for Christmas in front of a nice warm log fire. How I would like to unwrap her on Christmas Day!

Henry Walker was unaware of such electrical discharges. He sang the words mechanically. At home, his papers would still be stretched out on the desk when he got back. Nothing would go away, not even for Christmas. He would have to pack it up for the night, have a drink with Lucinda, try to enter into the spirit of things, but it would all be hard work. She had no idea how bad his business affairs were and he had no intention of telling her. Not now, while there was still some chance of survival. She was bound to need some more money for the shop, too. He had bought it for her as an amusement, in the vague hope that it might pay for itself, but had not counted on it running at such a loss. Did they never buy any clothes?

He looked round. Apparently not, or at least not of the type that Lucinda was trying to induce them to. She sold more wool than anything else. He thought that her present outfit was perhaps a little too showy for the occasion, and he had said so.

'It's part of my stock-in-trade!' she had said, and smiled that lovely smile. He had wondered what lay behind those stunning eyes. Was

4

she still being faithful to him? She did not always answer when he rang the shop from London.

Still, they had Christmas together. It might be their last Christmas here together. If it all went, the house would have to go, and the shop and would Lucinda go too? He slipped his hand into hers, and felt her lean against him in response. Did she respond so quickly to everyone?

The running man had his third wind by now, and was almost beginning to enjoy the run. There was a sense of liberation, of spring-heels, of giant strides, of stunning speed. Perhaps he was a little light-headed. He ran past the Christmas tree, which stood in front of the large tablet of the memorial, set in the wall surrounding the churchyard. There was a flat area, paved with level flagstones, with two municipal benches with their backs to the sorry litany of the dead. It was truly in the centre of the village, because here the High Street branched in a 'Y'. The left hand remained the High Street, the right hand became Church Row. The snow was first blue, then red, then green, then yellow, then multi-coloured as the tree went through its paces.

The sound of singing could be clearly heard over the gasping of his own breath. He took an even deeper breath and held it for a few paces.

'Of all the trees that are in the wood,
The holly bears the crown . . .'

Holly, the symbol of eternity, evergreen. Red berries, the blood of Christ.

'The rising of the sun
And the running of the deer . . .'

The man smiled to himself briefly. The running of the deer. In the snow? Was it really so? He looked up at the church clock, set in a gnarled tower. It was brightly illuminated on three sides. On the fourth was a sundial. The clock had been a present, so the little guide said, of some wealthy Georgian family that the man could not remember. It was black with gilt lettering, too large really for good proportion, and very noisy. They had intended to be remembered, that Georgian family, and he could not remember their name! Five minutes to midnight. Almost Christmas Day.

He nearly ran full tilt into a solid dark figure, tried to run around it at the last moment, but failed because one foot shot sideways. His outflung arms grabbed the other man, and they collided heavily. Each tottered in the other's arms, trying to keep their feet.

'Good God, Mr Gibbon, you gave me a fright!' said the other man in broad accusing tones. The running man recognised Wilkinson the butcher.

'I'm sorry,' he puffed, 'I looked up at the clock.'

Snow was beginning to fall in earnest now, obliterating the outline

5

of things.

'I wondered who it was,' said Wilkinson, 'pounding round like a racehorse. Before I had time to move, bang!'

'Are you all right?'

'I'm all right,' said Wilkinson. 'You reckon this does you some good, do you, or is it just an excuse to eat more tomorrow?'

'I think it does me good. Mind you, at the moment I'm not so sure!'

John Gibbon smiled ruefully, and rubbed a thigh. He was dancing on his toes as he spoke, trying to keep moving, trying to keep his breathing steady.

'Aren't you going to Church?' he asked. 'Everyone else seems to be there. Or locked up in front of the television. Except at the "Feathers". They're having a party there by the noise of it.'

'No I'm not going to the damned Church,' said Wilkinson, with startling vehemence. 'You won't get me inside that place!'

The running man was too surprised to know what to say.

'Did you sell a lot of turkeys?' he asked, by way of polite conversation. His feet were getting cold now. He must get moving again. The flakes were large but it was so cold that they were dry.

'We did all right,' said Wilkinson. 'Now I must be getting to that do at the "Feathers". It's the only place I know in this damned village where there will be any Christmas spirit and charity tonight. You'll learn when you've been here a bit longer, Mr Gibbon. Why don't you join us? Go home and get out of that sporting stuff and you could be with us in fifteen minutes. It goes on until two.'

'That's very kind,' said Gibbon, 'but I don't feel like it, not after a run. I shall collapse into a hot bath, have a whisky and go to bed.'

'Suit yourself,' said Wilkinson. The big man started to move off.

The running man jogged on. It was common knowledge how much Wilkinson disliked the vicar. He reflected that they always warned that village life was a seething cauldron of dark emotion and rumour. He had come to Brimshill aware of that, but hoping the place would still provide an escape from his own grief, from the failure of his marriage. An escape he was finding now, in his own way, through the hurting of his lungs and the rawness of his throat.

Perhaps he should have accepted the man's invitation? He had nothing better to do, now or tomorrow, and it was a time when his loneliness would put him at risk to self-indulgent grief. No doubt they had a high old time at 'The Feathers' on Christmas Eve! Instinctively he decided against it. It would all be too personal, too intimate. It would be a time for the exploitation of confidences, for probing, for un-innocent baring of hearts. A time that would be used to the full. He had no illusions about the citizens of Brimshill. They were very normal in their inquisitiveness.

Wilkinson was the kind of man he should avoid, in any case. A very unprivate individual, who liked no one and was given the same in

6

return. It was characteristic that Gibbon had run into him, for the man seemed to be everywhere at all times. If he wasn't in his shop, which commanded a view of both arms of the 'Y' formed by the two main streets, he was out in his familiar blue van. They said he was a devoted amateur archaeologist, a crank, and that his rural wanderings gave him the opportunity to combine his substantial butcher's business with his passion. The van could certainly be seen everywhere, in highways and byways, up lanes, on village greens and even on ridge ways, on ancient tracks. Wilkinson operated a shop from a stable door arrangement at the rear, wearing a boater. He even looked bluff and amiable. Acquaintance proved otherwise. Like John Gibbon, Wilkinson was a newcomer to the village, although he had been there nearly two years now. It was said that the origin of his feud with the vicar could be traced, literally, underground. That Wilkinson had found something the vicar had been looking for for years, some ancient site. Of course some people said it was a crock of gold, a Saxon hoard, even the Holy Grail itself.

Gibbon smiled to himself, and shook his head slightly in amusement. He was passing a row of unpretentious Victorian cottages on his left, of dull yellow brick with red arches over doors and windows. The moonlight made them silver and grey. On his right lay the high wall of the churchyard, a gnarled flint enclosure that contained the building and its buried dead like a pie in a pie-dish. They had all been stranded up there by the roads that passed on all sides. The carts of centuries had cut old hollow ways around the sacred land, wearing away, softening. Rain had swept the mud down hill to the river. The wall had been built to stop the erosion when the gravestones began to shift.

From above the wall leaned dark yews, heavy with snow, drooping with the exhaustion of ancients. They framed the lich-gate set deep in an opening in the wall. It was a dark place even on sunny days. Gibbon noticed that the gates were open for the service. A light sparkled in the gateway, for the guidance of worshippers. He could see that the footsteps of the congregation had already been obliterated by the continuing snow, leaving vague round impressions.

He speeded up in anticipation of the flat stretch that lay ahead when he turned right along Hundred Row. Here he ran directly beneath the flint wall, with the west front of the church just visible above it. The wind swirled violently, perhaps deflected by the church roof. On his left was Tudor House, a fine building, and Tudor Cottages, more picturesque than anything, all with fine gardens, with vegetables mixed quite properly with the flowers. At this time of the year, Brussels sprouts stuck up boldly like summer hollyhocks. They would be gone tomorrow! In the cottage windows, Christmas trees glittered. Three cottages, three trees, all in a row. It was all very

7

beautiful, and it would all be down hill now. He turned again and was on his way back, crossing Church Row and slithering on cobbles. He could hear the singing again. It was almost midnight.

Inside the church, Peter Luxford, the vicar, was aware that Mrs Philippa Crabbe was staring at him. He could not quite make out what her expression contained. He drew himself upright and sung even louder.

'The playing of the merry organ,
Sweet singing in the choir.'

He congratulated himself on the mellow tenor tone of his voice. He was in good form tonight. It always seemed to surprise people, perhaps because he was tall and thin.

What did Philippa Crabbe want? He must avoid her. But Lucinda Walker . . . Ah well, Lucinda Walker. Dear Lucinda. He was certain she could be coaxed to the party at 'The Feathers', and leave that dull devil of a husband behind . . .

But Philippa Crabbe. He had really wanted Philippa Crabbe. She had such a nice body. Not just average, but really nice.

Peter Luxford thought again what an exciting time Christmas was. A time of possibilities and promise. Of self-indulgence. The very garlands festooning the ledges reminded him that it was truly a pagan time. He sighed. He would have liked to have lived in those pagan times. The occasional tweak of conscience at his cassock was still an embarrassment.

His eyes roamed back to Lucinda. What vanity, he thought, but I'm sure she's dressed like that just for me. What an extraordinary sweet thing a woman is, he thought, and smiled, as he sang 'Amen'.

It was his last thought as the bullet smashed into his brain, hurling his body against the lectern. There was a stunned silence of that brief intensity that follows some unexpected accident, then a turbulent din, indistinct, like noises heard under water as ears rang with the deafening violence of the report. People moved to Luxford as though in slow motion, as though silent. He was very dead. Within seconds the noise returned. Screams, protests, orders. Pandemonium. Blood spattered everywhere. Brain.

John Gibbon was passing the Post Office and stores when he heard the noise.

He was aware of the shot. The sound seemed so immense in the clear night. It rang and bounced, echoed and re-echoed, though whether in his head or around him he could not say. He was aware that people were screaming. It seemed to happen immediately, a high strange sound that started as the organ stopped. He started to run, passing the Christmas tree and war memorial again, sprinting now, hoping not to slip, running back to the lich-gate, the only way to the church, the only path. The clock was tolling midnight. He noted the time, aware it might be important, aware that something

8

dreadful had happened. Surely, at midnight, on Christmas Eve, a shot could only mean some terrible thing?

Inside, the verger was trying to keep the congregation away from the body. He was an elderly man, and was standing over Luxford, hiding the man's destroyed head with the skirts of his cassock. A thick trickle of blood was spreading over the stone floor. It was congealing already, had the consistency of cooking oil. It seemed important to him that no one should step in it, and he was pushing at people with the flats of his hands.

Henry Walker was first there. He had knelt beside the body.

'You must let me see!' he said sharply, as the verger tried to push at him with some sort of protective instinct. 'Stop flapping, man. Keep them back.'

He looked quickly.

'Just stay where you are. He's dead.'

Walker stood up. The screaming had stopped now. People were either standing stock still in the pews, or had sat down. Only a few had gathered by the body. He looked over the congregation slowly, deliberately, the look of a man accustomed to speaking in public, knowing how to attract and keep attention.

'Everyone be quiet!' he ordered. 'Stay exactly where you are.'

He waited, and a hush fell.

'I am going to shut the door,' he announced, very collectedly, 'And no one must leave. He's been shot and I regret that he is dead. I ask everyone to co-operate to make sure that everyone stays put. The police will want it that way.'

Henry Walker walked down the aisle, away from Luxford's body.

'Are you sure he's dead?' asked Philippa Crabbe, her voice calm. She appeared little affected, but then Walker seemed to be taking it very coolly as well.

'There's no doubt about it.'

Someone sniffed loudly.

'The poor vicar!' exclaimed Cynthia Fry in a doom laden voice. 'Oh, it's so terrible. Who would do a thing like this!'

'I very much regret it must have been someone in here,' said Henry Walker, 'and it is for that very good reason that I intend to keep the door shut until we can get the police here.'

Then the screaming started. Mrs Hodge, a little plump lady with a tall thin husband, could take it no longer. It was she who had given voice immediately when it happened. Mr Hodge, tall, pale, well dressed, reached down and with complete calm slapped her across the face. Mrs Hodge stopped screaming as if a switch had been turned off.

'Sorry,' said Mr Hodge.

Walker had reached the door. He was wondering what he should do next. Lucinda joined him, still looking ravishing and unreal. Mrs

Crabbe had also moved. The choirboys were leaving their places. Meadows the Greengrocer joined Walker.

'Who's going for the police?' he asked.

He was shaped rather like one of his own pears, and had a yellowish complexion.

'I don't know,' said Walker.

'I'll go,' said Meadows.

'Why you?' demanded a slim dark man with venom. 'Trying to escape?' The man smiled while he uttered this last remark, or rather bared his teeth in a parody of a smile.

'Why don't you see to your brother!' snarled Meadows.

'Stop it!' snapped Philippa Crabbe. She knew William Luxford. She knew his evil tongue. She knew that Meadows hated the sight of him. William Luxford was the local antique dealer and as lovable as his brother.

'What a start to Christmas,' said a distinguished looking man wrapped in an extravagant tweed cape. It made him look like an ageing actor, and it was the effect he was trying to achieve, because that was what Harold Jeffrys was. His tone was one of scarcely concealed boredom. It brought immediate if unflattering attention to him. They stared hostilely, while Jeffrys feigned surprise and lifted an arm in an extravagant gesture as though to ward off a blow.

'I'm sorry,' he said, 'I didn't mean anything. But this will certainly affect every one of us here. Whether we like it or not, we are all suspect. I for one will be put off my Christmas pudding!'

'Why don't you go and sit down somewhere, you old fool!' snarled Luxford. 'This is the sort of time when we don't need you.'

'That's not so,' said Philippa Crabbe, stepping towards Jeffrys. 'I think this is the time that he should go for the police. Don't you all think so?'

She looked round at the faces fronting her. They were blank, uncaring, worried, shocked, everything but hostile to this suggestion. As she had anticipated, no one thought Harold Jeffrys likely or capable of murder.

'A good idea,' said Henry Walker, who knew nothing about the details of these people but was quick to sense that Philippa Crabbe did know, and was right.

'One person only must go.'

Jeffrys seemed flattered by this suggestion. He wrapped his cape about him, gathering his robes.

'I would be delighted.'

Gibbon was standing at the lich-gate, concentrating on what he was looking at. He was aware of the need to be observant, to discern and not merely to see. Snow had overlaid the path to the church porch so that it was quite clear that no one had entered or left by that route since he had heard the shot. He started slowly up the path, looking to left and right to make sure that no footprints were visible through the graveyard. He noted that the noise in the church had completely died away. The silence was worrying. In his imagination, he wondered if someone was being held hostage. He hurried now, trying to take giant strides, as though he was stepping over a newly-washed floor.

At this moment the church porch door opened. The feeble yellow light was so potent in his eyes that he held his hand to his forehead to shield them. Jeffrys fluttered out, waving a skinny arm to someone inside the church. He almost walked into Gibbon, and started back in alarm. Gibbon realised that the man had not had time to develop any night-sight and was walking in darkness.

'Who's that?' demanded Jeffrys, his over-educated voice fruity with fright.

'Gibbon. From Bridge House. You're Mr Jeffrys. What's happened?'

Jeffrys seemed reassured by this. He held out a hand and clutched at the other man.

'Where are you? Good. Stay there. There's been a murder in the church. Someone's shot Luxford the vicar.'

'Are you sure he's dead?'

'I haven't looked myself, I must say, but it appears he's rather obviously dead. I've been sent out for the police. To tell you the truth I can't see a thing yet.'

'Who shot him? Do they know?'

Both men were standing still on the path. They could hear the door being bolted.

'No idea. There was just this almighty bang. A smell of gun smoke everywhere, and people screaming. No one has stepped up, brandishing a gun or anything.'

'Was that the door being kept locked? I heard the bolts.'

'That's the idea. That Walker chap who works in the city, and Mrs Crabbe. They're going to stand by it until I arrive with the police.'

Gibbon thought uncharitably that they had obviously made the right choice getting this elderly fool out of the way. He hoped the man's eyesight had adjusted.

'Can you see now? Is your sight normally good?'

'There's never been anything wrong with my eyes.'

'Look down then. Can you see the path?'

'Yes.'

'Can you see any footsteps?'

There was a pause.

'I don't believe I can. . . . Yes . . . There is one over there, and another there.'

'Good. I want you to notice this particularly. I made these steps coming towards the church. If you look behind you, there are only

11

your footsteps. Please check and make sure you agree.'

Jeffrys looked round.

'Yes, I agree.'

If he reached any conclusion, he was keeping it to himself. Gibbon thought it unlikely that Mr Jeffrys had a lively brain.

'Then note that no one has come to or left the church.'

'That's true.'

'Then whoever fired the shot must be inside. Unless there's another way in or out.'

'There's no other way in or out. That's certain. Are you really wearing a track suit? On a night like this in the freezing cold?'

'Yes I am,' said Gibbon, annoyed by the man's lack of attention. 'I was out jogging. Keeping fit, you know. Now this business of footsteps is bound to be very important. I will turn around now and walk back to the lich-gate. I'm going to walk in the same steps that I took to get here, and I'd like you to try to do the same so that we don't wander all over the place.'

'I understand. You ought to be the one to go for the police. You'll be much quicker than me. I think track suits are very smart. You can jog to Mann's house in half a minute. Is it blue? I find it so difficult to make out colours in this light. There is a moon, I see . . . .'

Prattling to himself, Jeffrys followed Gibbon back to the lich-gate.

'You're right,' said Gibbon. 'I will be there in no time, if you tell me where to go. I'm a newcomer here. I don't know where the police station is. I don't think I've ever seen one.'

'It isn't a station. It's Mann's house. He's the constable. The one with the view over the pub car park. It has a white gate. There's a notice board thing beside his front door.'

'Wait here then, and note everything you see!'

'I will. Or I'll certainly try to,' added Jeffrys, spoiling the effect. He did not like being left alone in the dark. Gibbon seemed to have vanished. He caught a flash of his dark form crossing the road, heard his footsteps crunching softly. Snow was still falling. Mr Jeffrys, who may have been a fool in many ways, was certainly provident in others. Now was just the time, he thought to have a swig from the quarter bottle of whisky he carried for such occasions. For most occasions. He thought how hateful William Luxford was and how hateful Peter Luxford had been. It obviously ran in the family. This death was certainly no loss. He took a good gulp and leaned back against the woodwork of the porch. There must be half a dozen people who might have killed Luxford, he thought. All of them with good reason! Now one of them had. Or so it seemed.

Constable Mann had been dozing with eyes shut in front of the television when there had been a vigorous pounding on his front door followed by a brisk clattering of his letter plate. He had had a drink or

12

two and was surrounded by bottles both empty and full, well within arm's reach. His wife had already gone to bed, and he had promised to follow shortly but had remained where he was in front of the fire. She was unsympathetic and inclined to be cross when he dashed into the bedroom and started to pull off his everyday clothes and change into uniform.

'What are you putting that on for, for heaven's sake?' she grumbled at least half asleep, 'Can't you have the evening off even on Christmas Eve! Don't be late back!'

'I don't know what I'll be,' he said struggling into his shirt. 'There's that fellow Gibbon downstairs in running gear. He says there's been trouble at the church.' Mann looked disbelieving. 'He says someone shot the vicar!'

'I'm not at all surprised!' said Mrs Mann.

'It's impossible,' said Mann. 'He says he's been shot dead!'

Mrs Mann sat up.

'He's really serious. This isn't some sort of wild joke?' Mann shook his head. He looked quite shocked and pale. He pulled on his trousers, slipped his feet in his boots and was ready.

'I'll get up then,' said Mrs Mann. 'That's the end of Christmas if it's true. How do you feel? You look awful. How many did you have down there? I told you to come up!'

'I'm all right!' snarled Mann. 'I've never been to a murder before. It's shaken me, I can tell you.'

'You'd better clean your teeth,' said his wife. 'You don't want to breathe alcohol over everyone.'

'I shouldn't think they'd notice!'

Nevertheless he had scrubbed his teeth hurriedly. Then he picked up the telephone before taking to the road with Gibbon.

'I called the ambulance,' Mann called after Gibbon as they ran past the 'Feathers'. 'Just in case. O Lord I was almost asleep! Slow down.'

Constable Mann was having the greatest difficulty in keeping up with Gibbon. Apart from the fact, increasingly obvious, that Gibbon was fitter than he, the constable had boots on and these were skidding wildly on icy patches on the pavement. 'Hold on!' he shouted, 'It's all right for you!'

The Christmas tree winked at them, its fairy lights now unnaturally festive. Both men heard loud music and laughter. The party was still going on.

'They're having a good time!' puffed Mann. 'Tell me, did anyone see who did it?'

'No,' said Gibbon. 'But I wasn't in the church, I was running round it. Someone inside may have seen something. That old chap Jeffrys told me there was just an almighty bang and he didn't see anyone with a gun.'

He was pleased with himself for being able to talk and trot at the same time. His breathing was measured. It was curious how, even at a time like this, these trivial thoughts intruded. The constable on the other hand was gasping dreadfully. He had to give him credit for keeping up at all for Gibbon was striking a brisk pace.

'Jeffrys is an old fool,' puffed Mann. 'I wouldn't believe anything he said, on principle. Are you sure it's the vicar?'

'Yes, and don't speak so loud,' said Gibbon, 'He's waiting at the lich-gate.'

'I suppose they're crashing about all over the place in there?' asked Mann. 'Won't have the sense to stay put.'

'No, they're all in the church. Jeffrys is posted there to keep watch and to make sure no one leaves. Whoever did it is in there.'

'That's well organised,' said Mann with respect in his voice.

'I made sure he stayed there, but someone else had the sense to send him out alone. I can't take credit for that.'

'Done my job for me, I can see!'

They halted at the covered gate.

'I'm glad to see you!' said Jeffrys, who was standing hunched against one of the heavy posts. He was beating one hand in the other and looked very cold.

'You've been a long time!'

'I've been exactly ten minutes,' said Gibbon, looking up at the illuminated dial of the clock. It was exactly ten minutes past midnight.

'That's long enough out here. The snow's stopped again. Temperature's dropping, believe me. We're in for a good freeze!'

'Evening, Mr Jeffrys,' said Mann pointedly.

'Evening, Constable,' said Jeffrys. He was off-hand to say the least. John Gibbon needed no further information to know that the dislike was mutual. He wondered why. He would no doubt find out.

'Has anyone left the church?' asked Mann, businesslike.

'Certainly not,' said Jeffrys. He rearranged his cloak around him. 'I have kept the door under surveillance. Apart from some arguing or something, it's all been as quiet as the grave.'

Jeffrys was quite unconscious of the banality of his remark, or was accomplished at appearing stupid. Gibbon wondered which.

'Those are our footprints,' said John Gibbon, pointing them out to Mann. 'I walked almost up to the porch – you can see the big steps I took. Then Mr Jeffrys came out and we both walked back in the same prints as far as possible.'

'Fine,' said Mann. 'So there were no footsteps to or from the church before you came in through the gate.'

'None.'

'So you think that whoever did this is still in there?'

'It seems like it.'

'I would have thought that was a fairly logical conclusion,' said Jeffrys in tired tones. 'I mean, what's the point of standing there and guarding it otherwise!'

'You'd all better come in with me,' said Mann. 'Walk in your footsteps again. It may be important and in any case it's a wise precaution.'

They took giant steps to the church porch. Mann knocked.

'It's Constable Mann here!' he called.

The bolt was shot back, and they stepped inside.

Chapter Two

The atmosphere inside was strange. John Gibbon meant this in both senses. Firstly, people had been smoking, and the cigarette smoke mingling with a whiff of gunsmoke made an unusual aroma for an ecclesiastical building.

Secondly, there was tension in the air and it seemed to be centred about the little group of people who were standing close to the door. John Gibbon sensed that some sort of argument, as reported by Jeffrys, had indeed been taking place, and that someone had been trying to leave. This was immediately interesting.

His own appearance seemed to attract as much attention as that of Constable Mann. They couldn't know he had run to get help, and his sporty appearance was a little out of place amongst the furs and tweed coats and scarves.

'I ran to get Constable Mann,' John Gibbon volunteered. 'I was out jogging.'

He saw in their eyes that flicker of disbelief that is like a shake of the head, then they lost interest.

'Where is he?' asked Mann.

'Over there,' said George Fry, bulky and bossy. He was red in the face and had obviously been involved in what was going on. He waved a meaty hand in the direction of the pulpit.

'No one is to leave this building,' said Mann.

'Right,' said Henry Walker with considerable edge.

Mann crossed over to the body. It had been covered with a cassock. The vicar's feet stuck out showing the bottom of his

15

trousers, a band of white but hairy leg, surprising red and green socks and a pair of well worn black shoes. Mann raised the cassock cautiously, and peeped under it. It seemed to take him a moment to realise what he was looking at. He had steeled himself, but even then it was messy. There was no doubt that the man was dead. He replaced the cassock. 'He's dead. I have called the ambulance, but it will probably take some time to get here in the snow. I want everyone to sit down. I shall have to take statements before you can go home.'

'This is Christmas!' protested Fry. There was a chorus of voices, all complaining.

'How long will this all take?' demanded Meadows the greengrocer. 'I don't see how you can really stop us from going now. No one here killed the man. None of us saw anything. Isn't that right?'

There was a chorus of assent.

'I can't let any one go yet,' said Mann firmly. Now John Gibbon could see him properly in the light inside the church, he recognised a firm man who would not be pushed around. He would obviously use his personality as much as possible to keep these people in order before falling back on his uniform. A useful man as a village policeman. Mann had a thick hank of yellow hair that had fallen over his face. He was hatless, and he swept this back, mopping his forehead with the back of his hand. He was still out of breath from running. His eyes were dark grey and his face a weatherbeaten red. Mann's eyes moved everywhere, taking everyone in, nodding slightly as he caught an eye here or there.

'Let me explain things clearly, so you know how they stand. Mr Gibbon here was jogging round the church when the shot was fired. He ran round to the lich-gate. When he arrived there, there were no footprints in the snow either to or from the porch. The porch is the only way in or out of this church as you all know. You sent out Mr Jeffrys to get help, and he met Mr Gibbon. Mr Jeffrys stayed in the lich-gate and Mr Gibbon ran to get me.'

He paused. It was quite clear what he was driving at, but there were a number of people who obviously did not want to know.

'That shot was fired by someone here, that's what you mean,' said a man called Hazlitt. Hazlitt was always to be seen hedging and ditching. He was brown of face where the constable was red. He saw everything, said nothing. He had lived in the village for as long as anyone could remember. Fools ignored him, sensible people talked to him. He was an encyclopedia of local knowledge.

'That's what I must consider, Alf,' said Mann.

'Has to be,' said Hazlitt, 'Yet I didn't see anyone do it. That's the puzzle. And it were a good shot. I should say a rifle.'

This caused a stir. No one who knew him doubted Hazlitt's ability to tell what sort of gun it was. Hazlitt owned a few himself and shot them over local farms. With and without permission.

'Are you sure?' asked Gibbon, then wished he had kept quiet, because Hazlitt turned to him and gave him a long and searching stare.

'Of course I'm sure. You're that new fellow Mr Gibbon, aren't you? Well, apart from the hole it made, which is obviously a bullet, you can tell the noise when you've heard as many guns as I have. No revolver makes that noise. In any case you'd have to hold it up here, shoulder height, to aim like that!'

The brown old man demonstrated. The arm he stretched out was perfectly steady, the curled forefinger squeezed slowly, as the arm descended from just above horizontal to a level position. He was aiming straight at where Luxford had been in the pulpit. It was a chilling moment. Gibbon fully expected to hear another shot ring out as the gnarled forefinger closed.

Hazlitt dropped his arm.

'Even then, not many people could hit the target. I could though, but I don't reckon on anyone else hereabouts.'

He gave a short laugh. Hazlitt was enjoying himself.

'Never mind this fun and games,' said Meadows. 'What do you propose to do with us? If this was done with a rifle like he says, then it's all crazy. I mean, we might have seen someone standing around taking a pot-shot!'

'I don't understand anything yet,' said Mann. 'I do understand that there's a dead man in here and that he doesn't seem to have shot himself. Now will you all be quiet and patient. I will start with the women first, and I'll take names and addresses and a short statement from everyone about anything they saw or think they saw, then I'll let everyone get home. If you do it in an orderly way, it shouldn't take long.'

'Oh Lord, let's get *on* with it!' shouted George Fry. 'It's Christmas Day.'

'I shan't get my turkey in at this rate,' said a little middle-aged woman with a jolly face, 'And I was going to make the stuffing after I got back from the service!'

This welcome domestic note produced a thaw. People smiled, agreed, chatted to each other. Mann mentally thanked Mrs Harris for injecting the right note. He knew she was far too intelligent for it to be an accident.

'You'll get it done,' he said. 'No one will go without their Christmas dinner.'

'Except the vicar,' said Jeffrys. 'All right, all right, I didn't mean it unkindly. Why are you all staring at me!'

Jeffrys flung his cloak up in the air with his elbows and stumped off to sit behind a pillar.

Just tactlessness, wondered Gibbon? Or hate.

17

'Forgive my asking,' said the slim dark man that Mann recognised as William Luxford, 'But don't you think someone should inform my sister-in-law?'

This was said so slyly that Gibbon could feel Mann bridle. It was flung in to question his competence.

'That will be done as soon as the ambulance arrives and the vicar has been removed.'

'She'll be expecting him shortly.'

This was obviously true. Mann looked as though he would have liked to hit William Luxford to remove the clever-clever smirk that played around his lips.

'I'll go and see Molly,' said Mrs Crabbe, 'If you take my particulars first I can be on my way. I know her as well as any one.'

'What about him?' asked Mann indicating William and exacting a petty revenge.

'I don't think she would want that,' said Mrs Crabbe. 'I'll go by myself.'

'Thank you, Philippa,' said Luxford, 'What a charming way of putting it!'

'I'll take down anything you have to give me,' said Mann. 'I'll see people singly in the vestry. The choir had better take their things out now.'

'Why do you have to see us in there?' demanded Meadows. 'What's wrong with seeing people out here?'

'There may be something someone wants to tell me in private,' said Mann slyly. 'Something they wouldn't want others to hear if they saw a person doing things . . .'

'Ridiculous!' huffed Meadows.

'I think we should get on!' declared Mrs Harris firmly. 'Otherwise I shall certainly not get the chestnut done. Sausage meat is one thing but I do like a bit of chestnut if it's to be a proper bird, and it does take time. If we all get held up because of you, Ted Meadows, I shall ask for my money back!'

Meadows made a conciliatory gesture, half a shrug, half a mock flinch.

'Come on, Mrs Crabbe,' said Mann. 'And you can come with me, Mr Gibbon.' He nodded to Gibbon to step aside. 'Police procedure was never designed to cover these circumstances!' Mann made a face. 'It is drummed into us from the beginning that first we look to the injured, then we get the witness statements. I would appreciate if you would sit in with me, Mr Gibbon, just in case anything is said when I am on my own and then retracted. Normally there would be two of us, you see my problem? And I do at least know that you weren't in the place!'

John Gibbon nodded. They went into the vestry, passing the body again. Gibbon wished someone would cover those stripes of white hairy leg and the garish coloured socks.

'I'll take the notes,' said Mann. 'You just have to listen unless I ask you to confirm anything.'

It appeared that Philippa Crabbe had seen nothing at all. Mann had methodically taken her name and address although he knew them perfectly well, and had asked her the question he was to repeat so often.

'Did you hear or see anything, anything at all, immediately before the shot or immediately after or at any stage during the service?'

'Nothing at all. Everything was going as usual – we have the same service every year – then suddenly there was that ear-splitting crash. Shattering. I couldn't hear a thing for some time after that.'

'Where did the shot seem to come from?'

'It seemed to be right in my ear. It was so loud, it was impossible to tell. You know how the acoustics are in that building. Any noise hits you from all sides. We were just singing away then there was a crash like a blow on the head.'

Mann was taking notes, though what they were, John Gibbon could not see. He was using a Sunday school jotter and a ball-point pen. Gibbon found himself taking a considerable interest in Philippa Crabbe. She was stunning, for want of a more exact word. Although dressed in a brown tweed coat lined with some imitation fur material, she managed to convey clearly that underneath was a body of firm and distinct curves. Her hair was jet black and very glossy, her eyes a greeny-brown. She smiled easily, and dazzled John Gibbon. Yet there was nothing flirtatious about her. She gave the appearance of being a serious woman. He wondered what she would look like in an evening dress. He wondered about Mr Crabbe, if there was a Mr Crabbe? He guessed her age to be about forty and wondered, if she was single, what she was doing here.

'So no one made any abrupt moves, no one seemed to be concealing anything? I mean no one had a gun in their hands or anything obvious like that?'

'I certainly didn't see anyone fire a shot or conceal a weapon. You have to appreciate that we were all standing up, singing, and facing the altar. I suppose we all had a hymn book in our hands. When you are singing you are either looking at that or up at the rafters. You don't really notice anything else. I was staring at the rafters when the shot was fired. There's a carved angel up there I always stare at. It's a habit.'

'So you didn't look at Luxford?'

'I tend *not* to look at Luxford.'

Mann said nothing.

'So much discretion and tact!' Philippa smiled. 'I didn't like the man. You're bound to hear that from others, so you may as well hear it from me first. I thought he was unpleasant and unkind to his wife. I won't say any more because I'm sure you will hear quite a lot. I would really like to get away now, if you don't mind. I don't look forward to breaking the news to Molly, but the saving grace is that she didn't like him either. I hope you don't find that terribly shocking. You're new here, Mr Gibbon, but this is all historical fact to everyone else.'

'John,' said John Gibbon, extending a hand which Philippa Crabbe coolly shook.

'Philippa. This is a peculiar way to meet, but I expect you'll get to know everyone before this is all sorted out. You're lucky in a way. It could take you ten years to get to know them all, and instead you'll do it overnight.'

'Not the whole night I hope.'

She smiled at him.

'Come and have a drink over Christmas sometime.' She looked at Mann. 'This isn't for the notebook, is it?'

Mann shook his head.

'I look forward to it,' she continued. 'I understand you're on your own as well.'

Gibbon noted the 'as well'.

'Yes.'

'Painfully so?'

'Yes.'

'I'm sorry.' She started to get up. 'Anyway, I must get up to the Vicarage.'

'Have you *any* idea who might want to kill Peter Luxford?' asked Mann.

'I should think everyone here might, for one reason or another. That's the problem.'

She smiled at Mann.

'There's one last thing,' said Mann a little clumsily, 'I'm sorry to have to ask this, but would you take your coat off please. I have to make sure you aren't carrying a gun. I know it sounds silly,' he added apologetically.

'Not at all,' said Philippa Crabbe. 'I wondered when you were going to search for the weapon.'

'I can't be in two places at once,' said Mann. 'If no one goes out with it, it has to be in the church somewhere, and we will find it in the end. I shall have reinforcements in the morning. They'll go through the whole place.'

Philippa handed Mann her coat. She wore a cream silk blouse and dark ivory skirt. Mann patted the coat carefully all over. He eyed Philippa and John Gibbon wondered gleefully what he was now going to do.

'I couldn't carry a gun on me anywhere else,' said Philippa. 'And in particular, not a rifle if Alf Hazlitt is right.'

20

Mann handed the coat back with a rather redder face than usual.

'There are times when a woman comes in handy,' he said. To his consternation, Philippa Crabbe laughed, stifled it, put on her coat.

'I'm sorry,' she said, 'I didn't mean to be rude. I'm just trying to keep my sense of humour. Goodbye. Please call in, John.'

She smiled at both men and left. There was a silence.

'Divorced or separated?' asked John Gibbon.

'A widow. Not the Merry Widow type. A scholarly lady I'm told.'

'But quite something.'

'Yes sir,' said Mann. It was the first time he had used the policeman's formal 'sir' to Gibbon. He wondered if Mann disapproved of Philippa Crabbe, or of the social arrangements they had just discussed.

'But she's a little difficult to make out,' probed Gibbon.

'I appreciate your help,' said Mann, 'But I can't discuss personalities with you. I don't mean to be rude or off-putting, but this *is* my job and I am in the process of taking preliminary statements.'

'I understand,' said Gibbon, 'but you will allow me to help if I can?'

'Of course. But when the upper brass arrive tomorrow, all that may change.'

'Of course.'

'We'll have Mrs Harris in now. She's the one who's worried about her stuffing, God bless her. Her son's in the choir. And when it comes to the men, and certain of the women, I'd be very grateful if you would actually see them off the premises, when I ask you to see them out.'

Gibbon raised his eyebrows.

'Just in case anyone picks anything up on the way to the door that they shouldn't,' said Mann. Gibbon was impressed. And absorbed.

Mrs Harris told the same simple story as Philippa Crabbe. She had seen nothing at all, everything had been going normally, then suddenly there was an ear-splitting crack. She had been reading the words, or at least had been staring at her hymn book when it happened. It had seemed to come from behind her, she said, as though it was at the back. Mann was curious.

'Why do you say that?'

'There was a sort of double crack in it. I don't know what I mean. It wasn't two shots, but there was another sound mixed up in it, and it wasn't really beside me, so it could only have come from behind, couldn't it? I'm certain there was nothing funny going on in front.'

Mann asked for a list of everyone in front of her which Mrs Harris supplied.

'Can I have Tom in here as well?' she asked. 'He's in the choir. If you can have him in now we can both be getting off home together.'

'We don't need him, do we?' asked Mann. 'He's just a lad and we don't need to upset him.'

'Oh he might have seen something,' insisted Mrs Harris. 'Best to ask everyone.'

'All right,' said Mann and went out of the vestry to fetch him. Mrs Harris turned to John Gibbon.

'How are you finding things?'

'A bit exciting at the moment!'

'I should have put it differently. It isn't like this very often, believe you me! We've never had a murder in my time nor in anyone else's time. As for the murder of a vicar, that's unheard of! Mind you if you knew as much about him as I do, you'd be surprised he hadn't gone sooner! There I go, speaking ill of the dead! I like Eric Mann, don't you. He doesn't live his part all of the time. It's difficult being a village bobby, unless you can take your uniform off and just be yourself. Young Tom gets on with him too. I think kids respect him. Anyway, as you're here on your own over Christmas, or so I'm told, why don't you pop in and see us? You know where we are, in the first of the "semis". That's what they call us. The two Victorian houses just before The White House. I'm not pressing you am I? I shouldn't like to force you to do something you don't want to.'

'It's very kind of you. I know where you are. We're nearly neighbours.'

'Well feel free to call in.'

'Thank you.'

Gibbon was saved from the invitation becoming more precise by the return of Mann with Tom Harris. The boy had taken off cassock and surplice and was obviously in his good jacket and trousers. He seemed to be about thirteen or fourteen and sturdy.

'I've had a word with Tom,' said Mann, 'and he doesn't seem to know anything. Just repeat what you told me, there's a good lad.'

Tom was white-faced and seemed shaken, which was hardly surprising. He was a boy with a naturally closed face and a secretive look. Perhaps it was his habit of avoiding your eyes, thought Gibbon, perhaps it was just his age.

'I didn't see anything,' said Tom in broad local vowels. 'I just heard a tremendous crash, and then the vicar went over too, hard and fast, like a rabbit.'

'Did you see a flash or anything?' asked Gibbon. He saw Mann glance at him quickly, half puzzled and half annoyed. It was the first question that Gibbon had put.

'No.'

'Tell Mr Gibbon what you said about direction.'

'It was very difficult to tell, but it seemed to come right from the back. It was a long time anyhow until we could smell the smoke.'

'Do you know of any reason why anyone should do this?' probed

22

Gibbon, risking another of Mann's annoyed glances. He was rewarded with one. Rather to his surprise Tom seemed ill at ease at this question and shook his head without replying.

'Sure?'

Tom looked distinctly wary. He seemed to be appealing to Mann to stop these questions, but Mann reached out a hand and put it on one of the boy's shoulders.

'Come on now, Tom. Any reason why anyone should do this?' He looked hard at the boy.

'If there's something you know, you'd best say!' said Mrs Harris.

The boy turned pink. Mann removed his hand.

'I'd tell you wouldn't I?' he protested. 'There was always jokes about him and women and things like that! Lots of people didn't like him.' The poor boy really blushed. Mann relented.

'All right Mrs Harris, I think you can go now. Will you please just let me check out your coat. I have to do it the same for everyone.'

'Help yourself!' She offered her heavy black coat and handbag to Mann. 'Give him your jacket, Tom.'

Mann examined everything, returned them.

'See them both out please, Mr Gibbon.'

Gibbon was surprised, but did so. Mann's revenge for interference.

'Why Mrs Harris?' he asked Mann when he returned. 'I wouldn't have any suspicions of her. The boy seems a bit devious to me. He never looks you in the eye!'

'The boy's all right. See him blush! I just wondered about that simple motherly type . . .'

They worked through a succession of ladies with the same depressing lack of results. Gibbon received more invitations that he refused, Mann kept on filling in his notebook.

'Now we'll have Cynthia Fry,' said Mann with a slight smile. 'Without husband George. He's the one who's so keen to get home for Christmas!'

The clock struck one as Cynthia Fry entered at Gibbon's request. She sat down and twiddled the end of a silk scarf in her lap. She wore a soft tweed suit of a lavender mixture with a pink jumper. Her lipstick was towards the purple end of red and she had been lining her blue eyes with a band of even lighter blue, an effect that reminded Gibbon of certain birds of the parrot family. All this, combined with her well-blonded hair, had resulted in a colourful combination, – 'Christmassy' was the word, Gibbon supposed. If you wanted to be charitable.

'Hello, Mrs Fry,' said Mann, indicating one of the hard chairs they were all using. 'We shall try to be quick, but I have to get a description of anything you think you heard or saw while it's still fresh in your

23

mind. First impressions are important.'

Mrs Fry nodded her firm approval. These were sentiments with which she plainly agreed. She crossed her nicely shaped legs and dangled her deep maroon kid shoes. For a woman in her late forties, and somewhat given to bulk, she managed to be rather obviously well-maintained. Gibbon thought that she was certainly an interesting specimen. There must be something about her worth knowing. He saw now why Mann had permitted himself the slight smile.

'This is Mr Gibbon, who ran to get me,' Mann was explaining. 'And I mean ran. It was a lucky chance he was out jogging.'

'Hello, Mr Gibbon', said Cynthia Fry, fixing him firmly with her blue-on-blue eyes. It was rather like being pinned on a board, Gibbon decided. A woman of strong will and little apparent shyness. He found he was the one who looked away.

'Could you just tell us what happened, in your own words?'

'Well of course it will be in my own words,' said Mrs Fry. 'That's what they're always saying on television. I mean it's a bit silly isn't it, because whose words would you use?'

She raised an eyebrow at Mann, and smiled. It was not entirely a sweet smile. Gibbon imagined that she enjoyed scoring points. Her delivery was fast and assured. It could be nervousness.

'You know what I mean,' said Mann pleasantly. He was making an effort. 'Tell us what happened just before the shot, if you saw anything, and what happened afterwards.'

'Well I was singing of course. We all were. The Holly and the Ivy. I think it's one of the best carols, and very appropriate. I decorate the church, you see, so I was thinking about it. I had such a lot of trouble this year. There are so many birds. Fieldfares are the real problem, there are such enormous flocks of them. They come in hundreds at a time when they're migrating, and strip every berry off the holly.'

'It all looked very nice to me,' said Mann interrupting impatiently.

'Thank you,' said Cynthia. 'But it's always the same. If you haven't decorated a church, you don't understand how much work it is, and you don't understand the *skill*. I mean it isn't like sticking a few flowers in a vase at home. The whole *scale* of things is quite different and of course churches are often such gloomy places so that the placing of things is so important to pick up the light . . .'

'Can we get back to you standing there singing. Please?' asked Mann. 'What did you hear or see?'

'Well I heard a fantastic bang, of course!' said Cynthia, looking rather cross. Gibbon realised that in her twenties, Cynthia must have been stunning. He wondered what George was like. He must have a good deaf ear to turn to Cynthia's continual out-pourings.

'Is that all you noticed?' he asked. He had seen a tightening of Mann's mouth.

24

'Well, it was very loud. I jumped out of my skin. My ears were ringing so much I couldn't think. I didn't notice that Peter Luxford had fallen down at all, to tell you the truth. It was only when people started running towards him and pointing and so on that I noticed he'd gone.'

'So you saw nothing strange? Nothing that could be connected with the shooting?'

'Not a thing. I didn't see any guns or smoke. The whole thing is very bizarre. It's not the sort of thing you expect to get mixed up in on Christmas Eve, is it? Mind you, Luxford was a . . . well I shouldn't really say. You'll think it awful of me when he's lying there dead. Nevertheless, I'm sure there's a reason for it.'

'There will certainly be a reason for it,' said Mann. 'But just you go on. There's absolutely no point in not telling us anything that might help. If you know something, you have a duty to tell us or you may be withholding essential information.'

Cynthia's eyes sparkled.

'Well, what I was going to say, was that he was a man with a past, if you know what I mean. And a present too. How he managed to keep his cloth on his back is really a puzzle. You're bound to hear about it from other people anyway, and I should think you've already heard plenty about it in the village, Eric Mann.'

'I've heard about his womanizing,' said Mann, very matter-of-fact. 'But there's always a lot of gossip. As far as I'm concerned, he did his job, kept himself to himself, and the one thing he was really interested in was his archaeology.'

'Oh is that what you think!' said Cynthia with a laugh.

'What do you mean?' asked John Gibbon gently. 'I don't know anything about the village and people, I haven't had time to learn.'

'What Constable Mann says is true enough, but not with the emphasis he puts on things. The man chased every woman in the village, I should think. He was a disgrace. I'm not going to name names, but you will find out. He was mixed up in everything. As for keeping himself to himself, I should think that will raise a laugh or two. He was a terrible gossip!'

Cynthia Fry delivered this judgement with complete sincerity. Gibbon suppressed a desire to laugh, to puncture her air of self-satisfaction.

'Do you mean that someone may have killed him because of something like that?'

'Oh come on now, it's fairly obvious! It wasn't suicide, so someone shot him. I don't know how they did it without being seen, and no one says they saw anyone do it. Or if they did, they aren't saying.'

'You think that's possible?' asked Mann.

'It might be,' said Cynthia, slightly uneasy that she was being questioned so closely.

'Do you know something that you aren't telling us?'

'What an offensive thing to say!'

'I didn't mean to be in any way upsetting,' persisted Mann, 'But it might explain lots of things. You obviously do think it's possible that someone saw something and might not mention it.'

'All I'm saying is that with a man like Luxford, there must have been an awful lot of people in the congregation tonight who didn't care too much when he was shot. Maybe they would turn a blind eye. It was only a thought, you know, you don't have to start to build a case around it!''

Cynthia was colouring, and her voice had taken on a higher tone. She obviously wished she had never made the suggestion.

'I'm very grateful for the idea,' said Mann. 'I agree it's no more than a thought. It does seem strange, doesn't it, that a man can be shot in front of a full congregation without anyone seeing who pulled the trigger?'

Cynthia Fry was not going to add anything more to what she had said. She sat expressionless, staring at the middle distance. Gibbon sensed very strongly that behind the gossipy, highly-coloured exterior there was a guarded secret. He made up his mind to take the risk, and probe it cruelly, now.

'Did you have trouble with Luxford's attentions?' he asked.

Cynthia Fry sat up, her eyes blazing. She looked formidable, and Mann seemed to shrink, aghast.

'I know you're new here Mr Gibbon, but what a disgraceful thing to ask! What gives you the right to even suggest such a thing? Are you connected with the police or something? Is he, Constable Mann?'

Mann shook his head.

'I thought not! What a thing to say!'

Cynthia had turned quite pink. Gibbon watched her performance of outrage with calm fascination. Their eyes held each other. He tried to let her know through the calmness of his expression that he was not impressed by her outburst, that he would wait patiently and persist, that he knew she was doing it for Mann's benefit.

He thought he saw in her eyes a hint of pleading.

'I apologise if I've given offence, but you have said Luxford had a past and he was a womanizer. You're an attractive woman, so the question naturally sprang to mind. He might have been a nuisance to you in some way. After all, you do look after the church decorations . . .'

'Are you painting a picture of him padding round after me in the church? Is that the sort of nasty innuendo you're determined to put about in front of Constable Mann here?'

'Of course not!' lied Gibbon.

Cynthia looked at him evenly. There was a short silence. Gibbon prayed that Mann would hold his peace. Mann did. Cynthia fiddled with her silk scarf.

'He could be a very nice man,' she continued in a calm voice. 'It was that side of him that attracted women, I'm sure. He would be very gentle and understanding, and before you knew where you were his hands would be all over you. It's a great surprise from what they call a man of the cloth. You don't expect it and at first you don't believe it. He relied on that, I'm sure. Who's going to believe you if you say that sort of thing about a very respectable-looking vicar? I mean in this day and age they believe it about a choirboy but not about women. He was flattering, then a terrible pest.'

The twiddling of the scarf was rapid now. Cynthia Fry spoke in a low calm tone, her eyes on the movement of her hands.

'He really was a lecherous man, you see. He was never content with one woman at a time. He had to have more than one, so that he could taunt each one about the other. There was never anything lasting in it. I think he liked the idea of having a sort of harem around the village and tried to keep women dangling by making them jealous of each other.'

Cynthia sniffed. John Gibbon saw that she was becoming upset. He felt a pang because he knew he should say something comforting, and simultaneously knew that if he did they would get nothing more from Cynthia.

'So he did that to you,' he stated baldly. Mann was watching him now, leaving this to him.

'My husband doesn't know about it,' said Cynthia. 'I insist on your absolute discretion. I really don't know why I'm telling you at all!' she added with a flash of returning spirit. 'There are others you can ask about him, you know, but all the asking will make him a lot more trouble dead than he was alive. It looks as though he'll have the last laugh after all!'

She dabbed at her eyes with the silk handkerchief.

'We won't ask you any more,' said Mann, taking pity, 'And nothing you've said here need go any further. I'm sorry it's been distressing.'

'It's so humiliating,' said Cynthia. 'I don't know how I shall be able to look you two in the face again.'

Gibbon said nothing. He doubted if she was quite as modest as she liked to pretend. The look she had just given him was far from shy. He let Mann deal with the problem of asking for her jacket, and walked with her to the door of the church.

'Are you going now?' demanded George Fry, bounding up to them.

'My husband,' said Cynthia, introducing John Gibbon. George Fry merely nodded. He looked extremely annoyed and smelled equally of peppermints and beer. In appearance he reminded John of a cartoon colonel except that he was also plump.

'It's a bloody disgrace being kept in here on Christmas Eve!' said George loudly. 'Can't that policeman hurry up?'

There were various voices of assent. It was clearly very trying on the rest of the congregation who were waiting to be interviewed and released.

'He's being as quick as he can,' said John. 'He only asks a few simple questions.'

'And what are you doing in there anyway?' demanded George. 'You've nothing to do with the police.'

'I was asked,' said Gibbon. 'Someone has to be there with him. I just happened to be the nearest.'

George snorted, and seemed about to launch another attack when they heard the hee-haw of a siren.

'That must be the ambulance!' said John. They had all forgotten about it.

'Taken its time!' said Walker.

'Roads will be terrible,' said Hazlitt. 'Should think they must've got stuck more'n once.'

The ambulancemen came in with a tale of delays and drifts. Roads were blocked here there and everywhere and they had had to back-track and then finally dig to get there at all. Mann appeared from the vestry and while the rest of them stood back, the body was expertly dealt with, covered, lifted and disappeared.

Cynthia Fry followed them out.

'You make sure you have everything ready!' George was insisting rudely. 'I intend to have my Christmas dinner despite all this blasted nonsense. While you're about it, why don't you bring us back a bottle or two!'

There were assorted protests and shouts of agreement. Cynthia Fry shook her head. George looked very annoyed. Not a happy marriage thought Gibbon. William Luxford was allowed to go with his brother's body.

'Let's have Lucinda Walker next,' said Mann softly. He was standing beside Gibbon near the doorway.' After that I think we may be able to let most of the women go. After checking for the weapon.'

'Who's Lucinda Walker?' asked Gibbon quietly.

'The beauty,' said Mann. 'We may as well get the pleasant bits over first!'

He gave Gibbon a brief smile. Mann was thawing. He obviously approved of the interview with Cynthia Fry.

Lucinda gave them both a dazzling smile. It was one sustained smile that she rotated. The effect was like the beam of a searchlight that passed over them. John Gibbon was impressed.

'I don't think I'll be able to help you, I'm afraid,' she said as she sat down. 'I didn't see anything until the vicar fell onto the floor.'

Both men were studying her tight yellow dress. Lucinda flicked her stole carelessly over one shoulder and settled down in the chair. Her skin was a fine medium-dark colour that Gibbon realised was truly the colour of mahogany. Lucinda did not seem to object to this appraisal. She raised an eyebrow. Her fine eyes sparkled.

'That's been the problem,' said Mann. Gibbon thought it only polite to allow him to take command.

'No one saw anything and everyone was deafened by the noise. However, we're not so interested in that any more. We're rather more interested in who might want to kill him.'

Lucinda's mobile eyebrows were raised even higher. She made a droll face.

'I suppose Cynthia Fry has been talking!'

The remark was tart and her voice had a hard edge.

'Why do you say that?'

'Oh come on! She was the last in here, and suddenly you ask who might have wanted to kill him. I don't have any experience of murders or murder enquiries, but I should have thought it was obvious she's been dishing the dirt. She didn't like him much.'

'Why?' asked Gibbon softly. Lucinda turned to him sharply, apparently surprised by the very gentleness and innocence of the question. Then she smiled.

'She must have told you. You're just leading me on.'

'We'd like to hear in your own words why you think she didn't like him.'

In your own words. That exceptionally pedantic phrase.

'I don't particularly like Cynthia Fry. I think I should make that clear. In fact it would be honest to say I can't stand the woman and the feeling is entirely mutual. She's silly and bossy and prejudiced, to mention just a few reasons. All that pale blue eye make-up and baby-blue eyes stuff! She thinks innocence comes from a jar and I daresay she thinks you can put it on every morning!'

Both men were taken aback by this forthright speech. Lucinda beamed at them, satisfied with the result she had produced. Gibbon realised that she probably considered them both idiots. There was a great deal of tough common sense and candid thinking about Lucinda Walker. A woman accustomed to getting her way with men, a woman who was no great respecter of men! Gibbon knew that she ran the wool shop-cum-boutique called 'The Black Sheep'. How could anyone miss it, with Lucinda behind the counter? He had noticed it on his second day, with the shock of his separation fresh in his mind. The irony in the name impressed him. She had flashed him one of her smiles as he had looked briefly in the window, and he had moved on, embarrassed.

'I think you've made that point reasonably clear,' murmured Gibbon with sly humour. 'But why didn't she like Luxford?'

29

'Hell hath no fury, and all that sort of thing, Mr Gibbon. Don't you believe that? I thought it was a part of the bedrock of male education.'

John Gibbon was faintly surprised that she knew his name. Mann had not introduced him. He supposed she must have found out while they were all talking in the church. A disappointing explanation. Lucinda Walker was quite a person, as they say.

'Are you saying that there was some personal reason why she should dislike Luxford?' asked Gibbon quickly. He could see that Mann's face was disapproving. He might try to stop this fascinating gossip.

Lucinda Walker laughed. There was nothing malicious in it. It was the honest laugh of someone enjoying watching the bovine performance of two slow-witted men.

'What do you think?'

'We're not hear to listen to gossip!' declared Mann with a masterful ring of authority in his voice. At least he thought he had. Lucinda looked at him.

'Oh!' she pouted. 'You really ought to. It's what makes the world go round. That and love, and aren't the two things intimately connected?'

She laughed to herself again. Gibbon was worried about Mann. He was getting annoyed and was out of his depth with Lucinda Walker. He must not be allowed to be heavy with her.

'In the case of Mrs Fry, how intimately?' he asked.

'I can't have questions like that!' shouted Mann. 'This isn't the bar at "The Feathers". This is a serious inquiry!'

'It's important,' said Gibbon calmly. 'The man seems to have been fond of the ladies, as the euphemism goes. It may be very relevant. It may be the very reason he has been killed. We have to know as much as possible. It isn't the sort of thing that every woman will necessarily volunteer!'

'I'm not going to sit here and be a sort of dust-bin for unproved scandal,' said Mann. 'That's not a policeman's job. Just the opposite really.'

'Come now,' said Lucinda chidingly, 'You know that's not true. A policeman is supposed to keep his ears open for every little rumour. It's part of his stock-in-trade. He's supposed to lurk about in pubs and listen in dark corners!'

Mann was having difficulty in controlling himself. He was red in the face and his teeth were gritted. He wiped twice at the lank mass of yellow hair that fell over his forehead. He gave the impression to Gibbon that it would not be long before he arrested Lucinda for something or other to teach her a lesson.

'Can we please get back to what we want to know?' interjected Gibbon sternly. 'Back to who might want to kill him.'

'An awful lot of people,' said Lucinda. She seemed conscious that she had gone far enough with Mann. 'Cynthia Fry hated him, although she always looked after the church. Anyway, apart from her, I suppose you can list any woman as a suspect between the ages of sixteen and sixty.'

'We know he was a chaser of women,' said Gibbon.

'Oh he didn't just chase them,' said Lucinda, 'He caught them all right. He was very attentive, quite the smoothy. I suppose he had charm. He certainly had fascination value. After all, I think any woman is curious to know what a randy vicar gets up to!'

This outrageous remark made Gibbon grin, but it made Mann shudder.

'I don't think we should go on with this conversation!' he announced. 'Thank you Mrs Walker. I think you can go now.'

He had his hand on the door handle.

'As you wish,' said Lucinda. She got up, flicking her stole again. 'I think the secret of the whole thing is where I've said.'

'You've made your point very plain!' said Mann coldly. 'I sincerely hope you don't repeat any of the things you've said in here to anyone.'

'Nothing I've said is any kind of secret!' said Lucinda, very frosty in turn. 'I've only told you the utmost commonplaces. You'll find out.'

What about searching her, thought Gibbon. The only place Lucinda could possibly conceal anything would be in her stole.

'May we just look at your stole?' he asked.

'Of course,' said Lucinda, and handed it over. 'Looking for the weapon?'

'Yes,' said Gibbon, honestly. There was nothing there but fur. He handed it to Mann who patted it and handed it back.

'You're separated, aren't you, Mr Gibbon?' asked Lucinda.

'Yes,' said Gibbon, surprised. 'How did you know.'

'It's the very stuff of life. Just as I said. You must be alone for Christmas?'

'Yes'

'Why don't you pay us a visit? Henry and I always have a few drinks on Christmas morning. Oh Lord, it *is* Christmas morning! Why don't you call in at twelve. We have no children, you see, and it makes a sort of substitute.'

'Thank you very much. I think I shall do that.'

Lucinda smiled at him, but this time without the dazzling effect she had practised before. She had extended a genuine hand of friendship, and the mention of the absence of children had been from her heart. There was a great deal to Lucinda Walker, he thought. It would certainly take his mind off his own emotional pain, and enable him to find out a great deal about what made this place tick.

He showed her to the porch door. Henry detached himself from the other men and joined her. He was looking very tired and strained, Gibbon thought, even allowing for the lateness of the hour.

'John Gibbon, my husband Henry Walker,' said Lucinda as they stood at the porch. The men shook hands.

'I've asked John round for drinks at twelve,' said Lucinda. 'It's already Christmas Day.'

'I know,' said Walker. He seemed preoccupied but managed to raise a smile in a superficial way.

'I look forward to seeing you.'

It was intended to dismiss him, and he moved away to re-join Mann in the vestry. Curiosity made him move slowly, keep his eyes and ears open. He heard Henry saying that the whole thing was an impossible nuisance, that he really had so much work to do, Christmas or not. He certainly had no time to waste cooped up in a church in this stupid way. Lucinda replied that perhaps it would do him good to give it a rest. There was tautness in her tone that was shown in her face. Gibbon saw that a haunted expression crossed Henry Walker's face in turn, to be immediately extinguished when he noticed that Gibbon was watching him.

There was something in their affairs that was far from well.

'It certainly seems as though you'll be having a busy Christmas!' said Mann acidly. 'Busy enjoying yourself, unlike me. I shall be lucky if I get a proper knife-and-forker at all!'

Mann stretched and yawned. They were in the middle of interviewing the men, who were uncommunicative by comparison with the women. So far they had found no one who had seen anything, they had found no weapon, and as far as motive was concerned, whatever the males of the village knew about Luxford, none so far were prepared to talk about it.

George Fry was collected by Gibbon. He had to admit to himself he was looking forward to this. The clock had struck two and there were only Fry, Walker, Hazlitt and Meadows left. The best of the bunch.

Fry was very grumpy and smelled of whisky. Presumably he had managed to persuade Jeffrys to part with some of the contents of his hip flask. Unless they were all carrying them!

'Let's get this over with!' demanded Fry. 'Two in the morning!'

'I don't enjoy it either!' objected Mann acidly. He had a dull headache and the thirst induced by drinking. He longed for a cup of tea and was repelled by the smell of whisky. He moved away from Fry.

'If I had stayed in The Foresters, I wouldn't be here at all,' said Fry. 'That must prove something or other. I told the wife I didn't want to come to this blasted service, and look where it's got us. She has to come to look at her greenery and spray glitter and all that sort of thing! This is where coming to church at Christmas gets you!'

'Where's all the bit about the season of good will?' asked Gibbon with a gentle smile that made it difficult for Fry to respond to the criticism.

'I don't mind the good will bit at all!' protested Fry. 'And I most certainly enjoy the festive bit. What I don't enjoy is the religious bit. Is there anything wrong in that?'

He glared defensively at Gibbon.

'You won't get me to criticise anything,' said Gibbon. 'I don't mind how people see Christmas. After all, I was jogging round the church when this happened.'

'So you were,' said Fry, mollified.

'I was about to go to bed!' said Mann pointedly.

'Well I could have been lowering a pint or two.'

'After hours?' queried Mann with a quizzical look.

'Oh come on, Constable! Charlie Brooks always has a little private party. *You* know that!'

Gibbon was trying to make out George Fry. He was plump and had a sturdy frame and red face – a man who had spent much of his life in the open. He looked more like a farmer than anything else and had a strong twang of the local accent. He must be retired now, Gibbon decided. Cynthia Fry was obviously a good ten years younger than her husband, which explained much of what they had heard from her. George Fry looked a boor. Cynthia Fry certainly was not. George Fry obviously liked his drink. Cynthia Fry liked her church. A mis-match.

He caught George's rather watery brown eyes.

'I suppose I ought to introduce myself,' he said, probing.

'I know who you are,' announced George impolitely. 'We've all heard about you.'

'I don't know what you can have possibly heard,' said Gibbon mildly.

'Oh don't worry about that. Shortage of facts never stopped any one round here. They just make it up as they go along. We all know about your mad jogging anyway.'

'Thank you.'

'Well you have to admit it's a bit bloody cold for it! It's not my idea of fun.'

Gibbon was annoyed to see that Mann was controlling a distinct smile.

'It's healthy,' he said, wishing immediately that he hadn't because it was a defensive reply.

'So they say!' said George with a derisive snort.

'Well you'll have to forgive me if I don't know you except by name,' said Gibbon. 'I have hardly met anyone yet. Are you retired?'

'Yes,' said George, 'I suppose you could say that, but I keep active in my own way.'

'Mr Fry managed three farms locally,' volunteered Mann.

I was almost right about him, thought Gibbon.

'He knows everyone and everything that goes on locally, don't you, Mr Fry?' prompted Mann.

Doesn't know about his wife though. Or does he? Fry's face had a wary expression.

'Don't you give me that sort of chat, Constable. That's all soft soap so that you can keep up the questions. I want to be out of here as soon as possible, if not sooner and I'd be much obliged if you'd come straight to the point. I saw nothing, I can tell you that. As for who might have done it, I can tell you almost anyone could have. Including the verger! I could have done it myself. Luxford was an oily something-or-other and always interfering.'

Mann wiped back his hank of hair. He was trying hard to be casual. 'I wish I'd thought of bringing some aspirins with me,' he said. 'I have a bit of a head. I hope this isn't going to be difficult.' George snorted like the bull he resembled.

'The point is, no one saw anyone doing anything,' said Gibbon.

'I can't see the point of keeping us here at all. If no one saw anyone fire the shot, then you're a bit up a gum tree. Have you found the weapon? I shouldn't think so.'

'We haven't,' said Mann massaging the base of his neck tenderly. He found the spot from which his throbbing head seemed to emanate.

'Well, it can't have walked away,' said George, 'that was a rifle. I've had a good look round while you lot have been talking in here, and I can tell you there's no gun in the church. At least it isn't anywhere obvious. I didn't exactly want to start going through all that bloody greenery my wife insists on putting up everywhere. In any case, I think the shot must have come from outside.'

'Why are you so sure it was a rifle?' asked Gibbon. 'That's exactly what Hazlitt said.'

'Hazlitt's right. It *was* a rifle shot, it's as simple as that. You can't mistake it for anything else. A hand gun sounds quite different. The velocity is lower. I've been shooting around the farm for at least forty years now, and I was in the last war. I've used most sorts of guns, and that was a rifle.'

'Who do you really think might bear Luxford a grudge?' asked Gibbon, deliberately naïve. Fry snorted, not deceived.

'I think you must have got the message by now. He was not liked, as they say when they're being polite. Anyone could have done it.'

'But no one in particular?'

'He had some very particular enemies, everyone will tell you that, but if every one of them had homicidal tendencies you'd be

34

shovelling him up.'

Mann's face showed his disapproval. George Fry raised a hand before he could say anything.

'I know, I know, I ought not to be speaking like that, but the man was loathsome. You wouldn't put up with an animal with his ways and manners! You'll get no accusations out of me. It's my view that whoever did it deserves a commendation in any civilised society!'

'If you know something and are concealing it, that's a very serious matter,' said Mann, mustering his policeman's voice. Fry gave him a brief wintry smile.

'Look, I don't know anything, and I don't intend to make guesses. That is up to the police!' He stood up. 'Just search me please and let me go. I have visions of a hot toddy at this moment, and find it difficult to concentrate on anything else! Have you thought that in this room somewhere Luxford must keep the communion wine?'

George Fry had taken off his overcoat and handed it to Mann who dutifully patted it. George started to take off his jacket, but Mann shook his head.

'I think you're right about the rifle, and I don't think you've got one in there. I'm sorry we've taken so long.'

'Find the weapon,' said Fry. 'That's the thing to puzzle you.'

'How did Mrs Fry get on with Luxford?' asked Mann quietly, one hand on the vestry door handle.

'How do you mean?' demanded George savagely. He had coloured instantly and his eyes were furious.

'He had the reputation of being a nuisance with the ladies,' said Mann in his calmest tone.

'You watch what you're saying, Constable!' said George, emphasising each word with a jab of a stubby finger in Mann's direction.

'I'm sorry,' said Mann quickly. 'Your wife herself said that he had a bad reputation.'

'Don't you dare infer anything, Constable.'

'I don't think the constable meant to,' said Gibbon, realising he had better intervene quickly. Fry stared at him hard, then finally nodded.

'I'll let you out,' said Gibbon.

When Gibbon returned to the vestry, Mann was massaging the side of his neck and rolling his head.

'Troubling you?' asked Gibbon.

'I will know all about it tomorrow,' said Mann. 'Things like this should be tackled on a clear head. I should be sleeping the sleep of the just. Just had enough!' Mann gave a wry smile.

'You should be keeping fit like me. It gives you so many aches and pains you don't have time to concentrate on any one of them.'

35

'No thank you!'

'You can always jog back home with me.'

'You must be joking! It's all right for you. This all ends when you go home. It's just starting for me. As soon as I pick up that phone, all hell will break loose. It'll already have started. The ambulance has only to get to the hospital and then the coroner will be informed. Violent death, all that. By the time I get home the line will be smouldering gently with in-coming calls and the wife will be smouldering gently too! My word, I should have had a pint or two less. Or more.' He sighed deeply and shook his head as a dog does when drying itself. 'Perhaps it could have been a shot from outside.'

'With no footsteps, no place to fire it from? Someone would have had to climb the walls, and there's nothing to get hold of. Except round the window heads. It's just possible but very unlikely. If we didn't notice footsteps when we first arrived we shan't find any now. Not with the way it's still snowing.'

Mann sighed.

'I suppose you're right. I'm sorry to have had to involve you in this. As I have, let's get it finished. Walker next?'

Henry Walker looked ill. He had the grey resigned appearance of a man whose facial muscles have given up appearances. Even the way he sat down expressed collapse rather than relaxation. His legs stuck out in front of him inelegantly, his feet splayed as though they were too heavy. He was wearing an expensive black overcoat with a striped satin lining, a City garment that looked out of place in Burberry country. The dark blue suit that he wore below that was of an equally impeccable origin, as were the silk socks and black leather shoes. Mann felt like telling him to pull himself together, as though there was something wrong in treating such good clothes in such a sloppy way.

Walker's eyes moved from one man to the other. Gibbon thought that he had never actually seen eyes flicker before, as they write about in books, but Walker's eyes were definitely flickering. The man was a knot of tension. The extraordinary over-relaxed posture was an attempt to control himself.

'Can we please hurry this up?' asked Walker abruptly.

'We'll be as quick as we can,' replied Mann with irritating blandness.

'I have absolutely nothing of help to tell you, and I'm one of the last people here. I would be very grateful if you can let me get home. For some people Christmas is one long party. For others of us it's a time to catch up with work. I have things to do.'

'I'm sorry,' said Mann diplomatically. 'I don't like to hear of a man who has to work over Christmas.'

'I don't enjoy it either,' said Walker. 'I would be able to get it done better with a clear head.'

'What do you do, Mr Walker?' asked Gibbon. 'It isn't fair that you can't take a few days rest.'

Walker looked at him sharply, but seeing Gibbon's face was casually enquiring, crossed his legs.

'I have a company or two. I suppose that makes me a company director. One of those people that always figure in trials in the tabloids. What do *you* do, Mr Gibbon?'

Gibbon smiled slightly. However tired Walker was, he was by no means subdued by the situation.

'Apart from jogging you mean? Or interfering?'

'I don't know if you're interfering. Presumably you're the best judge of that. I assume you're helping Mann because he needs a witness.'

'Correct! And there's no need to be rude to Mr Gibbon!' said Mann firmly. 'He's been a great help to me and it is a matter of procedure that I have asked him to remain. No doubt he would much rather be tucked up in his bed. Like the rest of us!'

'I don't take offence,' said Gibbon. 'It's perfectly reasonable of Mr Walker. Apart from jogging, I'm recently separated from my wife and I'm trying to get over it. Jogging is one of my penances, if you like. At least it makes me forget about it for a time. Perhaps that tells you that I didn't want the separation. That's a start, isn't it Mr Walker?'

John Gibbon wondered how he was going to get through the drinks party Lucinda had asked him to. It had all the makings of an embarrassing occasion if Walker was going to maintain this level of hostility and Lucinda was going to be dazzlingly friendly.

'Apart from my private life, I was a librarian.'

Walker was surprised, and made a small expression of interest, pursing his lips and raising his eyebrows.

'I didn't mean to sound hostile,' he said. 'I'm just a bit fed up with all this. Sorry about your private life. I didn't mean to enquire into that.'

'It doesn't matter. Your wife already knew anyway.'

'Did she?'

This produced a further quick flickering of the eyes. Henry did not look particularly pleased.

'I must say I've never met a librarian before. And I never thought of them as being particularly sporty types.'

'I'm not a particularly sporty type. Can't stand them.'

'That's all right then,' said Henry Walker with the glimmer of a smile. 'Join the human race.'

'Can we get on with this?' asked Mann with a sigh of impatience. 'It was you people that were all in a raging hurry.'

'Sorry,' said Walker. 'My story is simple. I didn't see anyone fire the shot, I didn't see anyone acting suspiciously, as they always put it,

37

and I have no idea where the shot came from. On top of that, I had my eyes down on my hymn book and didn't really see Luxford being hit. Finally I don't have any idea who did it, although if rumour is to be believed it could have been any one of half a dozen irate husbands or spurned women. He seems to have deserved it. I just wish that whoever did it could have chosen a less public place, a better time and not caused such bloody inconvenience to all of us. Apart from that, I've no feelings on the matter!'

'I see.' said Mann in a voice heavy with disbelief. Gibbon felt like giving a small cheer. He too had been very unimpressed by Henry's fluency. It veered towards professional glibness and he was hiding something. John Gibbon thought he knew what, and guessed that Mann had got there as well.

'What do you see?' asked Henry, uncrossing his legs and pulling himself slightly more upright. It was a small gesture but quite menacing. Henry was evidently practised in boardroom body-language. John Gibbon found himself more and more interested in the man.

'It seems to me that you have quite strong feelings in the matter,' Mann persevered bravely. 'You can hardly describe your feelings about Luxford as "neutral", can you?'

Gibbon wondered how much he dare weigh in and help Mann. Mann was casting him a hopeful glance. Gibbon felt a rat but ignored it. He had more to learn over drinks with Lucinda than by antagonising Henry.

'Of course they're neutral!' snapped Henry. 'Luxford meant nothing to me. I didn't know the man at all.'

'Did your wife know him slightly better than you did?' asked Mann, throwing all caution to the wind and looking quite pale at his lack of discretion. Walker coloured slowly. To Gibbon who watched him it was rather like blotting paper absorbing ink. The pause was measured.

'And what the devil do you mean by that?'

'As she was responsible for the church flowers and things.'

Henry Walker re-crossed his legs, tugged at the creases of his trousers. He addressed his shoes.

'And that is of course all that you mean.'

'I'm afraid I don't understand *your* meaning,' said Mann guilelessly. He had obviously decided to plant the seed then retreat. 'I only wondered if she had heard at first hand about these alleged carryings-on. Told you anything that might be material.'

'No,' said Henry Walker.

'Oh,' said Mann.

'I think Mr Walker ought to be allowed to go, don't you?' said John Gibbon, to be rewarded by Mann with a black and furious look. Nevertheless, he had won Walker's gratitude.

Walker had already risen to his feet.

'I'll go then, if there is nothing more cogent you want to ask,' said Walker with cool anger.

'I can't think of anything at the moment,' said Mann.

'Good. I'm very pleased to hear that,' said Walker. 'It disturbs me however that it's taken you two hours to get to this momentous moment. Life must be nice when time comes in such abundance.'

'Would you see Mr Walker out,' said Mann. This time it was an order, not a polite request.

'I don't like the fellow's innuendo!' said Henry to Gibbon as they reached the door. He was whispering in case Meadows should hear. 'Thank you for getting me out.'

'I'm afraid I'm in bad odour with Mann now,' said Gibbon, disgusted with himself at the easy way he was playing his part.

'I don't think you'll lose any sleep over it! I'm off home. I look forward to seeing you – in a little less than ten hours,' said Walker glancing at his watch. 'Lucinda and her little drinks at Christmas! She's invited half the village, although God knows how many will turn up after this. All of them I suppose, so they can chew it over between them.' He sighed. 'To tell you the truth I never liked Christmas anyway. I suppose that reflects badly on me somehow!'

Walker summoned a faint smile as he opened the door, letting in a cutting blast of air and crystals of blown snow.

'I didn't like Luxford either. A nuisance to the end.'

Meadows was looking at Gibbon expectantly, so he nodded to him. Gibbon appraised the man for the first time. He had seen him on a number of occasions, had bought fruit and vegetables from him at his shop, but somehow those humdrum activities had never led to him noticing the man. Meadows in church clothes was different from Meadows in the shop. Meadows in the shop wore Fair Isle jumpers that by their colour distracted attention from his sandy hair, light freckled skin and blue eyes. He also had a small moustache – perhaps intended as a hint of a military past – that had remained a surprising shade of ginger and, although it was entirely real, appeared to be badly applied with gum to his round shiny face.

Now, dressed in a sober dark blue suit, Meadows' colouring blazed. He looked like a man who had just been tending to a fire. His hands were freckled and on the back of them were silky fair hairs.

Gibbon had no reason to dislike the man. He had always been kind to him in fact, slipping in the extra weight over the pound, yet there was something about him he found unpleasant. He toyed with the word 'revolting' but that was too strong. It was difficult to analyse. Maybe it was because he had fair eyebrows like a white pig!

Gibbon told himself to behave. This was no time to start to develop prejudices.

'I've been very patient,' said Meadows. 'In provoking circumstances!'

'I know,' said Gibbon soothingly. It sounded hollow to him and he wasn't surprised when Meadows refused to be shut up.

'You haven't been shut in this place with nothing but a bunch of lunatics!'

Gibbon looked at him, made an expression of politely contrived incomprehension and fortified it with a shrug, holding his shoulders high.

'Look at him!' said Meadows.

For the first time Gibbon was aware of a brown shape asleep on a pew. He recognised the jacket as belonging to Hazlitt. The man's body inflated and relaxed slightly. He was asleep.

'I think we almost forgot him.'

'And what about Walker! That man's as twitchy as a dragonfly. *And* I've been on my feet all day and stayed open until seven because it was Christmas Eve when a lot of people would have been in the pub a long time ago. *And* we had George Fry huffing and puffing and giving you eczema with his breath, *and* we had Luxford's loathsome brother in here with us. I tell you, this has been worse than the hippo house at the zoo!'

Gibbon was interested to know that William Luxford was considered loathsome by the piggy Mr Meadows.

'We'd better join Mann,' he said.

Mann was still looking sulky as the two men entered the vestry.

'Hello Mr Meadows,' said Mann. 'We'll be as quick as we can.' He went through the familiar questions and received the familiar replies. Gibbon said nothing. He was watching. Meadows was an uneasy man. He shifted in the chair, his eyes flicked to the door from time to time as though he were nervous at being confined. He was covering it with bluster and annoyance at being kept so late, and Gibbon was not sure if Mann was taken in.

'I think that's everything,' Mann had just said. 'No one seems to have seen anything.'

Gibbon watched Mann's hand move back to his head again. Clearly his headache was troubling him and he would have the whole of the next day with the detectives and whatever reinforcements that arrived. He felt sympathetic.

'Tell us Mr Meadows,' said Gibbon. 'Why do you think this happened? The facts tell us nothing, but you know most people in the village. If you had to guess, what would you say?'

Meadows seemed duly flattered that they should want his confidences. Mann looked hard at Gibbon, but thankfully held his peace.

'I mean, you said Luxford, the brother that is, isn't liked. Why are the Luxfords so unpopular?'

'You must know the vicar had a reputation for treating a certain one of the Commandments with not much respect.'

'What about his brother William?'

Meadows snorted. He also looked uneasy.

'Well, you said he was loathsome,' said Gibbon treacherously. 'It may have some bearing on the matter.' He noted Mann's head come up slightly. He understood what was going on.

'You don't have to quote me in front of Constable Mann,' said Meadows, flustered. He looked even redder in the face than usual, and his face was slightly shiny.

'This is no time for niceties,' said Gibbon firmly. 'Why don't people like William?'

'I hope this is all in confidence!' said Meadows. 'I'm in business in this village. I have to get on with people.'

'We know that,' said Mann. 'What is all this about William Luxford? I'm asking the questions now.'

'Nothing at all really,' said Meadows. He looked very uneasy. 'I don't like him particularly. He meddles.'

'In what way?' asked Mann. 'He runs that antique shop.'

'He got that antique shop off old Mrs Tomlinson. That should never have been turned over to antiques. It was the village store. Everyone knows that he used the vicar to work it on the District Council. It should have remained the store.'

'The vicar was on the District Council?' murmured Gibbon, asking the obvious to elicit more.

'He certainly was! And they said all sorts of things about Mrs Tomlinson and the way she kept the shop. There was a procession of Health Inspectors! That was what broke her in the end. You can't bring a place like that up to every standard! It was the sort of place where the firelighters were stacked with bread, you know how stores used to be, and she had her troubles with rats and mice so next the Vermin Officers were round. There was all sorts of talk of closing her down. Our beloved vicar of course was being so kind! He would see what he could do, all that sort of thing. He saw what he could do all right. She gives up, half dead with anxiety and brother William snaps up the shop and gets permission to change it to an antique shop. That's what makes a village die. When you get below a certain level of shopping, people go to the nearest town instead!'

'So you blame all that on the vicar really,' said Gibbon quietly. Meadows' blue eyes were round and alarmed.

'Now wait a minute! Don't you manoeuvre me into that! The village store was nothing to do with me. As a matter of fact I've had a good deal more trade since it closed.'

'And you never had any direct experience of this meddling of William Luxford's?'

'Look, I don't give the man the time of day if I can avoid it. As far as I'm concerned it was a bad day when we heard the name Luxford in this village, and that goes for both of them. That doesn't mean I shot the man. You know I couldn't have. I was in sight of everyone minding my own business, enjoying the service, so leave me alone, gentlemen!'

Meadows had risen to his feet and appeared to be very annoyed, even angry. Gibbon felt sure it was mostly an act. There was more to be uncovered than Meadows was saying, but whether or not it was relevant would be another matter.

Mann was reassuring Meadows that they hadn't meant to upset him, that of course he wasn't suspected of having anything to do with the murder. John Gibbon made a move to the door to let the man out.

'I can find my own way!' snapped Meadows. He was angry with Gibbon, at least.

'We have to ask you to take off your jacket,' said Mann, and Meadows suffered this indignity in silence. They allowed him half a minute to leave the church before waking Hazlitt.

Hazlitt had the appearance of having been woken from hibernation. He was rumpled, grumpy and there was a long pale weal down the left side of his face where his head had been in contact with the unyielding oak edge of a pew.

'On Gor, what a way to start the festive season!' he growled. 'You might as well have left me.'

'We let you sleep till last,' said Mann soothingly.

'You know perfectly well I didn't shoot the chap,' said Hazlitt. 'Why should I?'

Innocent blue eyes in a face as brown as stained wood. Very convincing. Plausible. Too plausible? Gibbon was not sure. On the face of it, Hazlitt was their most unlikely candidate.

'All right,' Mann was saying, 'You didn't shoot him, but did you see anything, or do you know why anyone else should want to shoot him?'

'You know as well as I do!' said Hazlitt summoning up a grin that expressed sheer enjoyment. 'That Luxford was fornicating his way around the entire village! They do say that farmers had to lock their heifers up at night!'

Hazlitt roared with laughter. Mann looked discomfited and Gibbon was unable to supress his own silly grin.

'That's no way to talk about a man of the cloth!' Mann asserted bravely. 'Did you see anything, that's what we want to know.'

'I saw him running his eyes over that Lucinda Walker! Mind you, you can't blame a man for that! Why do you think his wife didn't come? She doesn't come to services any more because she knows what he's up to. She can see the direction of his eyes.'

'Is that why you think someone killed him?' asked Gibbon

42

abruptly. Hazlitt looked at him sharply.

'If you want my honest answer, I don't know.'

'But you hinted that was the reason.'

'Oh no! You assumed that. I don't think that was the reason, personally like. I think there could have been other reasons. Mind you they do say that Molly Luxford had been talking about seeing the bishop about him, but that may all be tittle-tattle, and in any case she wasn't here, was she?'

'What other reasons?' demanded Mann with growing irritation. He tapped his notebook with his pen.

'Well, you'll find out soon enough. The man had a knack of making good enemies. Him and his brother. He had this thing about local history. Archaeology and that sort of thing. Him and Wilkinson for example, they was going at it hammer-and-tongs one day. I came upon them and they were having a real barney!'

'What about?' Mann was showing impatience.

'I don't know the cause of it, but they were at the roadside. Wilkinson had parked to serve Mrs Thistle and vicar drew up in his car. He was shouting about metal detectors and bloody amateurs and destroying every scientific which-thing and stuff like that. I couldn't hear it all. Not without being seen.'

Gibbon had to smile. Mann on the other hand was scowling.

'So he had had a quarrel with Wilkinson.'

'But Wilkinson wasn't here, was he? He'd be down the pub.'

'I met him in the street outside,' said John Gibbon. 'We talked briefly. I can vouch for the fact he was on his way to the pub.'

'Who else had he made enemies with?' demanded Mann. 'Never mind his sex life. What else was there?'

'Meadows wasn't too keen on him. But I can't see him doing anything about it. What's more, he didn't because I should have seen him if he did.'

'Never mind what you saw. Why didn't Meadows like him?'

'He used his position on the District Council. You must know that!'

'We've heard about that.'

'Got that shop for antiques. What's the point of antiques in a village like this? We don't need antiques, we need a decent store. I've never seen anything sold out of that shop anyway. It must be a front for something, or so they say. There can't be enough profit in it to provide a canary with millet. And Mrs Crabbe doesn't like him a good deal. I don't know why, but I dare say she has her reasons, for she's a sensible sort of soul, notwithstanding that they do say she had a little turn with the vicar.'

'Have you a single clue that isn't gossip or hearsay?' asked Mann. Gibbon wished at that point that the constable would keep his mouth shut and grasp the importance of this tittle-tattle. Gibbon vowed to keep eyes and ears open at Lucinda's drinks party. He was looking forward to it already. It had taken his mind off himself completely.

'This isn't hearsay,' said Hazlitt with spirit. 'This is fact as it is in a place like this. You should think of everything. Jeffrys don't like him either, or didn't I should say, and Jeffrys is a peculiar gentleman in some ways. What ways I'm not sure, and I won't spread rumour, but a nod ought to be as good as a wink to a blind man. You should try old Edwardes what lives next door to me! Hated Luxford's guts! But that was over the vegetable show. He always reckoned Luxford was a cheat and got his brother to go up to Covent Garden the day before and buy everything. Now I don't give that sort of nonsense any credit, but who knows? You get hot temperatures in a small oven, and it might be enough. Edwardes wasn't here neither. So what are you to make of it all?'

Mann sighed.

'I suppose we must make you show us you aren't carrying a weapon,' he said.

'Help yourself,' said Hazlitt, taking off his coat and then his jacket. Mann mechanically patted at all the pockets.

'And you're sure it was a rifle?' he asked.

'Certain,' said Hazlitt. 'Not a shadow of doubt about it.'

Chapter Three

John Gibbon had slept for five hours, then woke abruptly. The room was unnaturally light with the glare from the snow. He pulled the curtains and looked out on a magical landscape.

The sun was rising, with a slight lemon glow that touched every ripple of the static sea of drifts that stretched to a lost horizon where sky and snow merged. His bedroom looked out of the rear of the old house over flat meadows with scrubby hawthorn hedges and busy ditches, swift enough to grow watercress. Beyond, the ground began to rise to a coppice and a bluff. Rounded hills rolled above that. The contours of these were indistinguishable in the suffused glare. The sky was a pure blue, unadulterated with white; above the glittering fields of snow it was translucent, limpid aquamarine. Every tree in the ancient hedges had its hunched drift. Black crows, birds of the extreme cold and extreme whiteness, hopped and bobbed by the edge of ditches. Some circled like black scraps of rag. He would have a walk after breakfast, think about the events of the past hours, and enjoy the pleasures of sleuthing in the snow.

There would be tracks to unravel, to identify. The springing and burrowing of mouse and vole, the leaps of hare, the padding of a badger, the yellow eyelets where an animal had stopped to urinate, the flurries of fright and escape. The reddened snow of failure, the greatest of animal failures. Death.

He shaved in the low bathroom below black beams. He had to stoop while looking in the mirror. The lighting was poor. It was something he must attend to amongst many things in this ancient house. The bulb hung from one of those cords of twisted brown-fabric-covered wire, the bayonet holder was fractured bakelite. He supposed it was a fire risk. He should be attending to all those things now, but had not had the energy for it because of his loneliness and his pain. Now he had something else to think about, to give him an excuse for avoidance.

The face he looked at was tired. The eyes had bags beneath them and were red-veined. Yet he had slept soundly, and for once had not thought about Clara, Clara he had come to this place to forget. Clara the wife that was. At least the murder had driven it from his mind. He wondered how Mann was faring. By now, he imagined, the County officers would be at the church with the finger-print men. He wondered if Mann had got home at all. He also wondered if he ought to visit the church before going to the Walkers'.

He realised it was Christmas Day.

In the low-beamed sitting room he had put up and decorated a Christmas tree for himself, to remind him to be civilised. It was no use trying to avoid the seasons. He had expected no engagements. The death of this unpopular priest had had unexpected results as far as that was concerned. He had coffee and toast in front of a fan heater stuck in the vast empty fireplace that sucked the warmth from the room. Another thing he must do, have a plate made up for the flue to shut off the draught. The fire, when lit, burned well provided you could keep up with the wood supply. Yet another thing he must do – get in some logs from the coppice, hoping no one would mind if he helped himself. He would only be gathering winter fuel, how could they possibly mind that? It was a thing he had always done with Clara.

He wondered what Clara was doing now, in her house in outer suburbia. Was she up at this hour? Was she surrounded by dazzling snow? Quite probably not, as it was always so many degrees warmer in the city. It might even be raining there.

He threw away his second piece of toast uneaten, into the trap-like mouth of his new pedal bin. Everything was new. The wellingtons he

45

put on were new. They were green and fashionable and smelled strongly of rubber and he wished they were black and dirty. He thought that if he took a roundabout route he could combine a vigorous circuit of the village by footpath with a visit to the church. The sun was blazing now but without the least warmth in it. Ice crystals rustled across the hard crust of snow. A suitable penance before attending on the interesting Lucinda.

Mann had had a breakfast of sorts thanks to Gibbon. On his early morning homeward return, John had made a detour at the policeman's request to explain that he would remain on duty at the church all night. Would Mrs Mann please telephone County to find out when they would arrive, and could she please bring some aspirins to the church? Mann's wife had made a knowing face and she had thanked him in a resigned voice that revealed her feelings despite her rather emotionless face.

Now Mann had settled down to preside over the empty church until the reinforcements from Headquarters arrived from Wellsford. These turned up just after ten, as his wife had told him they would, and consisted of a detective with his fingerprint equipment, a uniformed constable who mounted guard on the door inside the porch, a dyspeptic looking Chief-Inspector called Mummery and a Detective Sergeant with the mournful expression of Buster Keaton who said his name was Frewin, and that as he had a wife, three children, a seven foot Christmas tree and a very nice twenty-one pound turkey at home waiting for him, he hoped this wasn't going to take long. Mummery, who resembled Mr Punch in features and was dressed in a black coat that was altogether too long for the current fashion, stamped his feet vigorously on the church flagstones.

'It's cold in here Constable!'

'You can say that again, sir! I've been here all night.'

Mummery ignored the appeal in this observation.

'We've seen the corpse. It was a rifle. Tell us everything you know and we'll get the detective here going on prints. I don't suppose any of us want to spend the rest of Christmas in this ice-box. Isn't there any heating?'

'It was on for the service,' said Mann. 'I suppose it's turned itself off on a timeclock. It started getting cold about two.'

'I suppose you let the verger go?'

'Yes sir.'

Mummery grunted.

'I would have hung on to the devil. That way he would have had to keep the heat on.' He sat down on a pew. 'Start from the beginning then . . .'

Mann sighed.

'From the very beginning?'

46

'From the time you were half asleep when this whole thing was happening, Constable. And the more you make a meal of it, the longer we shall all be, and the colder the turkey will get. And I don't like cold turkey, Constable. In a properly regulated village, murders wouldn't happen at weekends or on holidays and should be in May, June or September.'

Mann stared at Mummery, baffled. He believed the man was pulling his leg, hoped he was, but there was little indication of it as Mummery kept his face immobile. Frewin was equally deadpan. Mann began from the beginning.

The detective with the fingerprint kit and the uniformed constable began a systematic search of the nave of the church.

It looked like being a long business.

Gibbon's vigorous circuit was thoroughly enjoyable. He had thought it would merely be bracing as they used to put it, but the pale lemon sun had thrown aside all its delicacy and beauty and had decided to rise as a brash blaze. Iced twigs dripped. Puddles creaked. Moorhens ran about on ponds hopefully and fell and made fools of themselves. Gibbon observed it all with the pleasure of a countryman who has spent too long in the city but has now returned. He enjoyed the squeak of the snow beneath his boots, he pulled at the lower branches of drooping trees to start small snowstorms.

He thought about the events of the night. Over hedges, between houses insulated with snow he could always see the church tower. He had heard the clock strike nine as he started out. It occurred to him that there would be no Christmas Day service today. People would turn up from out-lying parts and be turned away.

Smoke rose from chimneys. He passed houses where children's voices were loud and excited, but which were still very private, intensely introspective. The day of the family, a day not to be disturbed until later. The time to open presents, to get that hearth alive with flame, even if it only happened once a year. A time to drink sherry and gin-and-tonic at nine in the morning.

He walked faster and concentrated on not thinking of Clara, of not thinking of her opening his present, but he could not suppress the images. She would be wrapped in her long dressing gown – a very average thing of powdery blue, but she looked very nice in it. She might be sitting on the edge of their bed. She might be looking at the Victorian brooch he had sent her. She had always liked moonstones, and he had spent a lot of effort in finding it. He knew it wasn't fair of him. Perhaps she would send it back, but he had to try. The thought of not sending her anything, not in any way being part of her Christmas was more than he could bear. It was blackmail of course, a crude appeal, an unworthy act, all those things that would be so easy to say. It would be there to remind her, whatever she was doing

47

today. Whoever she was seeing. Whoever might even be with her now.

He kicked at a frozen rut that hurt his foot, and swore. He was passing Lucinda Walker's shop. A sign hung out at right angles from the flint-and-brick wall. On it was painted an improbably fluffy black sheep with a self-satisfied smile. Lucinda Walker's joke. He wondered how she really got on in this small community. Being as dazzlingly beautiful might help with prejudiced males, but what about prejudiced females?

He looked in the window at expensive gowns draped over an improbable spinning wheel. The gowns were both silk. He smiled slightly. Another joke? He would have to ask her. Balls of wool were arranged in a huge rack of wooden pigeon-holes to one side. Lucinda had used white, green and red wool, so that she had created a holly leaf with two red berries. It was effective.

Bringing his mind reluctantly to the subject, he wondered who had shot Luxford.

It seemed unreal on such a morning that someone had with malice gunned him down in his own church, and someone amongst those ordinary people he had talked to last night. Who did he think it might be? The answer was that he had no idea. Luxford was clearly disliked, and sexual jealousy or fear of revelation seemed the most likely of motives. Perhaps a man was simply removing the nuisance? Perhaps it was a woman's work. There was no real reason to assume it had to be a man because he had been shot with a rifle.

Then there was the basic problem of the rifle. Where was it hidden? As he and Mann had agreed last night, it still had to be in the church somewhere. But that was only part of the problem. How had someone managed to aim and fire it while still remaining concealed? Admittedly everyone had been facing front, with their eyes either piously on their hymn books or lifted to the ceiling. There was that aspect of it that was clever. In such circumstances and at such a time no one would be looking behind them. He supposed the shot had to come from the very back of the church. Mann must have already thought that out. Perhaps they had already solved the thing, had even made an arrest while he slept.

He walked on past the newsagents, noticing properly for the first time that it said 'Fry's: Newsagent and Confectioner', and associating it with Cynthia Fry and George. At least he had met everyone now.

He passed 'The Feathers' with its cleared pavement, wet now with the slight thaw. At the limit of the stretch of exposed stones the snow was squelchy and pink with rock salt. The Christmas tree still winked in the upper window and the fairy lights were still on. There was the noise of beer crates being manhandled at the rear somewhere, and good smells of cooking. He crossed the icy street to the war memorial

48

and the municipal benches. Someone had switched off this tree, because it was municipal. He walked towards the lich-gate of the church beneath the towering walls of the graveyard. They were glazed with icicles and frozen weeping. The sun would never find its way here until May. He opened the gate and crunched towards the church door, aware how many sets of feet had now disturbed last night's unbroken snow. Feet led around the building in both directions. Police, he assumed.

Arriving at the eroded door he paused, feeling he no longer had any of the authority of the previous evening. He raised the heavy iron ring that served as knocker as well as latch turn and thumped it heartily. He found himself face-to-face with a man who looked like a hook-nosed undertaker with a heart condition and permanent drip on the end of the nose. Mummery.

'Good morning,' said Mummery dolefully, blinking out at the sunlight as though strictly nocturnal. 'What can I do for you?'

Past the man Gibbon could see the uniformed constable and another man peering under the pews.

'My name's Gibbon. I was here last night and assisted Constable Mann. Is he here still? I thought you might want a word with me. Also, quite frankly I thought I would call in to see if you had found anything.'

'Is that so sir?' said Mummery. His tone implied that this unhealthy interest automatically and without hesitation transferred him to the top of his list of suspects. Mann appeared to his rescue behind Mummery.

'This is Mr Gibbon that I told you about sir,' he said. 'I thought it would be good procedure to have another witness to my interviews in case it should be necessary. Mr Gibbon was good enough to do so.'

Mummery grunted and wiped at the drip on his nose with the back of his coat sleeve.

'Then I suppose you had better come in,' he said and backed into the gloom of the church interior. Gibbon was pleased to see that Mann had a slight smile on his face. He also looked very tired. 'We don't often approve of members of the public becoming involved in police procedures,' said Mummery. 'I'm sure you understand that. However, as you seem to have got involved from the beginning, I think we can stretch a point. Constable Mann had little choice.'

'Thank you,' said Gibbon politely. He had a strong desire to tell Mummery what he could do with his point once he had stretched it, but a look at Mann's earnest and relieved face made him hold his peace. He contented himself with staring pointedly at Mummery's wet coat sleeve. Mummery noticed, and his hectic complexion darkened ominously, becoming brick red.

'We're searching the church,' he announced loudly. 'Haven't found anything yet.'

'You haven't found the gun then?' asked Gibbon, more to be polite than anything. He immediately wished he hadn't as Mummery was now glaring at him. An unendearing man.

'No, we haven't found the gun,' he said with heavy irony. 'You will probably have noticed that this church, in common with many of its kind is full of nooks and crannies, not to mention floor grilles full of heating pipes, pews, draperies, tombs, ledges, screens, curly stonework, columns with bunches of foliage bursting out of the top of them like palm trees and altars like a timber yard!'

'Altar,' murmured Mann. He was promptly smitten by a glare that should have evaporated him.

'Now what I would like to know from you, Mr Gibbon,' Mummery continued, his flow unabated, 'is what was going on as you approached the church? As you seem to be the only masochist in this place who made the rounds, since our Constable here was sleeping off his alcohol intake, we'd better go through it with you for my benefit!'

It was Mann's turn to colour. Gibbon was uncharitably amused at his discomfiture and could not control a slight grin.

'There was nothing going on,' he said. 'I had jogged up the High Street and was coming down Church Row past the Post Office when I heard the shot. I ran round the war memorial, past the Christmas tree and up to the lich-gate. I know it was midnight because the clock was striking. When I got to the gate, I had a very good look round and saw the snow was completely untrodden. It was the first thing that occurred to me, I don't know why. I thought immediately it was important. There wasn't a trace of footsteps to or from the church, nor did I see any going round the church. Then I walked carefully up to the church door and the man Jeffrys opened it as I arrived.'

Mummery grunted.

'I don't like it at all. All this unbroken snow and lack of footsteps. It's all too contrived. Someone wants us to think it must have been done by a member of that congregation. I smell a set-up.'

'It had been snowing and it still was,' said Gibbon. 'It wouldn't have taken long for footsteps to be obliterated. Perhaps half an hour.'

'You mean someone could have come and gone who was not part of the congregation. Outside.'

'They could have. On the other hand, how could anyone have shot the man from outside? Where from?'

'That is precisely the difficulty,' said Mummery. 'The place is hardly overlooked except by one of those yews. You don't suppose he was lurking up there all the time? Dark things, those trees. They would give plenty of cover. A man could sit up there all night and come down in the morning. Unfortunately this didn't occur to our Constable!'

'If he had done that, there would be a hole through a window! Sir!' said Mann hotly. 'And there wasn't.'

'And just as well too!' growled Mummery, not to be put off by facts. 'We shall never know now anyway, what with all the feet that have tramped round since. A good cover, I would say. Our murderer makes it seem like a certain inside job so all the clues are cheerfully trampled outside! If we had thought for a moment that he had been shot from outside we would have put a cordon around the whole area, like we learned at Training College, wouldn't we Constable! But we didn't because Mr Gibbon here saw no footsteps so it had to be someone inside the church. Nice one!'

'But you said yourself there are no holes in any of the windows!' said Gibbon with rising annoyance. This Mr Punch was beginning to get under his skin.

'Then perhaps a window was open. I still don't believe this was an inside job. It narrows it all down too beautifully. How many people were here?'

'Twenty-three, sir,' Mann supplied. It sounded as though the words were being extracted from him under torture.

'Good,' said Mummery as though rewarding a dog. 'And what do we find out about them?'

'We find that none of them liked Luxford,' said Gibbon, more to spare Mann than anything else. He did not like Mummery's insulting manner at all. It reminded him of the insolence of a particular traffic policeman who had leaned on his window ledge after a speeding offence. He told himself he would not give him the satisfaction of being provoked.

'Didn't it surprise you that no one seems to have been surprised?' Mummery asked this question without any sarcasm. Gibbon had to acknowledge the point.

'Leaving aside all the details of who hates who in this place, and why, and God knows we shall have enough of those in due course – let's look at the broad strokes of the thing. No one shows any particular surprise after the initial shock. No one seems to think there is a maniac loose, no one asks for police protection. It's almost as if everyone expected it. That's the first point.

'Secondly, the whole thing has been done very skilfully. This isn't some impulse. We can't find the gun, no one saw who pulled the trigger. It's obviously premeditated and more than that it has been thoroughly planned.

'Thirdly, this must have been done here and at this time for a reason. If you want to shoot a rural vicar, you can do it any time and you can go out and choose your place. There's no need to take a chance. You can stalk him and wait for him in a quiet spinney, a country lane, that sort of thing. Particularly if you have a rifle and a little forethought. It should be as easy as shooting at a turnip. But here we have someone who clearly did it with forethought but who chose the most public place he could think of. Why choose the church on Christmas Eve?' he asked turning to Mann, who had, despite his annoyance been drawn in by this speculation.

'I suppose we have to assume he chose it simply because it would be crowded, sir,' said Mann.

'That's what I think,' said Mummery. 'But was it to show off, or was it to confuse? Is the man – or woman – an exhibitionist, an actor who enjoys committing the crime in such a classic setting? Or is the murderer a clever, rational person who has deliberately given us a church-full of suspects? It's all the stuff that Sunday newspapers are made of! Snow, midnight, no footsteps, the closed cell. Now that could be entirely accidental and unthinking. Or it could be someone who is playing games.'

Mann and Gibbon gave this consideration. It had not occurred to Gibbon that the whole affair might be contrived, but the more he thought about it, the more he was inclined to agree. The ingredients sounded unlikely when re-told by Mummery.

'I think your reasoning's sound,' he said. 'It wasn't done on the spur of a moment and I think it was done this way to confuse – by someone who got pleasure from the scenario. All of which puts a different light on the murderer. If there are different categories, I suppose that would make it a four or five star murder for callousness?'

'It's not all that callous, Mr Gibbon, compared with things I've seen, but it gets a high rating for theatrical effect. Stand back from it all, and what do you see? "Lustful vicar gunned down in his own church. Murder on Christmas Eve." Lessons and carols, only someone taught him his last lesson.'

Mummery paused. A wintry smile passed across his doleful face. Gibbon realised the man was truly enjoying himself.

'That's what we're supposed to see. And I never believe what I'm supposed to see when it's a trick!'

For all the equal theatricality of these trite utterances, Gibbon had to concede to himself that there was a lot of truth in what Mummery said. Those caught up in violent death became too absorbed by it to see the obvious, and that was where Mummery was necessary.

'Then if we expand on the reasons for doing this in the church, what do we come up with? Not only is it great theatre, but there will be a good collection of people present. Church-going people, worthy sort of people, not the ones in the pub who are all getting bottled. People who are withdrawn, in all probability, more private in themselves. People who will make our job of questioning difficult. If you go and shoot the man in a lane somewhere and we come in in force, you can be sure that at least eighty per cent of the population can account for themselves and be eliminated. The curiously successful thing about this is that everyone has an alibi because they were all watching each other in a casual sort of way, which means they are all suspects and the alibi is worthless. Everyone is implicated. I like it!'

'But going back to your first point, that no one seemed to be frightened by the killing in the sense that they feel that Luxford was a particular target and that there isn't a maniac at large, aren't you assuming that the reason for this murder must be in Luxford's sexual escapades?' asked Gibbon.

'That's what we're supposed to see. It may be the reality, or it may be the shadow. I feel very open-minded about it.'

'But where *is* the weapon, sir?' asked Mann. 'No one took a rifle out of here last night, and I believe the shot was fired from inside.'

'We shall find the weapon, Mann. To be fair to you, I don't think the thing left the church either. It will be well hidden. Everything so far has been done with intelligence and care. Our murderer is a planner. He creates confusion carefully!'

Gibbon looked at Mummery thoughtfully. The relish on the other man's face was rather disgusting. Gibbon recognised this was no time or place to be overly sensitive, and he supposed men like Mummery had to be hunters.

'We shall have to find out all about Luxford's sex life, Constable. Luxford as Lothario. Then we shall very possibly find it is all a red herring, but we have to know. Do we nominate you?'

Mann blushed, and wiped a hank of fair hair from his forehead.

'I don't know if they'll talk to me sir, being part of the village almost.'

'That should make you best placed. Perhaps we should co-opt Mr Gibbon here. Ask for his informal help again. I gather you were rather a hit with the ladies last night!'

Mummery's sarcastic tone was intended to enrage. Gibbon looked at him with studied calm.

'If this is your oblique way of asking for my help, I think you could put it more tactfully,' said Gibbon, affecting a mildly offended manner he did not feel. Mummery quickly responded.

'I have often been told I'm a tactless devil, Mr Gibbon, but I've always taken it as a compliment. Take it as a compliment from me please, that I would be very pleased if you would help us by telling us anything you discover. Purely as an informal arrangement of course.'

Gibbon nodded. He felt rather flattered. The feeling must have been detected by Mummery for he dashed it with his next words.

'It is of course because you're a newcomer here. You can justifiably ask questions that would seem suspicious in anyone else. New resident, eager to know the social form, eager to know who's who. And it will certainly help if, as I hear, the ladies like you because the ladies are going to be very important in all this. But all this will have to be a very informal arrangement. A little assistance from a member of the public! I know you're the man for it!'

Gibbon was spared any more of Mummery's clubbing compliments by the plain clothes policeman, Frewin.

'Excuse me sir,' the man called from a position towards the rear of the church, just in from the aisle, 'We've found a couple of things here.'

'Good.'

Mummery strode towards the plainclothes man with masterful determination that was spoiled by tripping over a hassock. Gibbon saw Mann grin and then erase it.

'Damned thing!' Mummery exclaimed, scowling round at the two men, daring them to laugh. He kicked the hassock. Gibbon calculated between the desire to ridicule this Mr Punch and the desire to become further involved in the exercise of unfolding a mystery. He had nothing else to do. It would occupy his mind, take up his time, give him a healthy interest – all the things a doctor would say were really better for him than his self-imposed discipline of jogging, which was more a punishment. He held his peace, kept a straight face.

'Careful . . . ' he murmured neutrally. Mummery for just a moment looked grateful.

The five men in the church converged as best they could within the constraints of the pews. The plainclothes man pointed. On the long wooden seats were thin cushions, not padded enough for comfort but just sufficient to prevent bruising of the buttocks. Each cushion was half the length of the pew and was covered with a nondescript material resembling bad tapestry, with a motif of ugly, rigid flowers in maroon and puce. Behind the cushion, just visible, was the slight shine of black leather, soft leather with large stitches. Mummery exercised his rights as senior man, pushed past the others in the awkward width of the pew and bent down.

'Looks like a pair of gloves to me,' he said. 'I'll take them out.'

The plainclothes man handed him a polythene bag which he had been holding ready. Mummery lifted the cushion. Beneath it was a pair of gloves as he had guessed. There was also an envelope that had been completely hidden under the cushion.

'Who's been leaving things behind then?' Mummery said, bending towards the envelope, not touching it yet. It lay about two feet from the gloves. Mummery let down the long cushion so that it rested on its side for a moment, then bent and flopped under the pew.

'It's addressed to the Reverend P. Luxford, gentlemen! A clue, no less! I would call that a clue, wouldn't you?'

Mummery grinned at his men, at Gibbon. His teeth were yellowed, like old bone dominoes, thought Gibbon. Mummery seemed elated, amused. He hummed tunelessly a few bars from 'The Sound of Music' and took a handkerchief from his trouser pocket with which he picked up each of the gloves carefully. He put them in the polythene bag.

'Hand size unhelpful. A small to medium man's hand, or a large woman's hand. We shall see.'

He handed the bag back to the detective.

'Now this is what we are all expected to want to see!'

He picked up the envelope by a corner, using the handkerchief again.

'Well now, there seems to be a letter in it. Who has been writing to the Reverend P. Luxford, I wonder, and leaving the letter in the church?'

With the greatest care he changed his grip on the envelope and took a pinch of handkerchief in his right hand so that he could just grasp the letter inside the envelope.

'Sergeant . . .'

The detective proffered another polythene bag. Mummery put both hands inside it, let go of the envelope with his left, grasping it again from outside the bag. He gently extracted the letter.

'It's signed Fry. Cynthia Fry. Does that mean anything?'

Chapter Four

The White House looked more cream than white in the whiter-than-white dazzle of the bright noon-day snow. Three dark hollies stood in a snow-laden hedge between the house and the road, then there was a wide stretch of grass intersected by a drive. Ornamental rose beds had been obliterated by small drifts, and a bird bath and a sundial in some reconstituted material stuck up like yellowed teeth. Gibbon made a face at them. Cheap and nasty, or at least nasty. Imported from some London garden centre by Lucinda, he assumed, then corrected himself. She had more taste than that. They must have come with the house.

The house was two-storeyed, a central block with identical short wings, and genuine late Georgian, complete with round-headed windows, a stuccoed front and brick rear. It would have looked more at place on the sea front than in this village setting. In the snow, the ripples and blemishes in the render beneath the paint were all apparent. Smoke rose from a chimney just visible in the slate roof above the long parapet. The cold and the lack of wind sent the smoke outwards and downwards until it hung like mist over the front garden. Gibbon appreciated the sweet tang of wood-smoke.

There were so many cars on the drive that they had been obliged to double park. Gibbon picked his way around them, thinking he was probably the only person there who had come on foot. He passed a tall window with thin glazing bars and had a view into the living room. An impression of people, candles lit, firelight and talk. The front door was open, so he walked into a small marble floored hall and hesitated. Everything about the house was a curious mixture of the trappings of good living and the blemishes of poor maintenance. The paintwork of doors and architraves was bruised and chipped, the joints of the marble floor were scoured and black, yet the rug on which he stood was Persian and excellent. Two niches on each side of him contained urns of good porcelain, but in each was a dying houseplant. The chandelier overhead was magnificent, but lacked one bulb and a barley-sugar was broken. Signs of what? Of lack of care or lack of money? Gibbon was an admirer of tattered style and would have been the first to appreciate any brave attempt to make-do in this fine old house, but there was something here that he felt to be pretence, not making-do. Lucinda had not struck him as lacking in vitality or invention. The house seemed to lack both love and money.

As if to prove him entirely wrong, Lucinda swept out from the living room in a cocktail dress of ivory silk that stunned him. She took his outheld hand, but rather than shake it, held it in both of hers.

'It was nice of you to come. Let me take your coat. I can feel you're cold.'

She released his hand and held her hands out to him, waiting. Gibbon felt unduly flustered. The ivory silk dress had a bodice on which seed pearls had been stitched in a deep filigree of white silk thread. Her skin was beautiful and she was a full-breasted woman. He felt he ought to avert his eyes, then thought 'Why should I?' and was ashamed to be behaving like a schoolboy. He struggled with his coat.

'It's heavy,' he said, folding it over his arm, not giving it to her.

'I'm strong,' Lucinda said, flashing a smile at him. She opened a door that revealed a small cloakroom under the stairs. She hung his coat on a peg while Gibbon took in the ivory silk shoes and the smooth darkness of her back and shoulders.

'Happy Christmas!' she said.

'Happy Christmas!'

'You can kiss me.'

Gibbon stared at her. Lucinda laughed.

'I knew you were shy the moment I saw you!' she said. 'You should see your face!' She pointed above herself. 'I'm under the mistletoe. Old English custom. You know! Just a peck on the cheek, surely, as we're new neighbours!'

Gibbon noticed the slyly placed branch. He bent forward and pecked her on the cheek. She smelled nicely of perfume. I must think of Mummery and do my duty, he thought, as Victorian English ladies were to think of England and do theirs!

'You're making fun of me. And before I've had a drink.'

'That is easily rectified, John Gibbon!'

She knows my Christian name as well, he thought.

'I think you'll know most of the people here, but before I take you in, tell me what you found?'

He pretended not to understand.

'Everyone knows you went back to the church this morning. You were seen! You have been spied upon, your every movement has been observed!'

'I suppose there's no use in telling you I was sworn to secrecy?'

'None at all.'

'Then I'll tell you the truth. We found nothing. No weapon has been discovered.'

He delivered the half truth with such conviction that Lucinda accepted it.

'Are they still looking?'

'They were when I left.'

'And do they still think it was someone in the church?'

'Should I tell you what they think?'

He had not meant to sound coy, but knew as soon as he said it that it did. Lucinda moved closer to him.

'Of course,' she said. 'We shall have no secrets from each other and I shall stand very close to you like this all morning and talk to you intensely and people will whisper and think all sorts of things! My husband, crazed with jealousy will retrieve his rifle from the font and you will die by the same gun that struck down Luxford!'

'I think they searched the font,' he reproved her. Lucinda laughed nicely. She had obviously been drinking – they all had – but he decided she was living on her nerves as well. The teasing was a form of obvious probing. Was the mention of her husband defensive? How much did he care for her?

'In any case, as a confidant of the police, I'm sure I should be taking a much more censorious attitude about all this. I should be telling you that this is far too serious a matter to joke about. I'm sure Mummery would approve of that.'

'Please don't say that. I think you're far too intelligent to be stupid, if you can forgive me for putting it so badly.'

Gibbon was embarrassed. Lucinda was serious now.

'In this place, brains are hardly at a premium,' she continued. 'Some of them are very *well-meaning*. In fact they are so well-meaning they crush you with it. Like being loved to death by a dinosaur or King Kong. The only proof they have of feelings is when all life has been extinguished and they feel guilt. Like shaking a broken toy. I'm going on too much! It's such a relief to talk to someone from outside that I'm starting to babble!'

'Not at all, not at all. I know what you mean . . .'

She really is dying here, thought Gibbon. How does she amuse herself, and what keeps her here? His mind raced ahead. How would he sustain this level of interest for all of them, what was he letting himself in for? He must not become involved in this way. He was playing the detective, and that had *not* been Mummery's intention. With Lucinda, he felt, it would be all too easy to become involved.

Why not? urged another part of his mind. You're human. You need love too. You feel sorry for yourself.

'And is this Mummery going to solve the crime?' asked Lucinda, obviously trying to bring the conversation back to less charged matters. Gibbon was relieved at her initiative.

'I think so. Eventually. He is the kind who will never give up.'

Lucinda nodded.

'Come on then, I'll introduce you to all the Well-Meanings. They'll cross examine you too. They're all waiting for you. I just hope it doesn't become too much.'

She detained him just at the doorway by laying her hand lightly on the back of his, for just a moment. It was a tender gesture. She liked to touch.

'Who do you think shot Luxford?'

'In all honesty I haven't a clue. Then I hardly know anyone. Let me ask you instead?'

'I don't know. It wasn't me, that's what I know.'

She moved away in front of him, leaving him no wiser. She steered him to the Frys.

'What would you like to drink?' she asked.

'Gin and tonic.'

She left him, with a quick smile. George Fry nodded to him, much as though they were passing in the street. As a greeting, it certainly lacked warmth. Cynthia smiled at him nervously, meeting his eyes then sliding away. She had been more restrained with her make-up, perhaps in deference to Luxford's death. She had used a dark blue around her eyes, and a dark, almost brown lipstick. Her blonde hair was still worn fluffed up as Gibbon had seen her last night. He wondered about the make-up and visualised her with her hair more natural, her skin unpainted and decided that Cynthia Fry was an attractive woman who hid behind these artificial dyes. George looked and behaved like a monster. He smelled beery again, or maybe he always smelled beery.

'I hope you're having a nice Christmas Day,' he said vacuously. George's eyes swivelled to him like gun barrels.

'Fat chance! Damned tired this morning, we were, I can tell you.'

He drank copiously from a pint mug of beer. 'What a damned nuisance the whole thing is. I gather you've spent the morning in the church as well. Have they found anything out?'

'No, I'm afraid not.'

'I suppose even policemen celebrate Christmas? Mind you, they'll be on double time, so I don't suppose they'll care!'

What a basic bastard, Gibbon thought. He had never liked the type of man – ignorant, wily and opinionated, relying on bombast and apparently succeeding.

'It's very cold in that church,' he said diplomatically. 'I wouldn't want to spend *my* Christmas Day in it searching it inch by inch.'

'Is that what they're doing?'

George's question was sharp and probing and very alert. Gibbon tested the act of telling himself he didn't loathe the man, then gave up, deciding he might as well enjoy a good hate. Clara had always accused him of being too diffident, of hesitancy in relationships, of marshmallow emotions, of a librarian pedestrian mind that filed and categorized but never judged. He wished he could tell Clara he loathed George Fry. There were many things he wished he could tell Clara.

'That's what they're doing.' He stared coldly at George. George was unabashed.

'You gave up the search and decided to have a drink, eh?'

'I'm nothing to do with the search.'

'I thought you'd been co-opted as a policeman. After last night.'

'Come on George!' protested Cynthia, 'Mr Gibbon was only helping out because he was asked to!'

Over Fry's head, Gibbon could see familiar faces. It appeared that social life was as restricted as Lucinda had said. The congregation of last night had been redressed and transplanted *en masse*, with only a few additions. Philippa Crabbe caught his eye and inclined her head slightly. She was talking to Meadows, who turned, seeing her movement, and gave Gibbon a cool look. He was glad when Lucinda appeared with his drink.

'Come on George,' she said, threading her arm through his with a wicked expression, 'Come and meet a friend of Mr Jeffrys. He seems to be a bit of a country man. We can't have husband and wife sticking together . . .'

It looked to Gibbon as though George tried to withdraw his arm, but Lucinda appeared to exert considerable torsion, and George was propelled forwards.

Cynthia turned to Gibbon with an amused expression.

59

'You have to forgive George. He was rather rude about the help you gave last night. I think Lucinda is about to give him what he deserves!'

'The friend of Jeffrys?'

'George hates Jeffrys at the best of times. You can imagine why. Harold is a bit, you know, and has his men friends down to stay from time to time. It's very naughty of Lucinda to take him off like that, but he does deserve it. Happy Christmas!'

They sipped their drinks. The room was crowded and warm. A log fire burned in a fine fireplace of carved white marble that looked genuine. The carpet they were trampling underfoot seemed to be silk. The decorations had to be Lucinda's. Twisted streamers of alternate apple green and silver spread out to form an impressive canopy from the ceiling rose of a central chandelier. Everything else followed this theme. A Christmas tree stood in one corner, decorated severely with only silver witch balls. Silver candlesticks held laurel-green candles. He understood why Lucinda was wearing an ivory dress with pearls. It was as near natural silver as her own taste would permit her to dress without becoming vulgar. Yet there was still the same problem with the room that he had observed in the hall. Old paper had been painted over, and the woodwork had been badly top-coated. By Lucinda? There was an element of window-dressing about it all, a feeling of paste and cardboard and tissue-paper.

He wondered if Lucinda had had any motive in taking him straight to Cynthia Fry.

'Can I ask you something,' Cynthia said earnestly, as though sensitive to his thoughts. His heart sank. 'I want to know what Lucinda said about me to you and to the police. She had the advantage of seeing you both after me, and knowing her, she'd use it! I know it may seem awful to you while I stand here and drink her drink, but she doesn't like me, and I don't much like her either. I have to stop rumours spreading, believe me. George is a jealous man. Can I trust you?'

Gibbon nodded. Cynthia drew him slightly to the side so that they stood together by the fireplace. She rested her elbow on the mantel so that they could talk close to each other and not be overheard.

'You're going to hear a lot about Peter Luxford and a lot about me and Lucinda Walker and others, so I may as well set the record straight. Rumour is like a woodpecker, making the whole woods ring. George knows nothing about this, so you must be sworn to secrecy, and that includes Constable Mann. Do you agree?'

'I agree,' said Gibbon traitorously. He crossed the fingers of one hand behind his back like a schoolboy, trying not to take this too seriously.

'Luxford and I, we had an affair. A real one, I mean, sex and everything.'

She looked intently at Gibbon, to see if he was shocked.

'I had guessed that,' he said solemnly. He was watching the person beyond the applied paint, the actor behind the act. She was no fool and no innocent.

'Well, thank God you're normal!' she said with a slight nervous smile. 'It's such a change to talk to people who don't shy like horses in fright at the very word. I haven't shared a bed with George for ten years. Would you? Look at him! He's revolting and a drunk, and those are only a few of his qualifications. When I married him, I thought he was sociable. That was the word I taught myself. Now for sociable read bar-fly.'

She drained her glass. Gibbon took it from her.

'What was that?'

'I have no idea. When you're married to George, you don't care, you're just grateful for the alcohol!'

My, my, Cynthia Fry! thought John Gibbon. He decided he liked her. More than that, he was attracted to her, and not just by her candour. He was also surprised at himself. Perhaps it was all this fitness, abstinence and jogging that was bad for his hormones, or rather, good for them. He went over to a lacquered dresser and poured her a gin and martini. She nodded when he told her what it was and said it would do.

'Why do you wear your hair like that?' he asked, trying shock tactics. She looked him straight in the eyes, pinioned him with their candour.

'To deceive George. He could never imagine that a woman with hair like this is capable of two consecutive thoughts or any other rational processes. I've tried hard to develop body armour. It's as good as a corset.'

Gibbon smiled encouragingly. He found it easy. Mummery had shown him only the first lines of the letter before declaring with satisfaction that it was evidence and therefore confidential.

'My dearest Peter,' it had begun, 'I have to write to you if I can't see you, although I know it's not discreet . . .'

Mummery had put the plastic bag and envelope in his inside pocket. To read later, he said, when it had been tested for fingerprints.

'It's the middle-class respectable ones you have to keep an eye on,' he had said with a leer.

'Do you like the village?' Cynthia was asking, bringing Gibbon back to the present.

'So far,' he replied, 'although I haven't had a long time to find out.'

'And are you a fitness fanatic, like they are saying? We've never had anyone who went jogging round here, let alone jogging in the snow. There's probably more obesity and ill-health in the countryside than there is in any town. So much for all the healthy outdoor life! If anyone round here prunes a fruit tree or digs a row of potatoes we all hear about it for weeks, and all about the back-aches and muscle strains and Lord knows what. I hope I'm not putting you off us?'

Gibbon smiled broadly, thinking how long it was since he had done so.

'Well, no one seems undernourished, and as for being a fitness fanatic, I'm not. I run to relax. I find it clears my mind of all the normal rubbish, and I think about the countryside, and how my legs are hurting and how my lungs feel as though they're on fire, and how beautiful the snow is when it becomes lemon-coloured in the sunlight. It's a very introverted occupation!'

'That all sounds a reasonable excuse! After all, no animals go out and exhaust themselves voluntarily.'

Cynthia had almost drained her glass again. It was time to get back to the subject that was uppermost in his mind.

'Tell me, what was Luxford like as a person? It's a very bizarre thing to happen, and it must be connected in some way to the nature of the man, and the way people reacted to him.'

Cynthia did not look at him. She stood her glass on the mantel.

'I don't think I really want to talk about him at a Christmas party.'

'I'm sorry, I've been tactless. But did he play golf or anything, or was he a weekend painter, a bridge player? Remember I'm new here and know absolutely nothing.'

'You're fishing. You know perfectly well that women were his chief hobby, and you'll hear plenty more about that. But as a matter of fact he was a very keen archaeologist. Amateur, but to the point of almost being considered professional, if there is such a thing. He wrote papers for journals, and I gather he was well thought of. In archaeological circles, anyway. He knew more about the district than anyone, although Wilkinson would have disputed that. Wilkinson would dispute anything.'

'Wilkinson the butcher?' John Gibbon had noticed him on the other side of the room and indicated him with a slight, warning nod of his head. Cynthia obviously knew he was there because she did not bother to look.

'That's him. It's an open secret that Wilkinson and Peter hated each other like poison.'

Peter, thought Gibbon. Does she still love him? Is it a term of endearment, or purely acquaintance? Shouldn't she be saying 'the vicar'?

'Why?'

'Rivals in the same field. Wilkinson is a menace.'

'Archaeology?' Gibbon deliberately sounded incredulous. Cynthia coloured violently, sensing innuendo of a sort that Gibbon

62

had not intended.

'Yes, archaeology! Don't take advantage of me, when I'm being honest with you. What the devil do you take me for!'

Her eyes blazed with sudden fury. It was a startling and revealing transformation.

'I'm very sorry! Please believe me, I was just surprised at a man like Wilkinson having an interest in a subject that attracts scholars. Nothing else!'

She was mollified, and indeed looked slightly ashamed of her flare up.

'Then you can get me another drink and we'll be friends again. I'm sure Lucinda can't afford it!'

An interesting aside. He wondered just how much they disliked each other, and whether it was only because of their own rivalry for Luxford.

'They don't seem particularly hard-up,' he probed. He indicated the decorations, silver candlesticks, the room in general. Cynthia made a disapproving face at him.

'You aren't an unobservant man. It's all a bit shoe-string. There's no depth to it. She was only bought that shop by Henry as a toy to keep her quiet. It loses money hand over fist. It has to. I don't think business is too good for Henry at the moment. The place is just running down. You've only really seen it in the snow, and the snow is as good as a coat of camouflage. The roof has slates slipped, the path's full of weeds, the conservatory out the back is all green mould and rot. It's Lucinda's training at window dressing. Make a little look a lot!'

Gibbon realised that Cynthia would be quite happy to keep him to herself for an hour or so. He took her glass from her, which she relinquished cheerfully, and got her another drink.

'I must circulate,' he said. It was a statement she immediately picked up.

'Is that your duty, or am I boring you?'

'In what way my duty?'

'Socially and for the police?'

'Perhaps,' he said, trying to make light of it. 'I've always wanted to be a super-sleuth.' She made a face.

'And I thought I had you all to myself! When you've done your rounds with all our good citizens, why don't you come back and have Christmas dinner with me? Us, I mean of course. There *is* George.' She laughed cheerfully. 'But of course after his first two bottles of wine George doesn't *exist*!'

Gibbon had an immediate and lurid vision of an unusual and interesting Christmas dinner, but had no taste for the involvement she obviously intended to follow.

'That's a delightful idea,' he declared, 'but I can't accept.'

63

'Can't or won't?'

'Can't of course. I have everything cooked already, and to tell you the truth I'm looking forward to having my Christmas dinner on my own. I'm a good cook so don't worry about me.'

'Oh dear. So naughty me can't even slip round and help you in the kitchen!'

'No!'

An interesting woman, Cynthia Fry.

In the hour that followed he managed to talk to almost everyone. The Harrises were there and Meadows, Hazlitt and Jeffrys. He met others as well whom he knew only as faces in the street from the short period of his stay in the village. They had as much curiosity about him and what had transpired in the church, as he had about them, but he was beginning to find his interest flagging. He shook off plump Mrs Hodge politely by simply getting another drink and not returning to her. Wilkinson was his aim. The fact that the man had not been in the church might make him irrelevant to the Luxford killing but Gibbon was intrigued by the tale of their shared interest and mutual antipathy. Twice he had also passed a fleeting word with Philippa Crabbe, who seemed determined to catch his eye. He would save a conversation with that delightful woman for later. He would also save Hazlitt, the Harrises and Jeffrys. Between that five anything that went unnoticed must be very small stuff indeed.

He nodded to Wilkinson, his full glass in his hand. Wilkinson returned the greeting.

'You've got yourself well mixed up in it all,' Wilkinson observed. He was clutching an enormous whisky in a cut crystal tumbler and looked very prosperous in tailored fawn and brown houndstooth slacks and matching chamois-coloured cashmere sweater. Gibbon noticed that his tan shoes had the unmistakeable stitching and glow of the hand-made object. Turkey sales for Christmas must have been good.

'I told you you should have come to the "Feathers". A few steps in the right direction and this would have been nothing to do with you at all and you could have spent Christmas in peace.'

He swigged from his glass.

'However, rumour has it that you fancy yourself as an amateur sleuth.'

He waited for confirmation or denial. Gibbon just smiled.

'What have they found in the church? They must have found the weapon by now. If it's there.'

'They hadn't found anything when I left.'

'Ha! Not as efficient as they think they are! Not unless someone walked away with it after all.'

'I don't think that was possible. I was there all the time and I don't see how anyone could have left with a weapon.'

'So it was an inside job, as they say? That narrows the field down!'

Or broadens it out. Gibbon wondered if Wilkinson was teasing him. There was a bantering tone in his voice, an amused attitude in the way he looked. The man looked fit despite his size and ruddy complexion and despite the boozy night he had apparently enjoyed at the 'Feathers'.

'It had to be someone in the church, didn't it?' pursued Wilkinson. 'The hush surrounding that conclusion is one of the loudest silences I've heard in a long time. After all the place was full of such respectable people. Has to be one of them!'

'I suppose so. It appears that no one liked Luxford very much. I don't think I've heard a good word said for him.'

'What do you want me to say to that?'

Wilkinson's rather florid face showed signs of truculence. Looking at him carefully Gibbon took in the man's large, heavy build, well camouflaged in his soft clothing. If he had to sum him up, he looked more like an ageing professional golfer who still kept his hand in and could go a good two rounds. A man who got out and about a lot. He was on the road for a large part of the day in his van, of course, and maybe his hobby had a lot to do with it. A man of hidden depths, Gibbon decided, and no fool.

'All right,' he said, 'I suppose I *am* probing. I've been told of course that you and Luxford didn't see eye-to-eye, to put it mildly.'

'I would be surprised if you hadn't. But as you have already observed, I'm not the only one. As a matter of fact I couldn't stand the man. He was an interfering, meddling nuisance.'

'In your mutual interest?'

Wilkinson snorted.

'I had nothing mutual with that man. As for an interest, he was a dabbler!'

'So amateur archaeology doesn't bring people together!'

'When two people are involved in the same thing in a small place like this, there just isn't room. Add to that the fact that Luxford never had any interest in the subject in my opinion until he heard about me. He was a vandal, a leech. He followed me around, you know, trying to find out what I was doing, then had the bloody neck to write it up and send if off to all the fancy journals. A bloody menace! He knew nothing, nothing at all. That's what made him so confident. There's no greater boost to self-esteem than pig-ignorance!'

Wilkinson's face was hard and angry. Gibbon watched him recover his composure with a deliberate effort and sip his whisky.

'You see, you've got me going,' he said with an awful attempt at a smile. 'Luxford was the sort of amateur that should be legislated out of existence.'

65

'He *has* been legislated out of existence,' Gibbon murmured. Wilkinson coloured.

'All right, a joke. I suppose you're trying to make a case for some violent quarrel between him and me, and that there was some reason I might want to murder him. It's not very likely is it, over three cists, two round barrows and a medieval village? It's not as though we've just opened up Tutankhamen's tomb or something.'

'They say passions run high in these things . . . .'

'Now don't take the joke too far. They say all sort of nonsense, particularly here.'

'I'm sorry. But believe me when I say I am slightly interested in the subject. I know that sounds like more prying, but having just arrived here, I was struck by the number of sites on the Ordnance Survey. I'm no sort of archaeologist, but I found it interesting. This must have been a busy area.'

Wilkinson eyed him for three seconds, apparently trying to make up his mind if Gibbon was genuine. He gave him the benefit of the doubt, but not altogether trustingly.

'It's a typical area. A place of continual habitation. The river, a ford backed by a prominent ridge suitable for fortification, gravel beds bearing flint, flat meadow land. Everyone lived here.'

'Have you any particular interest?'

'All of it. Bronze Age, Anglo-Saxon, medieval. It started with my father. He was a keen man. Used to take me out at weekends.'

'Have you found anything exciting?'

'Look, that depends upon what you call exciting! This is when archaeologists get very nasty.'

'I know, I know!' said Gibbon hastily, 'I didn't mean digging into burials and finding treasure and that sort of thing!'

Wilkinson looked at first mollified, then slightly apologetic.

'I'm sorry. This is a very edgy sort of conversation to be having at a Christmas party! Change the subject.'

They did. They chatted about Wilkinson's shop, about the age of Gibbon's house, about ridgeways and barrows. Gibbon was beginning to think it was time to move on when he was tapped rudely on the shoulder. He half turned to find William Luxford standing there. He was obviously drunk and was weaving slightly on his feet. He had a round fleshy face with small pursed lips that projected and seemed unnaturally wet. Strong lenses enlarged his blue eyes. He had multiple chins, although his body was not particularly plump. On his face was an expression of unconcealed hate.

'Don't listen to him. This man's a fraud!' Luxford said loudly. Gibbon stared at him. There was nothing else he could do. He sensed that Wilkinson was gathering himself up with fury.

'He knows nothing about barrows, the Bronze Age or anything else! As far as I'm aware, the extent of his published works is two letters to popular journals of the sort used by people with metal detectors, giving directions to all the other looters like himself!'

Luxford stuck his fat head forwards as though daring Wilkinson to knock it off his shoulders. Wilkinson clenched his fists and looked only too willing to oblige.

'Look, Luxford,' he managed to say, 'I know you've had a very upsetting time, and I'll let you off that last remark.'

'Oh bully for you!' exclaimed the poisonous intruder. '*I* don't need to be let off anything thank you. As for your own sins, I expect you know them better than anyone. It must be comforting to find a sympathetic ear in these parts. You realise, Mr Gibbon, that in talking to this individual you have probably sacrificed the goodwill of half the community!'

'I don't know what you're talking about,' said Gibbon. 'I don't think this is the time or place for this sort of acrimony.'

Luxford made an effort and focussed on Gibbon. His eyes were so enlarged by the lenses that it was possible to see the irises enlarging then contracting as they gauged the distance of their target. George Fry had heard the exchange and openly joined them. So had the Harrises, Philippa Crabbe and others. Lucinda looked up, and now darted over.

'Now, William,' cautioned Lucinda with the authority of the hostess. Henry appeared beside her. William glared.

'I suppose you're going to tell me I'm a naughty boy? Please don't bother, Lucinda, there has to be a limit to hypocrisy . . .'

'Come on,' said Henry with a masterful tone but tentative manner. Luxford ignored him and turned to Gibbon, seeming to pull himself together.

'Look here Gibbon, someone has murdered my brother, and quite possibly it was someone in this room. It's all very cosy standing here and having drinks with each other for Christmas, but who's the murderer? Happy Christmas! Ring out the bells! Yuletide greetings!'

'Perhaps you ought to leave,' said Gibbon quietly. 'It must all be very upsetting . . .'

'Oh, I'll go all right, don't worry!'

Luxford was infuriatingly airy. He gazed languidly around the faces that surrounded him.

'You had better!' blustered George Fry, suddenly pushing through and seizing Luxford by the arm. His face was puce with anger and he puffed like a small bull. 'If you don't go, I'll throw you out. We never needed your brother here and we don't need you either! You've been nothing but a bloody pest from the moment you arrived, and we don't need you here on Christmas Day spoiling things for the rest of us!'

Luxford looked down at George's hand that was clamped around his forearm.

'Take your hand off my arm!' he hissed. His voice was so venomous that George did as he was told. 'Perhaps everyone will note your unsolicited testimonial and friendly remarks towards the murdered man. Perhaps you have just nominated yourself as the principal suspect.'

Luxford went as far as to make a short bow to George. It was a silly, theatrical gesture, but in the mood that existed, it was highly provocative. Gibbon moved between George and Luxford before George could let fly. Luxford strolled to the hall.

'Did you have a coat?' asked Gibbon. Luxford paused to look at him.

'You see, I have the advantage over all of them,' he said, his eyes appearing to Gibbon to be very much that small variety of purple-blue jelly fish that is so often washed up on shores, 'I know I didn't kill my brother. I know I'm not a murderer. None of *them* can be sure of each other.'

Gibbon nodded at this piece of drunken illogic.

'I know how you feel, but it really would be better all round if you went home. We've all had a few drinks . . .'

'Oh, I've had a few drinks all right, but don't you go away thinking that it's just the drink talking. That would be very dangerous. They don't like me, you know, because I'm new here, and because the shop I have for my antiques used to be the village store . . .'

Luxford was looking for his coat as he spoke, raking about in the cupboard under the stairs. He found a dark grey coat with a fur collar and struggled into it.

'Village store! You should have seen the place! Salmonella corner! Rodents' refuge! The cellar was actually full of rat bones. They crunched under your feet when you walked. They won't like you either, because you're new as well. The women in this place hurled themselves at my brother. Some do, you know, its something to do with the cloth. It's a recognised risk for vicars and I'm sure Freud must have a chapter or two on it somewhere. Something to do with violation of the altar, no doubt. But just to hear them, you would think butter wouldn't melt in their mouths.'

Gibbon opened the front door, aware that there was silence from the living room and that all eyes were on Luxford's departure. He badly wanted to ask the man if he had a particular suspect. Another time. Outside, the snow was blinding. The assault on their optic nerves made both men stop and shield their eyes. Gibbon wondered if Luxford was fit to make his way home. Had the man walked or driven?

'I'll enjoy the walk home,' Luxford said, answering the question. 'Nice to get away from all that into the clean outdoors!'

He gave an extravagant wave, without turning round and

68

crunched off down the path, looking like a giant black mole in his black coat and fur collar. Gibbon closed the door and returned to the living room.

'Thank you for seeing him out,' said Lucinda, smiling in her devastating fashion.

'Yes, thank you,' said Henry, pale and more detached than anything else.

'Well you certainly stopped me from hitting the man,' rumbled George, 'I don't know if I should thank you for that or not!'

'Human pollution,' said Wilkinson. 'We mustn't allow him to upset us.'

'What an opinion you will form of us all!' declared Mrs Harris with a social laugh. Gibbon smiled at her.

'He'd been drinking too much.' Remembering her pre-occupation of the night before, he asked if she had managed to get the stuffing done. People were beginning to talk again. Henry Walker put a log on the fire then circulated with a bottle in each hand, pouring drinks. Being the host.

'I did,' she said, 'and the turkey's in now. I turned it on just before we left, and I shall have to watch the time. Isn't it awful really, here we are with a murder, and here I am preoccupied with my turkey!'

She didn't look as though she thought it at all awful. Gibbon re-confirmed his previous opinion that he liked Mrs Harris. There was real directness about her that seemed to be wanting in some of the locals! Her hair had been cut and set and she wore a pale blue woollen suit. It looked as though it might be her Christmas present. He envied Tom Harris his Christmas dinner. He imagined it would consist of an endless procession of courses, with every one of the trimmings.

'I was just hoping that Tom remembers to baste it. Young Tom,' she added in explanation, 'my son.'

'Fat chance at his age!' said Tom Harris senior. 'I like it crisp on the outside, too. Brown, almost . . .'

'Glazed, anyway,' said Mrs Mary Harris, 'with the chestnut stuffing crisp where it oozes out. It does tend to spread in the pan. You have to scoop it up and tuck it back in from time to time really . . .'

'You should have sewn up the neck like I told you.'

'Yes, I know dear, but I just didn't have time, what with coming here and it being Christmas morning and young Tom's presents. I did ask you if you would do it. Anyhow, it's just folded over and will have to take its chances!'

Gibbon decided that he objected to Tom Harris. It was perhaps a rather hasty judgement, but he didn't like his bossy tone. He clearly wallowed in her undivided attention, not to speak of her food, and was nothing but critical as a result. Wilkinson joined them and the two men started to exchange tales of drunkeness. Harris was very neatly dressed in a grey suit with a pink shirt and grey tie. His hair was in perfect order, and nicely greyed at the temples. He seemed weak to Gibbon, so bland as almost not to exist. The sort of man to make his wife's life hell.

'Shall I get you another drink?' he asked Mary.

'Yes please!'

When he returned they moved closer to each other to talk.

'I made him come to church,' she said by way of explanation, taking her glass of wine.' Jacob Wilkinson would have the whole village in there if he had his way. I'm no holy Joe, but I think it's nice to allow religion to intrude just a little into the occasion. It's good for children to remind them what it's all supposed to be about. We spend the best part of it gluttonising!' She sipped her glass and smiled. 'I'm no prude about that. Tom likes his food as you may gather, though he never puts on weight. Young Tom does too'.

'So do I. Don't you leave the party!'

'I wasn't going to, believe you me! Still, it wasn't very nice for the children. Tom does seem a bit upset. Fancy seeing a man gunned down in front of you like that! I asked him if he wanted to come here, but he wouldn't.'

She paused, sipped her wine again. She looked worried.

'He's a secretive boy, you know, and I think he was holding something back last night. Still it's very difficult to tell at his age. They deny everything and they're such accomplished liars. He's a good lad really but a bit wild and a rover, always out fishing or mucking about – I can't always keep track of him and I don't like to be too nosy.'

She leaned slightly nearer to Gibbon.

'He doesn't like Wilkinson, either. Asked if he would be here. I do wonder if there's something he knows . . . '

'Any particular reason?' asked Gibbon quietly.

'No. I think Wilkinson has a thing about his archaeology. He thinks all boys are out to steal things, which is probably true! Then Tom didn't like Peter Luxford either, or his brother, or quite a lot of other people, or that rather odd man over there behind you, Jeffrys. In his case you can see why. All the boys are told to keep away from him, but they're cruel and call him names . . . '

She fell silent.

'What do you make of this place?' asked Gibbon, indicating the surroundings in general with a circular motion of his glass. He was anxious to sustain this rich arterial flow of information.

'They can't afford it, I'm pretty sure of that. I think they could when they bought it and when Lucinda had the shop bought for her. I like Lucinda, but she'll never make a go of a place like that in such a small place. I think Henry wanted her to have it to keep her occupied. They say he's very clever in the City, but I believe business is bad. He never speaks about it. I don't think they really get on. Lucinda was friendly with Luxford and Henry went to see him. That made the fur fly a bit between the three of them.'

'You'll have to forgive me, but you know I don't even know what your husband does,' said John apologetically. 'Here I am, insinuated in your midst and I know nothing about anyone.'

'Tom teaches at the Polytechnic. He lectures in Computer Studies. It's one of those titles that sounds rather grand but is really very dull. For heaven's sake don't tell him that I said that!'

Gibbon smiled politely.

'And what about Phillippa Crabbe?' he asked. 'What does she do?'

It was Mary Harris' turn to smile, but her's was a knowing twinkle.

'She's rather beautiful, isn't she, and she's a widow! We do have some nice people here, not all Luxfords and Wilkinsons. I like her dress, don't you?'

'Yes, very much,' said Gibbon, momentarily embarrassed. Phillippa caught them looking at her, and smiled. She had opted for simplicity, ignoring the weather, and wore a deceptively simple silk dress in pale sage. Gibbon tried to suppress his thoughts about her figure, without success. I must be rallying, he told himself.

'I don't know what her husband did, but she's a very scholarly sort of person, though she certainly doesn't look it,' Mary Harris continued. 'She has so many interests, I don't know what she doesn't do. She paints, she reads, she writes little articles for the local paper on the countryside and that sort of thing. She's a very keen botanist, runs the Natural History Society and is probably the only one who actually knows what she's talking about. She obviously knows far too much for a little place like this but it's all the sort of things you would expect her to do to keep herself from boredom. Won't join the W.I. though, for which I can hardly blame her. I suppose they would once have called her a blue-stocking.'

Mary Harris paused.

'Now I've prattled on and answered all your questions. Will you please answer one of mine?'

'That depends.'

'What are *you* doing here? What are you running away from when you run, because that's what it looks like.'

'I suppose I have to answer that? Everyone has asked me. I didn't realise country people would find it so strange . . .'

'I really think you owe it to me, don't you?'

'To stop speculation!'

'Well, a man who lives on his own, runs to punish himself, seems to have enough money without working, appears to be unattached, is even attractive! What do you think? If it wasn't a terrible thing to say, I'd say you've taken over where Luxford left off!'

71

Gibbon looked amused rather than shocked.

'The common opinion is that you're a widower,' continued Mary.

'The common opinion is like astrology. It leaves plenty of options!'

'Then answer.'

'All right, I'm separated from my wife. And still in the hurting time.'

Gibbon looked hurt too as he said it. Mary Harris made a sympathetic face.

'It was clever then of Mann to get you involved in all this. It'll give you something to do.'

'Well I think he has a bloody nerve!' bellowed Wilkinson rudely. The man had gravitated nearer unnoticed and had overheard Mary's last remark. 'I know Mr Gibbon won't take this personally because he knows my views, but there's no room in police work for amateurs in my opinion!'

Gibbon resisted the temptation to reply to Wilkinson in the vein he deserved. There had been enough turbulence already.

'What *are* you supposed to be doing here in all reality?' Wilkinson pursued. 'Spying on us. Call it anything else you like but that's what it amounts to. The enemy in our midst, that sort of thing. It's not a decent sort of way to carry on. The police should do it themselves!'

'I only became involved because I was there,' replied Gibbon mildly. Wilkinson was evidently intoxicated. He snorted his disbelief, took another swig of the enormous glass of whisky he carried with him everywhere and showed every sign of being disposed to pursue this line of questioning. Gibbon forestalled him.

'I really must move around a bit,' he murmured to Mary. 'I promised to talk to Philippa Crabbe . . .'

Which was half true, because he had promised that pleasure to himself. Mary nodded and gave a slight wave with her free hand. She was smiling knowingly.

'I must move on . . . ' said Gibbon to Wilkinson. 'Keep on the move . . . ' He smiled in friendly fashion, knowing it was the sort of unconvincing grimace one would give to an accosting drunk in the street. Wilkinson would not be shaken off so easily. He followed him a little way and tapped him on the shoulder.

Gibbon turned sharply, prepared to be rude. He was surprised to see Wilkinson's face contorted into what he must have intended to be a smile.

'Look, I'm sorry if I was rude, Gibbon. It's only the drink talking. I have an idea. You're a man on your own, and so am I. Not that I regret it for a moment. I always think that women are like French cooking. They get to be altogether too much if they become part of your daily diet. Why don't you join me for Christmas dinner? I'm not so uncivilised that I don't enjoy eating and not such a fool that I don't get a woman in to cook it for me! I strike a happy balance you see. Mrs Edwardes comes in and takes pity on me for a considerable consideration, and she is excellent at dealing with meat!'

Gibbon was temporarily flummoxed. He had not expected this kindness in the least, but remembering Wilkinson's invitation of the night before to the 'Feathers', he began to wonder if he had misjudged the man. Another one alone and lonely. It might even account for his surly manner. Mummery would have wanted him to accept, but he did not feel strong enough, not today.

'I have my own dinner on at home,' he lied, 'It's very kind . . .'

'You'll never see turkey or beef like it. It's mine! It's the best!'

'I'm probably missing the best opportunity I ever had, but I really can't.'

'A drink later then. In the "Feathers".'

'I might do that.'

'Good man.' Wilkinson seemed to take his refusal well. 'Don't worry about it.'

'I was going to talk to Philippa Crabbe . . .'

'Watch out there.' Wilkinson's face darkened again. 'She's a peculiar woman.' He turned away, releasing Gibbon. A second dinner invitation, thought Gibbon. Popularity or curiosity? He knew the answer, he thought with a wry smile.

'Hello,' Philippa greeted him warmly. She moved slightly apart from others near. 'I've been trying to catch your eye.'

'I'm sorry. The new boy has to do his rounds.' Philippa nodded.

'I know. You'll have made all sorts of friends and enemies by now. This sort of party accelerates the process. There's no such thing as indifference.'

'You're very serious about everyone.'

'Perhaps I'm right to be.'

'What do you mean by that?'

'Undercurrents and things.' She was slightly flustered.

Gibbon looked at her so sharply that she made a wry face and obviously felt obliged to continue. For a moment she looked about seven years old.

'Have they found anything in the church?' she asked.

'Not so far.'

'No weapon, no clues?'

'No,' lied Gibbon, watching Philippa carefully for any reaction, but she accepted his reply at face value.

'I don't understand how they haven't found the gun. If it was a rifle and no one took it out, it obviously has to be concealed somewhere. I'm sorry to say such trite things, but I'm sure we're all puzzling over it. I suppose the police are searching?'

'They are.' He remembered that Philippa had had the task of breaking the news to Luxford's wife only a few hours ago. He asked

73

how she was.

'Molly's a stronger woman than most people would think. Of course she's shattered by the shock of the whole thing, especially at this time of the year when there is so much on in the Church, but she is hardly grief-stricken. I think everyone knows there was no love left in that marriage. I believe Molly simply stayed on because it didn't seem right to her to drag the Church in to any scandal.' She paused. 'But this isn't what I wanted to talk about.'

Gibbon waited.

'I don't want any of this repeated,' she said, carefully looking into his face, 'and I don't really know if I can trust you, as you are in league with the police whatever you may say. I don't mean that unkindly, it is simply a fact.'

She gave him a small nervous smile to take the edge off the remark.

'I don't know what to say to defend myself against that,' he said. 'And I can't promise not to pass something on if it's relevant. I hope this isn't a murder confession!' he said jokingly. Philippa Crabbe looked at him seriously, so that he felt flippant and chastised for being so.

'I am only asking that you use your judgement if you won't promise to keep it to yourself. It isn't earth-shattering but it is very personal, and I'd much rather tell you myself than have you hear it from others. There are no secrets in this place. Old Alf Hazlitt says its as water-tight as a chicken run, and I think that sums it up.' She moved slightly closer and lowered her voice. 'We're being watched now, be sure, and I'm shy about my little confession.'

She took a sip of her drink to help herself.

'When my husband had died and I moved here I was a classic example of the lonely withdrawn widow. Luxford pounced almost immediately, and I simply could not see what was happening. Perhaps grief made me blind. I think that the fact he was the vicar had a lot to do with it. I obviously don't read the right sort of daily paper. Despite all indications to the contrary, as they say, I couldn't actually believe he was doing what he did. It's all that damned dog-collar nonsense they teach us at school. They were always trotting vicars round our Primary school and I suppose all we little girls fell for those young clergymen.'

She sighed and smiled wrily.

'He was so confident of himself – I suppose with good reason – that it was like trying to stop a bulldozer by slapping it. He was also clever enough to appear to take a deep interest in things that I was doing, claiming them as his own interests. I fell for it like a schoolgirl. I've always been a keen botanist and of course I took that up. He must have stayed up at nights reading the right books because he certainly fooled me! It was lovely to have someone to walk the countryside with, someone nice and safe like the vicar! Quite simply I allowed

74

myself to be seduced with indecent speed knowing perfectly well he was married. He showered me with gifts and trinkets – God knows where he got the money – and did up to the day before yesterday. I sent them back. Molly knew about it. She told me, but we never discussed it. She certainly didn't blame me. I didn't know I was just one blade of corn in the whole field. That's my confession and I wanted to tell you myself.'

Gibbon felt very angry and very sorry at the same time. If Luxford had still been alive, he would have added himself to the potential list of murderers.

'I'm very sorry,' he mumbled feebly. 'You didn't have to tell me all that.'

'But I did, just to clear the air. You see, I don't think his lecherous past has anything to do with his murder.'

Gibbon knew he was goggling at her, and sipped his drink to give himself time. Was he too impressionable? Be cool, Mr Gibbon, be cool.

'Go on.'

'Luxford had too much money for a country vicar as I said. The sort of things he tried to give me were expensive. Bracelets, always gold, brooches – usually pearls and precious stones. Always good. Perhaps if you ask around you'll find he treated his other women the same way.'

'Did he have inherited money?'

'I don't know. Molly always said he had nothing at all, but perhaps he wasn't telling her. It isn't unknown.' She smiled at him brightly. 'Now the reason that I'm grimacing at you like this is that people are beginning to pay too much attention to us. I think you should move on!'

She seemed nervous. Wilkinson was certainly scowling at them belligerently and Lucinda, he saw, though apparently engaged in conversation with Jeffrys, looked away quickly when his eyes turned towards her.

'I think you're right. Perhaps we can talk again another time.'

Philippa nodded and moved away. Gibbon skirted the snorting Wilkinson and raised his glass cheerfully to Alf Hazlit who was warming himself in front of the fire.

'Happy Christmas,' said Hazlitt, raising his own in return. The old man's brown face had turned a fiery colour. He seemed quite content where he was, and Gibbon had noticed he made no attempt to mingle and talked only when spoken to.

'Going to freeze hard tonight?' asked Gibbon.

'I should say so. It's crisp out there and we shall have a moon like a dinner plate.' He nodded, as though to himself. 'Have you solved it yet?' he asked suddenly, looking up at Gibbon with sharp grey eyes full of naughtiness.

'That's not my job!'

'I don't know, if we have to wait for Mann to do it we shall all be a deal older. He's a good lad, but about as sharp as a telegraph pole. And just about as nippy on his feet! Hazlitt gave a chuckle and drank from a pint glass of beer. Gibbon wondered if Hazlitt kept himself apart from these other people on purpose. He was the old original after all, a true son of the village while they were all interlopers. Or did they avoid Hazlitt? Village snobbery? He certainly seemed to be happy to be direct.

'For a start, they haven't found the gun yet, have they? So I hear, anyway.'

'No, they haven't found it.'

'Well, I reckon it's still in there somewhere. There's more hiding places than there's fleas on a hedgehog. I'm certain no one left with it because I was watching particular.' Again the mischievous look. 'So, between ourselves, who do you think done it? I've been watching you having a good talk with the ladies. A rare source of information!'

Gibbon could not repress a grin, and Hazlitt took his familiarity further by nudging Gibbon with his free elbow. He then put down his pint mug on the mantel and picked up a very large tumbler of whisky that had up to now been concealed behind him. Hazlitt had got himself organised.

'Oh my Lord yes!' he said, as though reading Gibbon's thoughts, 'I don't drink beer by itself at Christmas. She pours a good drink does Lucinda Walker, and knowing the state of their affairs I thought I'd better take it while it was going!'

Gibbon ignored this indiscretion. He was beginning to understand why Hazlit was left to his own devices.

'Why don't you tell me who *you* think did it?'

'Well for a start it could have been any of the ladies, couldn't it? Without putting too fine a point on it, there seems to have been a few opportunities for blackmail, for instance, and he was certainly a nasty enough beggar for that! On the other hand, it could have been one of the husbands!' He grinned round the room. Gibbon prayed he would keep his voice down before they were next to be shown the door.

'Or his wife,' the man persisted. 'I should have thought she'd had enough of him!'

'What about you?' asked Gibbon to teach the man a lesson. Hazlitt grinned again, showing that his front top teeth were attached to a plate.

'Why not me! The bugger reported me to the police for poaching, as a neighbourly act. Have you tried one of those sausages?' he continued inconsequentially, indicating a plateful speared with green plastic swords. 'Wilkinson's. Very good too. Have one?'

Gibbon shook his head. Hazlitt, who seemed thoroughly

76

ambidextrous in matters of food and drink, took three with his left hand, inserted them all in his mouth at once and munched happily. He flung the sticks neatly in the fire where they caught quickly, producing a smoky orange flame.

'Well, did you?' pursued Gibbon.

'I wouldn't tell you if I had!' said Hazlitt, not at all offended. 'But why should I shoot him in church? I could pick him off any time!'

'So you have a rifle?'

For the first time Hazlitt stopped grinning. He looked cautious, then annoyed.

'I don't!'

'Then how could you pick him off?'

'Look here, mister, you mind your own business! You'll get so sharp you'll cut yourself. Never you mind what guns I may or may not have, just you concentrate on one thing. That shot came from high up and behind us all. It wasn't anyone sitting in the pews, that's for sure!'

'Why are you so sure?'

'Because there was no smoke, for God's sake! All you people are so clever you can't see what's in front of your face. The church should have been full of it, but it wasn't. After quite a long time a bit of smell came trickling in, but if you've just fired a gun in a room you know all about it immediately.'

It was blindingly obvious when he said it. Gibbon wondered if Mummery had thought of it.

'Who was it then? No one saw anyone do it.'

'Ah that's the clever bit, isn't it? You see, I reckon everyone in that church had a good reason for putting the bugger away, and quite a few people who weren't there had just as good a reason too. In fact you'd have a right problem finding someone in this village except his fart of a brother who would do more than give him a drink if he were drowning! You should be asking yourself where he got his money. We'd all like to know that.'

'I've already been given that advice.'

'Philippa Crabbe, I'll bet! Do have one of these here sausages. I don't like to eat alone.'

He offered one to Gibbon, who took it out of politeness while Hazlitt repeated his performance with three.

'She's a cool one,' he continued, 'and Luxford deserved what he got for the way he treated her alone. In fact I reckon if we could prop him up again, we would all have a go so as not to feel cheated! Happy Christmas!' he finished ferociously, washing sausage down with whisky.

'All right then, of all the good reasons, what seems to you the most likely?'

'Ah well now!' Hazlitt refreshed himself again. He seemed able to drink an enormous quantity. 'Though he were a randy goat, I reckon

77

the men hated him just about as much as the women, and I don't think a woman shot him. And I include Jeffrys among the men for the purposes of this description!'

From the corner of his eye, Gibbon saw Lucinda Walker and Wilkinson talking very close together. Lucinda looked very angry and Wilkinson's face was hard. What did it all mean?

'Is there anyone you think didn't kill him?' he asked in mock desperation.

'Well I don't reckon you did,' said Hazlitt. 'You haven't been here long enough yet!'

Gibbon had exchanged a few words with Jeffrys then excused himself and left. Others had gone before him, and the talk was of turkeys and puddings and wines. Lucinda had made a last minute attempt to invite him to dinner, but Gibbon had seen her husband watching with anxious eyes, and had refused. He would manage well enough by himself in any case.

Snow had melted on grasses and on thin branches, then refrozen, encasing them. It reminded Gibbon of those twigs of herbs in tall bottles of Italian liqueur.

He crunched down towards the three dark hollies that guarded the gate, noticing the steps of birds, the holes made by some sort of shrew or mouse, the linear steps of a cat. Nature left an abundance of clues. Every movement was there for those who could interpret them. Surely humans were no more difficult?

Instead of turning homewards at the gate, he turned right and then crossed the High Street towards the church gate. He must tell Mummery what Hazlitt had noticed about the shooting; but what else was he to tell the man? His mind was crammed with information, but like an over-fed sieve it threatened to block altogether. He needed time to analyse it all, to form clear impressions from shadowed suspicions. Why had it been done in the church? Was it vital to the whole affair or was it a blind? What was there about all these people? Or had he become so suspicious now that he was detecting suspicion where none existed?

He opened the door of the church to find himself confronting Mummery. The man must have heard him approaching.

'Back again, Mr Gibbon!' Mummery declared. The man sounded almost jovial. 'I can see you can't keep away from this!'

'I came back because of something that was said to me. At this drinks party of Lucinda Walker's . . .'

'Oh we know where you've been,' said Mummery. 'Festive, was it?'

'Yes, fine,' said John impatiently. 'I was talking to Hazlitt, the old chap, who was there. He reckons he knows where the shot came from and it seemed to me to make sense. I think I have some idea where

78

you might find the gun.'

'Oh we've found the gun,' said Mummery. 'That didn't take us so very long.'

Chapter Five

Mummery's casualness was as silent as an elephant crashing through the bush. Gibbon examined his wooden face. Was there a hint of triumph? Old Hook Nose had the faintest of up-turns at the corners of his mouth.

'Would you like to see it?'

'Of course I would!'

'I think we can allow that, don't you, Constable Mann?'

Mann was standing in the half light, half gloom towards the West end of the church. Gibbon could dimly see the two detectives beyond him. They were chafing their hands together, not from glee but from the stone cold, and moving from foot to foot. The walls and columns radiated iciness, or rather, Gibbon thought, were enormous consumers of heat, radiators in reverse, sucking warmth from anything near them. No one had put the heat on, Gibbon realised, because there was no one to say that it was authorised.

Mann did not advance towards them and Mummery waved his hand rather flamboyantly in the direction of the gloom. Gibbon preceded him down the aisle. To the rear behind a Victorian font with gross carving was a blackened high oak screen of imperforate panels. In this was an open door through which a feeble light shone grey on pitted stone slabs. Over the screen the same chill and unwelcoming light trickled like dirty water from the West windows beyond. One of the detectives, the man in plain clothes, opened the door further by pushing on a massive iron ring, making screeches and echoes.

'Like a horror film, isn't it?' said Mummery with satisfaction in his voice.

Gibbon walked through into the vestibule beneath the tower. The place was characteristically depressing and musty, a repository for hassocks and cassocks. Three of the latter were suspended like hanged men from iron hooks forming a row on the wall. The row had

79

optimistically been numbered from one to twenty in spiky script that had been gilded. A heap of dusty red hymn books leaned against a heap of dusty black bibles for support. A poster promoting the Mothers' Union had been pinned to one wall – the pins were rusted and the poster ten years old.

Gibbon glanced up. Above them was a boarded floor supported on exposed joists. Mummery caught his eye and nodded. To their right was another door set in a pointed arch. Up to the ringing floor.

'Yes?' he queried, feeling the excitement of the others.

'You'll see.'

'That's what Hazlitt suggested.'

'Was it now?' said Mummery thoughtfully. 'Hear that, Constable Mann. Isn't he the clever one? Meanwhile, as it's bloody freezing in here and my stomach is starting to digest itself and it's Christmas Day, shall we get a move on!'

He plunged forward through the lancet-headed doorway. Gibbon waved Mann on, but Mann made a droll negative face, shaking his head, and in turn waved on Gibbon with elaborate courtesy. Gibbon entered and found himself in the vertical stone tube of a spiral stair. Two winds of claustrophobia and he found himself on the wooden ringing floor. Bell ropes dangled in the gloom with pulls like animal tails. Mummery didn't pause but turned right again up another flight of identical stairs.

'Where does this go?' asked John Gibbon, knowing the answer, but for the sake of conversation. His words echoed hard in that small stone space.

'You'll see,' came Mummery's reply. Three winds this time, then they stepped out on to a small platform, little more than a tree house to Gibbon, supported he knew not how, and railed off from a fearsome drop to the ringing floor by only posts and two horizontal timber rails. Beside them in the gloom hung bells, sullen and ominous. The only light worked its way in through the slats in three lanceolate windows higher up. Somewhere above them came an explosion of sound that Gibbon recognised as pigeons flapping. He found his heart was beating fast, but decided to put it down to the climb up the stairs. So much for all his jogging.

'He had an eye for a setting, this character,' observed Mummery. *He* wasn't puffing. Gibbon was impressed. Mann hadn't even arrived yet. Gibbon hoped this platform was strong enough for all of them. He became aware of a slow greasy sliding noise followed by a heavy metallic 'clack!'. To the side was the clock, its mechanism turning. A pendulum swung backwards and forwards below them with exaggerated laziness. The platform shook as Mann and the two detectives added their weight to it, and Gibbon found himself searching around for a firm hand hold lest the whole lot should drop.

'There you are!' said Mummery.

At first Gibbon had difficulty making out what the white object was that Mummery was pointing to. It seemed to be a bandaged roll of something. He squeezed past Mummery in the small space and found that he was looking at a bundle strapped with masking tape. It was a rifle, taped to a horizontal rail, and so wound round and around that only the barrel and the firing mechanism projected. From the trigger hung a piece of cheap white string with a frayed end.

'Don't touch it,' said Mummery, 'but look down the sights.'

Gibbon crouched down carefully and squinted along the foresight. He was looking through a trefoil opening, one of several at high level between the rear west wall of the aisle and the tower. The view was quite clear, for the lectern stood in a pool of light even in the daytime. Hardly surprising, Gibbon reflected, as electricity was still a modern fad in the life span of this old building. There was no doubt about the direction of the gun.

'It doesn't point exactly at the lectern,' he observed. 'Slightly to the right.'

'It's been fired,' said Mummery, 'it was well taped to be in position at all. Someone knew what they were doing.'

'Fired by the string?' asked Gibbon. Mummery nodded.

'Simple but efficient. I think whoever did this enjoyed it. If it didn't work, it wouldn't matter. A real beauty. Murder by clockwork.'

He waved Gibbon towards him and taking his arm, pointed towards the darkness below the lanceolate windows. For some time Gibbon could only see the white snow that was sifting through the slats. As his eyes adjusted to the dark he made out the slightly darker outline of a bell. From below the hunched shape hung a thin white line.

'What bell is it?' asked Gibbon, thinking he knew the answer.

'The hour bell for the clock. It was tied to the clapper. No wonder you heard the shot at midnight!'

The five men scrambled down again to the vestibule. They were already suffering from a chill to the bones that made the flagged floor seem slightly warm.

'Have you ever seen anything like that before?' asked Gibbon.

'No, Mr Gibbon, not like that. I've seen people tie things to guns before to blow their own heads off, but I've never seen that. Mind you I've never been to a murder in a church either so this thing is full of firsts!'

Mann shuffled his feet and snuffled a bit. Mummery ignored him.

'And what did you learn while you were out enjoying yourself, apart from the fact that Hazlitt seems to know too much?'

'I found out that practically everyone had a reason for doing him a serious mischief. At least. He seems to have been as popular as Attila the Hun.'

81

'And of all the multitudes that were crowding round to kill him, did it strike you that any were more likely than others?'

'Don't be sarcastic about it!' said Gibbon angrily. 'I had to be a human sponge to take in everything I heard. Give me a day or two to sort through it in my mind. There are a dozen things worth following up. You don't just expect me to go to drinks with them all and come away saying. 'That one's the murderer', do you?'

Mann snuffled and shuffled again.

'All right Mann!' said Mummery rudely, 'you've made your point and you can go.' He had only deigned to notice him to avoid answering Gibbon. They all knew that.

'Yes, sir. At this rate I shall get my Christmas dinner in.'

Mummery sighed noisily.

'I suppose you all want to go now. And I shall have to stay behind and shut up shop. I'm afraid you'll have to stay for a bit, Sergeant.' The uniformed man sighed. 'I'll get someone here to take the gun away as soon as possible, remembering that this is Christmas Day and most people will be sitting down to their dinner between now and this evening!'

The two men set out together, glad to hear the church door pulled to behind them.

'I thought I was stuck there!' said Mann ruefully. He flapped his arms around his ribs and blew out a cloud of white breath. 'It's bright out here! A fantastic day! Hurts my eyes. That church is a cold and gloomy place.'

'I never liked churches much myself,' said Gibbon. 'It's always seemed strange to me that as places for worship – celebration if you like – they should always be so sombre and depressing. It's a strange idea of joy!'

They were standing at the lich-gate. It cast a monstrous four-legged shadow on the snow. Mann opened the gate and closed it again, dropping the iron band that secured it back over the post. He looked sideways at Gibbon.

'Are you going back to eat?'

'Oh yes.'

'What I mean is, are you having a Christmas dinner? I don't mean to intrude, but as you're on your own . . .'

'That's very kind of you.' Gibbon was touched. Mann must have been looking forward to his food like a wolf. 'I really thank you very much, but even on my own I have a turkey on.'

It was a lie. It was supposed to be cooking, but he had not had the time or the inclination.

'Won't it make lonely eating? By yourself?'

'I shall be all right. At least I don't have to worry about the washing up. I can lead a pig's life and leave it.'

82

Mann smiled slightly, was not entirely convinced although Gibbon guessed he would like to be. Why should Mann put up with such a disruption?

'Are you sure?'

'I'm sure. It was very kind of you to ask. Come on, I have to get back to cook's duties.'

They trudged down the High Street. The snow was noticeably softer and the air temperature had risen. A trickle of thawing water ran down the gutter. Icicles dripped on gutters. Here and there on south-facing roofs, small snow-slides had started, showing dark patches of slate or tile.

'What are you going to do now?' asked Mann. 'About this murder?'

'I suppose I'm officially released now?'

'That's up to Mummery.' They had passed Wilkinson's and were now walking between two cottages and the Walker house. 'Did you get a good drink?', said Mann, nodding in the direction of the house.

'There was plenty of drink, although I got the impression they could hardly afford it.'

'So rumour says. Did you learn anything there?'

'I learned too much there.' said John with a smile.

'Well, who *do* you think could have done it? The thing seems so peculiar.'

'It's worse than that, it's the sort of thing that Sunday papers are made of. It's a very peculiar way to carry out a murder, and that's what impresses most. Why was it done in that way? If you wanted to shoot the man, then surely do it quietly, somewhere remote. Someone wants us to believe that it was done by someone in the church. They must have intended to come back and get that gun when you had given up looking for it. After all it was reasonably well-concealed, and if there had been no guard put on the church it could easily have been removed over night. But does that mean it was done by someone who was *not* in the church? It could all be a giant red herring. Perhaps they never intended to remove the gun. Perhaps we were intended to jump to the conclusion it was someone not at church.'

'I agree with all that. Someone is being clever with us.'

They stopped outside Mann's house. Smoke billowed from a chimney, and there was an orange glow of firelight behind net curtains. The moving colours of television flickered across the ceiling within. Gibbon told himself to stop feeling sorry for himself.

'But all murders seem bizarre until they're explained,' he said. 'Think of the things you read about. This will have a mundane reason at the end of it all. We'll all be disappointed.'

'Do you think so?'

Gibbon raised a hand in farewell. He was pleased to see Mann

83

tramping down his own path, pleased to see the front door open before he got to it. The man deserved it. He was only mildly miserable himself.

Continuing over the bridge he paused to stare at the frozen stream that was actually the upper reaches of a river. Bullrushes rattled, their stems fixed solid in ice. The footmarks of a bird were visible on the surface. He saw the black shape of a coot moving further upstream. The only bird that would be running about in this sort of weather. The thought of it made his feet ache with cold and he stamped them, found this ineffective and kicked the parapet instead. This simply hurt. He should be jogging, his frame of mind was no good.

What was he to do about this murder? He had no standing in the thing at all, but he believed Mummery would be happy enough to use him for local 'errands'. He would like to remain involved. The whole thing intrigued him, he admitted. The pre-planned taking of life by one individual of another was such an alien idea, especially when so elaborate. There was undoubtedly an unhealthy thrill in knowing that someone he had met in the last twelve or fourteen hours had done it.

With or without Mummery's approval he would continue.

He heard a skittering, rushing noise and looked up to see a boy hurtling towards him on a new bicycle, both feet on the icy surface of the road to keep his balance as it half-rolled, half-skidded down the slight slope. The boy made the mistake of braking at the hump of the bridge and paid the price. The bike swung round in a swift arc, the front wheel spun quickly and there was a yell and a crash. A dramatic puff of snow flew up and cleared. It was Tom Harris, unhurt and grinning with embarrassment rather than humour. He examined his bike carefully, wobbling the handlebars to and fro, then picked up the front and turned the wheel.

'All right?' asked Gibbon, not wanting to contribute any more to the boy's embarrassment by taking too close an interest.

'Think so.'

'Front wheel not bent?'

'No.'

'Are *you* all right?'

'Takes a lot to bend me!' Voice filled with pride.

'Christmas present?'

'Yes.' The boy was examining the frame for scratches. He wetted his thumb with spit and rubbed it over the bright transfers on the metal. The bike had racing handlebars, derailleur gears, slim alloy mud guards, toe straps on skeleton pedals.

'A great bike.'

'Yes.'

Tom Harris met his eyes for the first time, smiled and slid away again too fast. Grey eyes, withdrawn, not windows of the soul but reflecting mirrors, thought Gibbon. There were reflecting strips on the pedals.

'I hope you looked after that turkey! Your mother was very concerned!'

Tom stared at him, perplexed.

'Your mother told me this morning at the Walker's. I met her there.'

'Oh.'

Tom seemed to be a master of monosyllables. Gibbon remembered Mary Harris' expression as she had told him about young Tom. Secretive, she had said, a bit wild, a rover. A liar? A boy who didn't like Wilkinson.

'Was it all right?' he pursued, more to continue the conversation than anything else. Tom surveyed his bike, apparently satisfied that no damage had been done.

'It was all right.'

'Maybe you're a good cook?' He knew this sounded fatuous but he was floundering in the attempt to keep the conversation flowing. Tom had already swung one leg over the bike ready to depart. He polished the new bell with the cuff of his jacket.

'I hate looking after food. It's boring. You have to just sit there and tip fat on it. All this grease oozes out and you spoon it all over it. Think how much grease people eat!'

'In a life-time!' said Gibbon, pursuing this line hopefully.

'Just think of it!' said Tom. 'Must be as much grease as a solid haystack. Even more. As much as a house! I mean, think of a block of lard as big as a house! And it all goes through you.'

'If you start thinking like that, you'll never eat a Christmas dinner. In fact you'll give up eating altogether.'

'Naw!' Tom was scornful. 'I like eating. I don't like fat and grease.'

How was he going to get any information out of him?

He opted for the direct approach.

'You must have had a fright in the church.'

'Made me jump,' said Tom reluctantly.

'Who do you think killed Luxford?'

Tom froze. It was the only way to describe his sudden rigidity. Gibbon mused that he had always thought of it as a cliché until then. For three seconds he was motionless, then his fingers squeezed the brake levers. He looked down at the snow, scuffed a toe in it, making a flat arc. Gibbon was afraid he was about to jump on his bike and cycle off.

'How should I know? What's it to do with me?'

Tom's voice was higher, more protesting. The foot moved back and forwards, uncovering yellowed grass then earth.

'You might have been giving it some thought. I certainly have.'

85

Gibbon deliberately turned away from him to lean over the stone parapet of the bridge. He watched the spindrift of ice particles running over the frozen surface of the river. He listened for the sounds of Tom making his escape. There was silence, then Tom spoke, trying to sound reasonable, but still reluctant.

'It could have been anyone. Nobody liked him.'

'Was he that unpopular?' Gibbon tried not to sound too naive. Tom was no fool.

'You know he was.'

'Why do you sing in the choir then?'

'My mum makes me! She says my dad did and I must too. I hate it. I hate wearing those silly clothes. They make you look a poof!'

'What sort of a person was he? I ask everyone that because I'm trying to form a picture. It's very difficult when you never met someone alive. People forget I never knew him . . .'

He half turned so that he could see Tom.

'Well he was always pestering women . . . ' said Tom, embarrassed.

'I know that bit. How could be afford it? It seems he always had plenty of money and they don't pay vicars so much.'

'I don't know.'

'But he always had money?'

'I suppose so.'

'You know he had!'

'All right, he always had money!'

'Why are you shouting? It's a simple enough question and there may be an answer there. What do you know about this archaeology business and about him and Wilkinson? I'm told you may be able to tell me something.'

'Who said anything about that! I don't know what you're talking about.'

Tom swung a leg over the bike, sat on the saddle, the other leg propping him upright. He was ready to fly. A coot made stupid noises in the sedges. The two looked at each other.

'I'm *not* prying!' insisted Gibbon.

'You're not a detective,' countered Tom. 'I don't have to answer questions.'

'No, you don't. But boys like you get around and see things. Wilkinson doesn't like you, and I don't know why, and you didn't like Luxford. Or Jeffrys. There's quite a lot of people you didn't like, isn't there?'

Tom snorted.

'Jeffrys likes boys!'

'I see.'

'No you don't see! You don't know nothing!'

Tom pushed off on his bike in the direction of Bridge House, did a

86

wobbly 'U' turn and then gained enough speed to shoot past Gibbon who remained where he was, propped on the parapet.

'This is a dangerous place!' called Tom dramatically, pedalling back towards the centre of the village.

'Food for thought.' said Gibbon aloud. He started to walk homewards. To a frozen turkey. Perhaps he would fry some bacon instead, and sit down to try to work some of this out. There was plenty of malt whisky and he would light a good fire and pretend to be comfortable and not thinking of Clara. Or Lucinda. Or Cynthia Fry. Or Mrs Philippa Crabbe.

Why not think of Mrs Philippa Crabbe?

Mrs Philippa Crabbe was thinking about him. He had no sooner closed the door and started to take off his snow-caked shoes than the telephone rang in the hall.

'I hope you don't mind my ringing,' she said. 'In fact I've called a couple of times already.'

'I was out walking,' said Gibbon.

'Please say "no" if you really wouldn't like to, but I wondered if you would like to join me for Christmas dinner. That all sounds terribly forward as they used to say, but I'm alone as you know and I wondered if you had had time to make any preparations for yourself? I didn't have the opportunity to get back to you at Lucinda's and I didn't think it would be a good place to ask anyway. I asked Molly Luxford along, more as a courtesy than anything. She wouldn't come. I shall have to go and see her later.'

Gibbon was tempted and paused. He had to call Clara. Was he in the mood to see Philippa with that agony hanging over him? He would much prefer to keep that pleasure to another time.

'It's very kind of you, but I've got everything prepared,' he lied.

'Can't you turn it off?'

'Please don't think me rude, but I'd rather be by myself.'

'Are you sure?' She sounded so disappointed that he felt a pang of weakness. He controlled it. Think of Clara.

'I'm afraid I am. Perhaps we could arrange something for another time?'

'Yes. That would be nice.'

'Thank you very much for asking. I feel terrible refusing.'

'Don't. It was only a passing thought. Happy Christmas.'

'Happy Christmas.'

She rang off. Gibbon went in to the kitchen and opened the fridge. Bacon and cold meat. Eggs, sausages. He opened the freezer and lifted out the turkey. He put it down on a worktop. It made a noise like an oak log and rolled sideways, trying to crash onto the floor. He looked with distaste at the bulging bag of plastic filled with the swollen mass of ready-frozen turkey. He realised he should have taken it out the day before. Christmas dinner had been doomed from

87

the start. Wiping away the frost from the fine print on the polythene, he soon confirmed it. Somewhere in there, it informed him, were the giblets in a plastic bag. He threw the whole thing back in the freezer.

In the sitting room he poured himself a monumental whisky and drank a large mouthful. It tasted vile, like varnish and turpentine. He was tired and needed something to eat. It warmed his belly. He was trying to find strength to ring Clara.

The telephone rang. He swigged more whisky in sheer panic and went back to the hall, staring at the receiver. His heart was thumping as though he was running. He felt a total coward. After six rings he picked it up.

'Is that John Gibbon?'

It was a voice he recognised but could not place.

'Yes?'

'It's me, Jeffrys.'

'Oh. Hello.' He set down his whisky glass. What was the old fool doing occupying the line? Clara could be ringing him even now. The whisky was already going to his head. Good.

'It struck me that you would be all alone today. I wondered if you would care to join me. After all I'm another fellow spirit so to speak. I usually eat in about half an hour. I like dining at four because it is already almost dark and there's nothing good on television until after eight anyway. I've plenty here.'

How many more? thought Gibbon. The Frys, Wilkinson, Mann, Philippa. They were determined to push food down his throat as though it was a pagan ritual, which he supposed it was anyway.

'That's very kind of you, but to tell you the truth, I was just about to eat,' he lied. He was becoming good at lying.

'Oh.' Jeffrys sounded very put out, as though the hand of friendship had been smacked.

'I'm sorry, but I had no idea . . .' babbled Gibbon, wondering why he was bothering to apologise. 'I mean, you didn't give me a lot of notice.'

'I suppose if one wants to be pedantic, that is perfectly true.' said Jeffrys huffily. 'After you left the Walkers' it occurred to me, you see. We hardly had time to chat through anything there, and after our little adventure at the church I thought it might be nice to meet more socially.'

'It would, it would,' said Gibbon, wildly apologetic and feeling sillily insincere. The old devil was trying to make an assignation! Gibbon had another swig from his whisky glass, noting the immortal truth that it was tasting better with every drop.

'The trouble is, you see, that everything's just ready, and I would really prefer to eat it here by myself.'

'I could always come round,' said Jeffrys reproachfully.

'No!' said Gibbon firmly. 'I really just want to be here by myself.'

88

'Oh all right.'

'Happy Christmas.'

'Happy Christmas.' Jeffrys sounded tearful. Gibbon wasn't having that. He put the phone down and laughed to himself wrily. So sought-after so suddenly. For what? While he felt stronger, he dialled Clara's number. It rang and rang. Who was she out with? Or in with. His jealousy was sudden and all-consuming and terrible.

The phone was picked up. Clara answered.

'Hello?'

'Happy Christmas.'

'Hello John. Happy Christmas.'

He was listening. For noises in the background, sounds of music, of happiness, of other people. Her voice was cool and kind. He could not bear the kindness.

'Thank you for the present. It was thoughtful of you, but you shouldn't have sent one. We agreed we wouldn't.'

Yes they had agreed, but what did that mean. Anything was fair.

'Please keep it. You know how you like moonstones.'

There was a long pause.

'It wasn't fair of you. You know that.'

'Yes I know that.'

'No more.' A command.

'No more.' An acceptance. He could hear no background noise. Was that itself suspicious? Surely there should have been something. It was the sort of silence that falls when everything is turned off, when everyone holds their breath. An insistent hush.

'I had to ring.'

'I understand John. But please don't make it difficult. Happy Christmas, and look after yourself. Please don't ring me up again, it's only upsetting for us both.'

'I'll write.'

'It would really be better if you didn't do that for a bit either. I won't read them you know.'

'Why not?'

'You know why not.'

'I hate you Clara!'

'I expect you to. Let's not fight. Not now. Put down the phone. Let's say Happy Christmas and leave it at that!'

'I can't!'

'Well I will. Happy Christmas, John, as best we can in the circumstances. Please don't call again.'

'Clara!'

But she put down the telephone. He wanted to cry and shout with rage at the same time. He put down the receiver, picked up his glass and poured another monumental whisky for himself in the sitting room. He must light a fire. The hearth was full of fir cones and ornamental bits of wood and grass. He picked up a box of matches from the mantel and set fire to them to relieve his feelings. The cones burned fiercely with the intense glare of fireworks. The grasses flared, carbonised and drifted up the chimney. Small worms of sparks ran over the soot on the fireback. He should have accepted Philippa Crabbe's invitation. Jeffrys' he could do without. He felt very sorry for himself. Even the logs were outside in the snow and the dry material in the grate would soon be consumed.

The telephone rang.

He assumed it was Clara, and ran to it.

'Hello?'

'Hello John Gibbon.' It was Lucinda, warm, slightly teasing.

'Hello.'

'You sound disappointed. That isn't a good start.'

'I'm sorry.'

'Don't apologise. You were expecting someone else . . .'

'No!' His denial was too abrupt. He could imagine her smile at the other end of the line.

'I don't believe that! Anyway, if you haven't got any alternative arrangements around there that we don't know about, I wondered if you would care to join us for dinner in about an hour.'

'I couldn't. Not after all your trouble this morning.'

He said it before he realised he had not given his standard excuse. The whole village seemed determined to invite him. Why turn this one down? It would take his mind off Clara. If he remained in the house, what would he do? Drink himself maudlin, eat nothing, wallow in self-pity. Would he enjoy that or not? Would he prefer Lucinda's company?

'I wouldn't have asked if it had been any trouble. You left before I had a chance to mention it and I've only just got things straightened out. Henry's doing some work and doesn't want to be disturbed for the time being so perhaps you can come round and have a glass of something in the kitchen while I'm cooking and stop me being bored!'

'You promise it would be no extra trouble at all?'

'I promise it would be a pleasure.'

'How does Henry feel about it?'

'Henry will hardly notice!' She laughed. 'That's his way. We can't have you sitting there all alone.'

'I've turned down other invitations. I've told them all I was cooking my own dinner.'

'But you aren't are you? Come on, your secret's safe with me. You can skulk in without being seen.'

'I'll bring a bottle or two then.'

'That would be nice. I look forward to seeing you in an hour.'

'I' not 'we'.

90

The fire was only embers now. He stirred them round with an iron poker. What about that letter in the church, he thought. What about the gun? All this socializing had certainly taken his mind off the main points. Perhaps he should have accepted Cynthia Fry's invitation in the first place. 'My dearest Peter, I have to write to you if I can't see you . . .' The elaborate arrangement of the gun in the clock tower. Was that because whoever arranged it could not bring themselves to pull the trigger but was happy to have it done by remote control? It was someone who got their timing right. A clever piece of work. Cynthia Fry with something to hide? Did Luxford's easy living come from blackmail? George exuded money in a quiet way. Did he know about his wife? George looked quite capable of the whole thing. George is a jealous man, Cynthia had said, and he believed it. George was a thoroughly dangerous man, and nobody's fool. The chances that Cynthia had managed to keep her affair with Luxford a secret were very small in this village. There was so much rumour and gossip being passed around in confidence that they might as well have printed it on broadsheets and pasted it in the windows of the Post Office.

Was Philippa Crabbe just as likely for the same reasons?

Or Molly Luxford, whom no one had seen? The wronged wife. She would know exactly where her husband would stand, know exactly the order of service, and been absent from the service. Wasn't that unusual for a vicar's wife? It wouldn't be unusual he supposed for a vicar's wife who could not face the other women in the congregation.

And what about Lucinda and Henry Walker? Henry had said he disliked the man. Similar reasons?

And Wilkinson, for reasons of rivalry, or something else?

And Jeffrys? Whatever the unspoken reason.

And the Harrises? Even Tom?

And Meadows, because Luxford had had the Village Store hunted out of existence for his unpleasant brother?

And what about unpleasant William? What did he stand to gain with his brother out of the way? Would it transpire he was sole beneficiary? Were the multitudes of reasons simply a useful diversion for another manoeuvre altogether?

Or was this all a blind? Had they been deliberately forced to examine all those involved at the church because in fact they had nothing to do with it?

Mummery had said that someone was playing games with them. Was it a double game? Snow round the church. Murder at midnight. Christmas Eve. Games or distractions? Or was there a reason for the time and place besides the obvious one that everyone was accounted for therefore everyone and no one was guilty.

What about the company at the 'Feathers'? No one had considered them at all. They would have to come in to the reckoning now. Except that someone had to have access to the church to rig the device up. And Cynthia and Lucinda had access for the flowers. Who would notice them, when they were carrying branches of holly and armfuls of ivy?

He had better get ready for dinner with the charming Lucinda.

The house had been tidied and the carpets bore the criss-cross marks of a vacuum cleaner but the smell remained. Lucinda came to the door clutching joss sticks which were all lit.

'I'm standing them about the place to kill the smell of smoke. I've had the windows open, but it's so cold.'

Gibbon took off his coat and Lucinda helped him although he murmured it was all right.

'I like taking off a man's coat,' she said. 'Enjoy it!'

John hoped that Henry Walker couldn't hear the amusement in her voice.

'Relax, John Gibbon. I won't eat you, you know. Have a drink!'

She stood a joss stick upright in each of the urns in the hall so that the smoke wreathed around the yellowing vines.

'Plants don't like me,' she observed, noticing his glance.

'Water?'

'I do all that. They just die.'

She had changed again. The ivory silk had given way for red wool with a white neck and cuffs. How could she afford to be so appropriate?

'You like it?'

'Father Christmas!'

'Of course. I saw it two months ago and thought it would be nice.' Her lipstick was the colour of holly berries, her dark skin was slightly made up to emphasize her cheek bones.

'You look very lovely.'

'Thank you.'

She took his hand as she had before and led him in to the sitting room. He resisted the desire either to disengage himself or clutch her tighter. He ascribed the last feeling to the numerous whiskies inside him.

'Where's your husband?'

'Safely away in his study, my dear. You mustn't be so obvious, and you mustn't be so shy!'

She kissed him firmly, and John kissed her back. She pressed herself firmly against him, breasts to his chest, belly to his belly. It was she who gently disentangled them.

'Happy Christmas, John Gibbon!'

She was laughing at him slightly, watching his reactions, but there was affection in it.

'Happy Christmas, Lucinda Walker.'

'That was your present.'

92

'I liked it. Do I only get one.'

'You attend to that fire, and I'll pour a drink. What do you want?'

'I suppose I'd better have another whisky.'

'So you *have* been drowning your sorrows.'

'I suppose so.'

'The woman in your life. I knew there was somewhere.'

'She's out of it now.'

Lucinda made a face. 'Do I ask about it, or not?'

'Not.'

'Well not today anyway.' She held two joss sticks in her teeth while she poured drinks. She put a bowl of olives and some cheese straws in front of John and then handed him his drink.

'I think you should eat something. Kissing you nearly made me fall over.'

'Oh, I'm sorry . . .'

'Don't apologise, don't say you're sorry! Rule one. Now tell me what's happened.'

She perched on the arm of a chair and motioned to him to sit down beside her. He wondered whether he should tell her about the gun.

'Nothing really.'

'John Gibbon, we all know about the gun. Don't play dumb.'

He was astonished and it obviously showed, for she chuckled.

'How do you know?' he asked. 'Who told you?'

'Charlie Brooks watched them taking it out to their car. He saw it from an upstairs window in the "Feathers". He watched them through binoculars, trying to wrap it in a cassock and all that nonsense but he says the barrel was sticking out! *Everyone* knows about the gun!'

'Well that's that!'

'What we want to know is where they found it.'

'I can't tell you that.'

'But you know?'

'Yes. But I can't tell you.'

'Really?'

'Really.'

'Spoil sport.'

'Why is he a spoil sport?' asked Henry Walker. He had entered the room unheard. John Gibbon automatically got to his feet. He felt ridiculously guilty at being found in this man's armchair with his wife perched at his side.

'He won't tell me where they found the gun.'

Henry Walker flapped a hand at John to sit down. He was dressed in a suit again. It was obviously his natural habitat because he looked completely at ease in it and had that knack of never crumpling it that seems to come to City men and lawyers. He scarcely looked festive. There were grey rings under his eyes.

93

'But it *was* in the church?' Henry Walker asked.

'Yes. I can tell you that.'

'And do the police have any idea who did it?'

'I'm afraid I can't answer that. Not because I'm not allowed to, but because I simply don't know. They haven't told me anything.'

Henry sat down in an armchair.

'How do you like our village?' he asked.

'It's a very pretty place,' said John ambiguously.

'Oh the place is all right.' Walker was sour. 'What about the people, the sturdy people?'

'That's rather difficult to summarise. There's quite a mixture, as you'd expect.'

'Lucinda says they're dull.'

Henry threw in the remark rather churlishly, Gibbon thought. Lucinda straightened slightly where she sat.

'They are. Try selling them something out of the ordinary!'

'Lucinda persists in trying to stock that shop of hers with fashion that would sell in the King's Road and is surprised when they come in to buy hanks of wool or two reels of white cotton.'

'I'm only trying to educate them, darling!'

Oh God, thought Gibbon, this is squaring up into a family fight.

'Perhaps it would be better if you tried to *sell* them something. The place isn't supposed to be a charity, though I must say from the books it certainly gets run as one.'

'Speak for yourself, darling! The Stock Market hasn't turned out to be quite the Klondike we all hoped, has it!'

'I didn't know you were a broker! What do you deal in?' yelped Gibbon frantically. Henry crossed one leg elegantly over the other, his eyes still on Lucinda with a calm steely expression.

'Commodities.' Gibbon prayed the man would have a drink or something. He was practising his concentrated super-relaxation again, and it was agony to watch. 'I'm not a broker.'

'It must be a difficult market, with things as they are.'

'You could say that.'

'Disastrous is the word that springs to mind,' murmured Lucinda.

'Darling, give it a rest,' whispered Henry.

So Cynthia Fry's observations had been entirely accurate. He sprang to his feet so that Lucinda wobbled and had to put her own legs on the ground to maintain her balance.

'This is a lovely room, isn't it,' he said, and grinned.

'You're right,' said Henry. 'You don't want to hear us quarrelling about money. That's all very boring and very rude. Lucinda asked you and we must be better behaved. I'll get changed and we can sit down and eat. Is the table set?'

'Of course,' said Lucinda. 'John can help me in the kitchen and can look over the table. Will you be ready to carve in ten minutes?'

'I should think so.'

Henry Walker left the room and Gibbon found himself drawing a breath of relief.

'I'm sorry,' said Lucinda. 'We shouldn't have let you in for that. Not at Christmas.'

'Shall I go?'

'Oh don't be silly! Henry hates my shop and business is bad, very bad, at the moment and of course he wants me to make money or sell it – but I won't. If I sell it I shall have nothing of my own here and he'll just close up and move. He doesn't care where he lives. He moves every two years on average. In any case he thinks he's going bankrupt.'

Gibbon stared at her aghast at her callousness. Lucinda put her hand on his arm.

'Don't look at me like that, darling! No I don't have a heart of solid rock, but when you've been nearly bankrupt as often as we have it's no big deal. It's hardly an event at all! Come through with me, I must look at the bird. If I don't get it right, that man there will just cut it into chunks to teach me a lesson. He's tougher than he looks, don't worry about it!'

Gibbon followed her into the kitchen with a mixture of horror and fascination.

'Is this the way you always keep going?'

'Mostly. He keeps his temper quite well. Sometimes it can get really bad, but I wouldn't have asked you round if I thought it was going to be a bad day.'

Gibbon roared with laughter. Lucinda looked genuinely puzzled.

'Never mind!' he said. 'Just my twisted sense of humour. Give me something to do!'

'Kiss me.'

Gibbon stared.

'Don't stare. Kiss me.'

Gibbon did what he was told.

'Now you go and look after the table and make it look nice. Henry wouldn't know a sugar shaker from a candle. You know, John Gibbon, you do things for me, that we could do better in bed!'

She waved John off towards the room next door. He knew he was reduced to astonished obedience, but didn't care.

'I am a man of steel!' he said to himself with a laugh. He surveyed the table which she had obviously spent hours preparing. There was nothing whatsoever to do. Garlands of ivy interlaced with holly formed runners down the centre. Silver glittered. Glasses shone. Paper chains in the same dark holly green hung in swagged profusion from a central ceiling rose and radiated out to positions on all walls. The napkins were the same holly green as the tablecloth. To pretend he could add or subtract anything was either a courtesy or a seeking

95

for compliments.

He wondered if Henry had killed Luxford. If Lucinda had behaved to him as she had just behaved to John Gibbon, then no doubt Henry had a lot to be jealous about! He even felt jealous himself.

'Pretty, isn't it?'

Henry stood beside him. He had entered noiselessly from a side door that led to the hall. Pretty was not the word Gibbon would have used.

'She has flair, there's no doubt about that, but she has no ability to run a commercial enterprise. You've probably noticed that. Look here, Gibbon, I know all about her sex life. I married her for it, after all. It's just that it's got a bit out of hand. I suppose I'm preoccupied and they say worry makes you impotent. I'm not that yet, but she has a heartily uncaring attitude to my money worries. I have to put up with her adventures, but I didn't kill Luxford although I would have done it cheerfully.'

'There's absolutely no need to tell me this,' said Gibbon. 'I keep trying to make it clear that I'm nothing to do with the police.'

'Well just believe me. I want to tell someone. I shall have to sell that shop if I can. She doesn't know how bad things are. To say I'm one step ahead of bankruptcy is to give me more credit for speed than I actually have.'

'I'm very sorry to hear that.'

'Oh, so am I! I'm not a very pleasant person at times as you may have noticed, and I'm certainly not as tough as Lucinda thinks I am. She's the tough one around here. Just make sure you don't become a victim.'

Gibbon didn't know what to say and was spared the need to answer as Henry held a finger to his lips and slipped out the way he had come in. John returned to the kitchen.

'It all looks splendid in there. What do you expect me to do? Shall I sharpen a knife or something? That's the great male act to avoid actual labour and claim dominion over the dinner!'

'Claim dominion over anything you like, darling!'

The door bell rang. Someone pushed the button for several seconds.

'Oh sod!' said Lucinda, caught with the turkey half out of the oven. She pushed it back in again and took off a pair of oven gloves made like puppets. 'What a noise. Who's that at this time of day?'

John listened from the kitchen. There were several voices. He recognised Mann's, Mary and Tom Harris. They were excitable; Lucinda was asking them to come in to the hall. She called for him and for Henry.

'Hello Mr Gibbon,' said Mann. He looked pale and tired and was back in uniform. The Harrises were agitated. Mary Harris had been crying and was dabbing at her nose with a handkerchief.

'What is it?' asked John.

'Young Tom Harris has gone missing,' said Mann.

'What?' The force of his exclamation made them all stare at him.

'I saw him about an hour and a half ago,' he explained. 'He was on his bike down by the bridge. I spoke to him.'

'He hasn't come home!' said Mary Harris woefully. 'He was just going out for ten minutes. That must have been when you saw him. He hasn't come back for dinner.'

Gibbon looked at Mann. Mann correctly interpreted the question in the look.

'The lad hasn't run away or anything. There was no quarrel, nothing like that.'

'He was delighted with his bike. He just wanted to try it!' Mary explained in anguished tones.

'I expect he's wrecked it, and doesn't dare show his face!' said Tom Harris unhelpfully. Mary Harris moved further away from him.

'I have to organise a search,' said Mann. 'I can't call anyone else out. Every police station is on skeleton staff, so it's self-help. It could all very well be a false alarm, but the lad may have fallen off and injured himself. It's very slippery out there. Will you please help us Mr Gibbon? And you too, Mr Walker?' he said to Henry who had appeared on the stairs and heard the last bit.

'We were just about to eat!' protested Lucinda.

'So was I, Mrs Walker!' said Mann gloomily. 'We must get moving. It's a cold night.'

'Hurry up, please,' begged Mary.

'I'll come right away,' said John. Henry nodded too.

'I should bring a bottle of something strong,' said Mann, 'and wear everything you've got. Have you all got torches?'

Mann's efforts had produced a small search party. In addition to John, Henry and the Harrises they had been joined by both the Frys, Mrs Tomlinson in a pair of hiking boots, William Luxford, who was being ignored by everyone, Alf Hazlitt, Brooks the publican and Wilkinson. There was a lot of beating of arms and puffing into cupped hands. The moon was alarming and clear, grey craters clearly visible in the dry cold air. A presence. Almost within reach.

'We'd best go back to the bridge first,' Mann had said, and they crunched off down the road shining torches into shadows and over hedges. His unspoken thought was obvious. Boys try ice for fun. Although he walked fast, Gibbon easily kept up with him. They soon outdistanced the rest and arrived at the bridge. The ice was intact and gleaming on each side.

'It was here you spoke to him?' asked Mann.

'Yes. He hurtled over the bridge and braked, skidded then

97

crashed. But he was quite all right. We passed a few words and he checked his bike – that was his main concern – and he pedalled back towards the village.'

'He could have come back for another go,' mused Mann. 'You know what boys are. Speedway skids over the bridge, jumps . . .'

'Might have gone out on the ice!' said Hazlitt who had joined them.

'We thought of that. It's not broken.' Torches shone on it, rotated.

'The bank's as flat as a pancake on the upstream,' said Wilkinson. 'He could easily cycle along there.'

'Whatever, let's hurry!' urged Hazlitt. 'In this cold . . . .'

'Lets get organised then,' said Mann. 'Come on!'

He split them into two parties, each taking a side of the river, working upstream. He told them, unnecessarily, to keep their eyes open for cycle tracks and not to walk over anything they found. Gibbon stayed with Mann as a matter of course. The Harrises followed with Luxford bringing up the rear. The others took the far side. Torches shone here there and everywhere, bringing glittering life to icicles on sedge, illuminating candied branches that were accustomed to trail in water but had now become stilled as the eddies froze and they became united with ice. Bubbles moved mysteriously below the frozen surface, uniting then multiplying like amoeba. At another time it would have been magical. The searchers were black bundles, crunching, talking.

'Where's Mummery?' asked Gibbon.

'I managed to contact him. He wasn't at all pleased!' Mann poked some crystallized brambles aside with his stick. 'He says he'll join us.'

'Where's he coming from?'

'Oh he hasn't left the village. He's staying at the "Feathers".'

'I didn't realise that. I would have thought there was nothing much to do until he gets his pathologist's report and one on the gun and bullet.'

'That man sticks it out.'

'There's nothing this side!' called Henry Walker. They had reached well upstream to the ford and had been looking for nearly half an hour.

'Back to the bridge then!'

Tom Harris senior stopped in front of Mann as they were retreating.

'Did you try to get Jeffrys out on this?'

'I asked him.'

'And what did he say?'

'He said he wasn't up to it.'

'Don't you think that's strange?'

'No. Why should I? He's not a youngster.'

'That man likes young boys! You know that! Don't you think you

98

should have got in to his house to make sure Tom wasn't there?'

'You have no grounds for saying that, Mr Harris! That's ridiculous. I expect your Tom is perfectly all right.'

'Don't,' said Mary Harris, putting a hand on Tom Harris' arm. He shook it off.

'He could have been lured into someone's house while we're all out here tramping over the countryside!'

'Why don't you go home then, Mr Harris, and wait there?' said Mann rudely.

'I'll go round to bloody Jeffrys' and see if he's there, that's what I'll do!'

'You'll do no such thing!' commanded a voice from the direction of the bridge. It was Mummery in wellingtons with a long black coat and a scarf wound four times about his neck like a surgical collar. 'Good evening, Constable Mann. From back on the road it looks as though Martians have landed.'

'This is Mr Harris. And Mrs Harris,' Mann introduced.

'How do you do. Let's all get back to the road and split up. Mr Harris, I understand your concern. I doubt very much the wisdom of either of you being out here at all. I really do suggest you return home. Suppose he's sitting there now wondering where everyone is?'

'I left a note,' said Mary Harris, 'saying we were all out looking and to go to Mrs Mann and tell her when he turned up.'

'Humph,' said Mann. 'Nevertheless, I think you would be better off.'

'No,' said Mary Harris. 'I won't go.'

The next sweep took in the stretch of road out of the village beyond John Gibbon's house. Here there was excitement as they found tyre tracks criss-crossing the snow and leading much further from the village than they had expected. Tom had paid no attention to his mother's ten minute limit. Then the tracks stopped and returned. They shone their torches into hedgerows and into ditches. An owl leapt out of a tree giving them a shock, and Hazlitt captured the pink eyes of a stoat in a ditch where it froze for a moment staring at them before bounding off in flowing jumps.

They returned to the village and split up to cover the High Street and Church Row. On the way back Mrs Harris called in to their house to find that Tom had not returned. The mood of the searchers was becoming more sombre. They had been out now for another forty minutes. The possibility of Tom lying somewhere in this cold with a broken leg was being openly voiced. Mummery tried to avoid speculation by keeping people spaced apart. There was nothing to be seen in the two main streets and no one had really expected it. Tom's cycle tracks were clearly visible in both directions on Hundred Row.

'The boy covered some distance!' growled Mummery. 'For all we know he could still be cycling up and down!'

He spoke to Mann, although Gibbon could hear him. There was no note of optimism in Mummery's voice. He was now grim.

'Do you think this has anything to do with . . . ?' began Gibbon.

'Don't even voice that thought, Mr Gibbon,' Mummery hissed. 'I wish the Harrises would go home! Can't somebody take them?'

He gave instructions to the searchers to split up into two parties again, each to walk down Hundred Row out of the village in opposite directions. Mummery, Mann, Hazlitt, Wilkinson, Walker, Gibbon and Mrs Tomlinson trudged westward. They had only gone about two hundred yards before drifts became deeper. There were no car tracks in this direction as the road was blocked between here and the main road. Mummery, Mann and Gibbon saw it simultaneously and began to run. There was a single tyre track suddenly, with no returning grooves. Over the hedge beside them cattle began to run too, startled by the noise and lights. Mann fell, cursed and picked himself up. Mrs Tomlinson was calling 'Wait for me!', but the men ran on.

The bike seemed to have been flung deep into a drift, or to have run into it at speed. In front of the drift was a frozen sheet of glassy ice where water had run from the earth bank at the side of the road and frozen. Tom Harris lay on his back on the ice. When Mummery tried to lift his head he found to his horror that it was stuck firm by the frozen blood in his hair which had made a patch of red ice. No bigger than a lollipop John thought. Tom was dead.

'Everyone just stand quite still now,' said Mummery. 'Let's get a clear picture of what we're looking at.'

He shone his torch around as Wilkinson, Walker, Hazlitt and lastly Mrs Tomlinson joined them. Mrs Tomlinson gave a cry and looked away. The rest were silent. First one cow then another shoved their heads over the hedge and snorted, rolling wild white eyes.

'The only witnesses I suppose!' said Mummery drily. The torch beam took in the bicycle again, embedded some ten inches in the drift so that only a pedal and a handlebar still projected. It looked as though it had been dropped into a mould. The road ahead of them was white and unmarked. The light turned back to Tom. Mann had taken the initiative and was unbuttoning his coat. They all watched as Mann covered the body.

'It would seem he slipped on the ice,' said Mummery as though ruminating to himself. He bent down to the body and propped his torch so that it shone directly onto Tom's head. 'He must have come down with a terrible crack. One of you go back to the village and get an ambulance. Mrs Tomlinson, you'd better go back as well. Thank you for your help. Mann, I must give you the unpleasant task of finding Mrs Harris. Bring her here, and I suppose you have to bring the husband. You will have to tell them what we've found but try to be tactful. I suppose we shall have to wait hours for an ambulance.

100

Wilkinson, your shop is probably nearest isn't it? You do the phoning.'

Gibbon was impressed at Mummery's grasp of who was who. He was surprised by his next move.

'Mr Gibbon, you can stay here with me until the ambulance arrives. Mr Walker and Mr Hazlitt, I want you to go home. Will you kindly go with Constable Mann now and retrace your steps as carefully as you can. Do not stray off your original course here, and above all don't walk on any bicycle tracks.'

Within moments the party had gone. There was silence except for the movement and continuing snorts from the cows. They were champing at food, presumably hay put out by the farmer. Mummery switched off his torch. Gradually their eyes became accustomed to the moonlight. Gibbon waited for the other man to speak, his eyes still on the black coat covered shape on the silvery ice.

'Well that alters things, doesn't it, Mr Gibbon?' said Mummery. He pulled a bottle from his coat pocket, undid the top.

'How?'

'The boy was murdered. Would you like a swig?'

Gibbon wondered if he was really surprised. Mummery misinterpreted his lack of response.

'You seem shocked.'

'I suppose I am. I'm not accustomed to this.'

'One shot, now one killed with a blunt instrument. There has to be a connection.'

'How do you know he was murdered? How do you know it wasn't a fall?'

'We're supposed to believe it was a fall, but the shape of the wound makes it impossible. Whoever hit him overdid it. The skull is depressed inwards. You don't get that from cracking your head on a flat sheet of ice.'

'So it's two murders.'

'Yes. And there's another thing that has changed. You've been present at both of them, Mr Gibbon. I think you have to join the list of suspects now, don't you? Particularly as you seem to have been the last person to see Tom Harris alive!'

Gibbon stared at him. He had wondered if that particular gem would be produced, but was still surprised it had been done so quickly.

'What we have to ask ourselves,' Mummery continued, apparently addressing the cows, 'is whether these two things were done by the same person? The method is very different. Could it be an opportunist murder? Someone wants to get rid of young Harris here and takes the opportunity because he believes we will think the same person committed them both?'

'I don't believe in opportunist murders. Have you ever come

101

across one?'

Mummery paused, readjusted his scarf around his neck.

'No. In all honesty I can't say I have.'

'Could this have been done by a person of either sex?'

'It could have, but it's more likely to have been a man. Tom Harris was hardly small for his age was he? A woman would have been taking a chance. Unless it was a big woman. Or completely unexpected.'

'A lot of qualifications.'

'Perhaps the two murders were committed by a husband and wife team. That might make a lot of sense in the circumstances.'

The Frys, the Walkers. Gibbon could see what Mummery was driving at.

'How was this done?' he asked. It was a question that needed asking while they stood there in the moonlit cold.

'No tracks again, just like the church. Now there's a similarity!'

'I know, that's why I asked.'

Mummery snorted.

'Well if you noticed, you tell me how it was done.'

'I have no idea. Someone could stand on this ice and leave no trace.'

'They could indeed. And if there's cows in the field next door, that will be well tramped. Someone knew that all right. Someone was thinking clearly and moved fast, but that doesn't necessarily make it premeditated either. It would be nothing for someone in dark clothes to jog across the field for example, would it, Mr Gibbon? Especially keeping close to the hedge.'

John had had enough of this cocktail of innuendo and questions.

'Why choose jogging? Do you seriously mean that you suspect me in some way? Apart from adding me to your list!'

'It was only meant to be a figure of speech, expressing semi-rapid motion on the feet!' said Mummery blandly and untruthfully.

'Well, you can stuff your figure of speech!' Gibbon felt suddenly angry. Perhaps it was the man, perhaps it was the cold and the cruelty of a young life taken so violently, the head frozen to the ice like a lollipop. 'I've better things to do than have these cat-and-mouse conversations about whether or not I killed this boy that I hardly even knew and have spoken to only twice. If you don't mind, I'll go back to the village . . .'

Seeing that John had already started on his way, Mummery wiped his painfully exposed nose with the end of his scarf and mumbled a half apology through a sniff.

'Wait a moment Mr Gibbon! I didn't intend to be personal. Come back here for a moment . . .'

John stopped, looked at the gaunt man beckoning to him, at the covered body, and was struck by the surreal nature of the scene.

'Would I be talking to you in this way if I *really* believed you'd done this? Wouldn't I have the Constable here as a witness?'

Gibbon sighed and retraced the few paces he had moved.

'All right. But frankly I'd rather not be here when the Harrises arrive. I'm not very good as a witness of distress. Perhaps I can be allowed to be spared that.'

'I don't like it either you know,' Mummery said, sounding both offended and dignified. 'It's my job and I do it, but I don't have to enjoy it. It drives policemen to drink you know. The public never think of that.'

'Now don't try to make me feel sorry for you.'

Mummery wiped his nose again.

'I don't want you to feel sorry for me. And talking of being driven to drink, would you like that swig you didn't take before?'

Mummery rummaged in his coat pocket and produced the bottle again. Gibbon saw this time that it was a flat half bottle of whisky. Mummery unscrewed the top, wiped the lip of the bottle and offered it to Gibbon. Gibbon was grateful he hadn't wiped it with his scarf. He wiped the rim again with the palm of his hand and drank from the thing quickly so that the whisky shot into his mouth without the glass touching his lips. He handed it back to Mummery who was clearly not so fussy, merely applying the bottle directly to his mouth and gulping twice.

'That's better!' Mummery executed a series of shaking movements that seemed designed to distribute the spirit to every part of his body. He screwed the top back on, put it away and gazed soulfully at the white moon.

'I hope the ambulance gets here first,' he said, 'It makes the business so much more impersonal if the body's all tidied away inside the vehicle, wrapped in blankets, comfortable looking . . .'

'You hate this bit, don't you?'

'Yes Mr Gibbon, I do.'

Far away a beam of light rotated like a cone of white glass, momentarily glared in their eyes then was lost in distant darkness. A blue pulsing was visible, reflected from the snow icing of far-off trees. The source was invisible.

'That'll be the ambulance,' said Mummery unnecessarily.

'Can I go now?'

'Aye. Thank you for staying for a while. I never really had a chance to ask you how you got on this morning. With your social whirl. Perhaps you could tell me about it sometime. You must have picked up a lot of gossip. In this sort of place it trembles there like leaves in autumn, just waiting for someone new to give the trees a good shake!' He gave Gibbon a fleeting twitch that was undoubtedly a Mummery smile. Gibbon realised that Mummery was actually suggesting they should meet and talk.

'Perhaps you would like to come round and see me after this has been seen to. Have a drink?'

'Oh, I don't want to put you out! Drop in at the "Feathers". I'll be about, I'm not an early bird.'

'No, you come to me. It'll be much more comfortable, and we can talk without being overheard.'

'I look forward to that.'

Brilliant lights shot vertiginous silhouettes of branches across the white snow. There was an illusion that the whole ground was rolling, undulating. The twin blue lights of the vehicle made the scene theatrically chill. Mummery walked quickly towards it, hand uplifted, to stop it well short of the spot.

'God, I suppose it's run over all the bicycle tracks,' groaned Mummery. 'And I never thought of that! I'm too old!'

John Gibbon stood aside and watched the quick efficiency of the two ambulancemen. They were momentarily delayed by the frozen blood, but one of them produced an implement, perhaps a penknife, from his pocket and there was a hard scraping and chipping. Then the body was expertly lifted onto a stretcher and draped with a blanket. As John walked away, he saw Mummery reaching inside his coat again for the flat bottle.

As he made his way carefully back down the road, his mind was racing with a purpose he had told Mummery nothing about. He had felt himself warming to the lonely man, but not so much that he would risk exposing himself to ridicule by explaining his theory.

Gradually the flashing blue light faded and the moonlight became the stronger force. His eyes recovered their night sight, and he could plainly see the bicycle marks in the centre of the road. One set only. There was no doubt about it. The ambulance had cut two snowy ruts that had left the tyre marks intact. Mummery would be pleased. He broke into a trot, hurrying in case he should encounter the Harrises being brought to the scene, anxious to be away from all that anguish and anger.

He regained Hundred Row before it entered the village and slowed down to a fast walk. His breathing was a little harsh, but not bad for the distance he had just run. He was definitely getting fitter. Seeing figures in the street outside the 'Feathers' he lingered, crossed over to the pavement beside the church, walked past the lich-gate and waited by the war memorial until the coast was clear. He then crossed back and walked quietly down the High Street towards his own house. He wondered why he was being so secretive as he did it, but could find no logic in it except that he wanted to test this thing for himself, without interruption or discovery. Or, if he was right, without being observed by the murderer.

Passing Mann's cottage as softly as a felon, he was now out of the village proper and in moments was standing on the bridge. He waited until he could see quite clearly, for the last street lamp by Mann's gate had made everything dark.

The sedge rustled suddenly, making him jump, but it was only a buffeting wind that set the crystals rattling like sand. His eyes watered so that the cold seemed to shimmer. He could now see clearly the trampled path they had made in their earlier search upstream. Moving towards the other side of the bridge he looked carefully at both banks. Tussocks and the snow-filled hoof marks of animals made a deeply indented surface, but the snow looked unbroken. He looked carefully down the hedgerow and no more than twenty feet from the end of the bridge parapet he found a gap in the hawthorn hedge that was suspiciously free of snow. Easing himself through this, with one foot on a stump so that he could look before jumping, he saw a line of footsteps that veered back towards the river.

Gibbon eased himself through the hedge, plucking off the sharp twigs of hawthorn that clung to his clothing. He pondered over the quandary of what to do next. He must leave the footprints intact for Mummery but at the same time he wanted to follow them to their destination to prove to himself that they did lead to the scene of Tom Harris's murder. He decided the best way was to walk a parallel course about ten feet away. He jumped down softly from the stump, wishing for the mixed blessing of a torch which would have made his task so much easier yet made him so much more visible to anyone who might be still watching. It was a possibility he had to consider, and it was alarming. Anyone who could destroy the boy in that way was quite capable of clubbing him on the back of the head. It made Gibbon feel chill at the nape of the neck. It was better not to think about it, but he must stay alert, listen, be full of stealth.

The trail of footsteps both came and went. He didn't have to be a Boy Scout or Indian tracker to see that. They appeared to be the same imprints in each direction although only close examination in daylight would reveal enough detail to confirm that. There was just enough light to see that there were no particular ridges or corrugations in the compacted cake of snow at the bed of the impressions. Gibbon felt gently with his fingertips, confirming with the subtler sense of touch that the walker had worn almost smooth soles. What did that mean? That they had deliberately chosen footwear that left no identifiable marks, or that they only had unsuitable shoes? No boots would have left such a mark. The size of the impression would be some help. If it was a woman's foot it was large, if it was a man's it was average. That must eliminate some of the village.

He began to follow. The trail led to the river in a straight line and crossed it, faint on the surface of ice. Whoever it was, they did not appear to have hesitated at the edge of the ice, and surely this meant they had sound local knowledge. Gibbon would not have dared to set off across this glassy stretch without testing it step by step. Who would have advanced with such certainty that it would hold? Hazlitt? George Fry? It was the sort of thing either man would know.

But he was being too creative. He deliberately made himself stop and think like any country person with eyes that see country things. It was very simple. The river widened here to almost three times its normal width between the banks to left and right and would therefore be much shallower. It was evidently a cattle crossing under all the snow and it should be obvious to anyone that it would freeze first and freeze hard. He walked over it himself making the ice emit squeaks and tiny crackling noises that indicated perhaps that a thaw was imminent. It certainly did not seem so cold.

The tracks led diagonally away from the glassy surface on the far side, and up a slope in the field that was quite steep and obscured all forward vision. Beyond the slope, flickering above it like some pale Aurora Borealis was the blue rinse of light from the ambulance. It defined the ground from the sky and tinged the horizon of the slope pale blue where snow particles danced in the breeze. The moonlight seemed yellow by comparison, the shadows grey as ash. Gibbon climbed the slope slowly, mindful how visible he would be as he breasted it. As he reached the brow, crouching, he saw that the footsteps were directly in line with the distant road and ambulance. The beams of light were sharp as a laser and swept the intervening fields. Next in front of him was a wire fence and beyond that was the field containing the cattle that had been so curious of Mummery. He climbed the wire fence awkwardly. The surface now was heavily pitted and diaphragms of ice crackled and popped under foot. It was squelchy beneath. A number of long wooden shapes lay on the snow, each surrounded by a dark circular area that from a distance looked like black pits but were no more than the churned area of frozen mud around wooden troughs. Beside these were also the remnants of hay bales, put out as animal feed. The absence of snow in these areas was a relief. Gibbon would be almost invisible as he crossed them.

His quarry had done the same. The footsteps led from one black roundel to the next. Island hopping. Was this a fortunate coincidence or expert knowledge?

A cow snorted loudly, making him jump, heart pounding. It sounded exactly like an attack. The animal stretched out its neck and lowered its head. Gibbon stood still, afraid it would bellow. Instead it tossed its head violently to one side, executed a following manoeuvre of no elegance with its body and threw wild legs in the air behind it. He could now see other dark shapes on the ground that raised their heads and stared at him. They had formed a huddle as if to keep out Indians but presumably for warmth. He skirted them quietly.

106

Gibbon moved further away from the footmarks so that he could more quickly reach the cover of the hedge. He could hear voices, but not recognise them. The footmarks disappeared, trampled out by the cows. He carefully examined the undisturbed zone at the foot of the hedge where drifts had formed as deep as his thighs. His quarry must have moved in close as he was doing. He found the footsteps again, deep and unmistakeable at the edge of the drifts. They continued in the direction of the ambulance, which was now very close. Gibbon pondered for a moment whether or not he should contact Mummery now, but as quickly decided against it. If the Harrises were there in their grief this was no time to bob up through the hedge announcing his private detective work. He couldn't imagine that Mummery would thank him for it, and in any case he had further things to do before he reported to Mummery.

Satisfied, he retraced his steps back to the fence, trying to walk on his own tracks. At the wire fence he stood very still, looking and listening. Everything was very quiet. The cows chewed softly, snow crystals rattled softly like sand on paper. There were no noises of a stalker, a murderous footpad on his tracks. There was no reason why he should have been seen, except for the cunning of the unknown person who had slipped through the night to kill a boy. That cunning was of the night, silent, more animal than human. Knowing and frightening. He had confirmed the route of the second murderer and now he would try to confirm the reasons which he believed he partly understood. At least he understood now why Luxford had died, and if he was right, why Tom Harris was responsible without knowing it. He walked carefully back to the river, then back to the hole in the fence, easing himself out onto the road after making sure the coast was clear. Having regained the road he walked normally, like any man taking a healthy outing, and made for his house. There he went straight to the kitchen cupboard where he kept a powerful torch. He must move quickly, if he was to establish the next piece in the puzzle while Mummery was still engaged with the dead, and before Mummery decided to drop in for that drink. He remembered too that he had half-promised to meet Wilkinson.

There was no police guard on the church. He had noted that as he passed it the first time. What had happened to the uniformed sergeant? Presumably the man, who was not local, had at last been sent home to celebrate the ruin of his Christmas as best he could. With the discovery and removal of the gun there was little more to be gained. They had dusted for fingerprints and done all the usual routine things. Mummery had in fact decided that with the bell tower firmly locked and sealed, the interesting bit was well out of bounds.

Gibbon felt even more guilty slipping watchfully through the lich-gate than he had crossing the fields. He felt like a grave robber or at the very least a profaner. When he turned the heavy iron ring on the porch door the noise of the latch clacking up was like that other shot. It echoed inside the building as Gibbon froze, convinced the village must hear it and come streaming from their houses with weapons to arrest him. He opened the door carefully, remembering that the hinges were well oiled and that it should be noiseless. It was. He pushed it to behind him, not daring to latch it again but balancing the heavy bar on the keep, using both hands.

The interior of the church was black and he stood still. The windows gradually showed as grey clearings in an ancient forest of columns. Afraid to move without light, he switched on the torch and shone it round. As he knew, the wooden stand for offerings and the 'Pocket Guide, 15p' and 'For the fabric', were just inside the door. On the other side were the faded brown postcards that no one bought and the Mothers' Union board.

He had noticed a tall pair of steps among the garments and hymn books in the vestibule beneath the tower that morning, presumably for changing light bulbs. He shone the torch low, aware that the light might easily be seen from outside, and made for that room. Thankfully the door had not been fully closed and he was able to open it without too many of the screeches and screams it had earlier given. A quick playing of the torch over the wall and he found them. They were an old pair with both leaves of solid wood connected at the bottom by two lengths of grey rope. When he tried to pick them up one-handed they were far too heavy and the further leaf swung away from him, banging on the wall. He switched the torch off quickly, waiting for the noise to die away, listening for what seemed a long time but was no more than two minutes. He needed both hands for this. He thought for a moment then turned the torch on again, laying it on the vestibule floor so that it shone from there out of the door and died down the aisle, outlining its ancient irregularities. Then he picked up the steps using both hands, turned them on their side and carried them through the door and down the lit path of the aisle to the side of the lectern. He opened the steps to the full extent of the pieces of rope and stood them beside a heavy drum column.

('Part of the aisle and all of the columns date from 1183 and the foundation of the Norman church on earlier Saxon foundations. The fine columns from that period are variously decorated with chevrons and zig-zags, the capitals mainly being plain. Note the rich decoration of the arches which resembles that of Waltham Abbey . . .')

Gibbon then returned for the torch. Holding it in one hand he moved the ladder around slightly, directing the beam at the column. He swore softly as the light momentarily flickered across the interior of the church. He must be careful. He tried climbing the ladder with the torch in one hand but the ancient steps wobbled. It would be easier to lean them against the column and use them as a ladder, and this he did. Satisfied, he climbed them and began to examine the column closely. High up, just below the capital he found what he was looking for and was examining it with satisfaction and excitement when the ladder was abruptly buffeted sideways. He felt a brief lurching motion as it described an arc sideways, a rush of air then an explosion of pain and nothing.

Chapter Six

It was very warm and there were faint dry rustlings and murmurings as though the wind stirred. Scraping like dried leaves sounded loud, inside the head, inside the ear drum. Bright light intruded, sun that could not be avoided. Eyelids transparent and red, eyes that hurt, deep in the back of the head where there seemed to be a centre of pain. Then sleep, vertiginous and unpleasant, falling and spiralling in a black tube that was infinite but cramped at the same time so that he tried to fight, to swim, to grasp something, but it was so smooth his hands ran down walls like polished jet. Then the spiralling stopped and he was floating.

A vigorous rocking feeling woke him. He opened his eyes to protest as it would unbalance his delicate poise, to explain he was afloat on the surface of the sea using only the pulse of his wrists to balance him. A figure in a blue shirt with a white bib was rocking him and he didn't understand. She smiled and rocked him again. He briefly understood she was making his bed. He slept again, cleverly keeping his balance.

Waking, he saw the uniformed sergeant whom he recognised from the church. He peered at the man through half-closed eyes that were heavy and covered with something sticky. The sergeant was smiling and talking to a nurse and neither of them saw him. It was dark, because there was only a low light. His head hurt and was strangely numb and he could not hear what they were saying. He wondered if his hearing was impaired. Silent film, silent film, he thought. He remembered falling, and slept again, restlessly.

When he awoke again his ears seemed much better, as though they had been drained of fluid. He saw Mummery looking at him, sitting only a few feet away. The man smiled briefly and leaned further forward, studying him. It was like the nervous tooth display of a chimpanzee, which is not intended to be friendly. The thought made him smile. He found that difficult as his face seemed to be made of ham rind.

'Awake are we, Mr Gibbon?'

'I seem to be.'

The words that came out were as dry as a cricket. They were unrecognisable as his own. There was a bustle beside him and a rustle and a nurse who had been sitting unseen to his left walked past the end of his bed and came alongside him in front of Mummery. She was holding out a glass of orange which he sipped when she pressed the glass to his lips, without moving his head. A lot of it ran out of his mouth and down his chin. The nurse held a wad of tissue there to catch it. His lips weren't up to much. He tried to remember what had happened to him and who Mummery was and gradually it returned. The nurse gave him time, smiling, applying the glass again and again, dabbing and mopping. He remembered the church, the ladder, the violent shove, the fall. He had survived it anyway. It was the first thought he had had about his condition. He tried moving his hands as it seemed a good start, and discovered he could only move his right. His left hand and arm were encased. Something was broken. He moved his right hand up to the side of his face. The nurse nodded encouragement. The fuzzy, unconnected sensation was explained. His head was turbaned in bandages, over his brow and over his ears. The nurse stopped administering the drink.

'What's happened to me?' he asked. The words came out much better now, but slurred because his lips still would not work properly. He touched them lightly with his right fingers and found they were puffed and tender. His jaw ached.

'You have a fractured left arm, a crack on the skull and a few fairly colourful bruises,' said Mummery. 'You're not a pretty sight but considering everything you're very lucky.'

The nurse tutted and shot a reproving glance at Mummery.

'You're allowed ten minutes,' she said. 'And I mean ten minutes exactly.'

'That's what they say in films!' Gibbon managed to joke. The nurse gave him a nice smile, and he tried to return it, but his face was a water-filled balloon and refused to crease. There was a short silence.

'Well, what happened?' asked Mummery.

'Someone knocked the ladder away. Who found me and got me here?'

'Never mind that bit now – the important bits first. How do you know the ladder didn't slip? We have to know that.'

'Because it was shoved.'

'How can you be sure?'

'You know all right when you're clinging on to it. It was pushed. Hard. Away from the column. Slipping is a slow sort of thing, you feel it starting to give. This was just wham!'

'Did you see anyone?'

'Not a chance. It was all dark as ink and happened so fast. I can remember flying through the air. That's all.'

'What in God's name were you doing there anyway?' Mummery's voice was officially stern. 'If your torch hadn't been seen, you would probably have been dead. Remember young Harris. Whoever shoved you off your perch probably meant to finish you, and he nearly managed it with the fall. It would all have looked like a silly accident.'

'I don't think you're supposed to treat patients like this when they're in a state of shock,' said Gibbon tartly. He was in no fit state for a lecture, or a reminder of his recent perils. His head was already throbbing.

'All right, that was tactless.' Mummery was trying to be penitent. He immediately spoiled it. 'I'm only trying to get it into your thankfully thick head that you have had a very narrow escape from someone who certainly doesn't want to wish you Happy Christmas! I have a man outside this room permanently just to make sure. That's how seriously I take this.'

'I take it pretty seriously too, you know!' protested Gibbon. He was trying to grapple with the astonishing idea that someone unknown, against whom he had no personal grudge whatsoever, had tried to kill him. He found it very difficult.

'The official story for the moment is that you were putting up some decorations in the church that had come down and slipped.' Mummery sighed. 'It's not a very good story but at least it's simple and people believe that sort of thing. Now what *were* you doing?'

Gibbon had been exploring his mouth. At least he had all his teeth!

'Well, when I saw Tom Harris lying there murdered, I suddenly had a theory, and it seems that I was right because someone saw me and someone realised what I was doing, so I was pushed . . .'

'Look, Mr Gibbon, in the politest possible way, stop babbling. What did you do when you saw Tom Harris was dead, and what is this theory?'

'When I left you I went back down the road to the village and went back to the bridge again . . . wait a moment, where is this place?'

'This is the County Hospital, now will you please get on with it? We only have six minutes. You went back to the bridge . . .'

'I went back because I realised that was the obvious way to get to the spot where Tom Harris was murdered if you didn't want to be seen. You must get there quickly. There are clear footmarks from a

111

gap in the hedge over the river. It's frozen solid. I walked well clear of them so as not to confuse anything, so you can get good impressions. I felt the footprints but there didn't seem to be any identifying marks. You can certainly get the foot size though.'

Mummery sighed theatrically and rolled his eyes to heaven.

'You really are a trial aren't you, Mr Gibbon!'

Gibbon was angry. He stared at Mummery blankly.

'What does that mean!'

'Wait a moment.'

Mummery rose to his feet and stood close to Gibbon's bedhead. He pulled open a curtain that Gibbon had not noticed or realised was shut. Brilliant sunlight doused the room. Gibbon shielded his eyes with his one hand.

'How long do you think you've been here?' Gibbon looked blank. 'You've been coming and going for three days. It's lovely out there. While you've been bye-byes spring has sprung, or at least tried to. Lambs aren't exactly leaping yet or daffodils popping from buds, but the sun has been really warm. Balmy breezes from the south. The whole thing. What you don't know is that there isn't a scrap of anything white out there except litter. No footsteps. No nothing. The thaw had already started when we were looking at Harris's body.'

'I did hear the ice creaking.' Gibbon remembered crossing the river. 'So now we'll never know . . .'

'So what did you do after finding these footsteps and doing your white tracker bit?'

Gibbon ignored the man's annoying sarcasm.

'I followed them to the spot in the road where Tom Harris was lying, keeping out of sight, then retraced my steps, went to my house and got a torch. Then I went to the church. I made sure I wasn't seen!'

'Well that worked well, didn't it!'

Gibbon had to admit to himself that Mummery was right. He had been woefully amateurish and naïve. The killer was a professional, not taken in by his skulking and concealment.

'What did you go to the church for?'

'To see if I was right.'

'About what? For heaven's sake I know you're not feeling well, but tell me.'

'To tell you the truth I feel a bit stupid. What I thought was that Luxford might not be the target in the first killing. Harris might have been the target and Luxford the accidental victim. That was why they persisted and got him second time. That all fitted well enough.'

Mummery was looking at him as Caesar must have looked at Brutus.

'Why didn't you tell me this?'

He delved in his coat pocket and Gibbon knew he was going to produce his half bottle of whisky. He unscrewed the top, took a swig,

112

looked at Gibbon, shook his head, and put the top back on and the bottle back in his coat.

'I didn't have all the pieces then and I wanted to be able to prove it.'

'Do you see why we have a horror of amateur detectives?'

The question was rhetorical.

'I got to the church,' Gibbon continued, 'and found the ladder to look at that column. You see when you showed me the gun and we were looking down the barrel it struck me that the slightest movement would have pulled it off target and that there was a great risk in the timing. Luxford had to go to the lectern at a set time for everything to be right. What if the gun was aimed at someone who would be stationary throughout? That would make a lot more sense. I saw that the gun had been strapped in position with masking tape. Now that stuff is very strong, but it stretches slightly when exposed to moisture for a period of time. It had loosened a bit, I thought, and that bit would be enough for it to kick a couple of degrees when fired. There's a bullet scar high up on the side of the column. Just a smear of metal. Being circular, it gave it the slightest deflection. I think it was meant for Harris and that merest touch, almost an act of God if you like, killed Luxford. A few more millimetres and it would probably have ricocheted away harmlessly.'

Mummery walked to the window and down to the end of the bed.

'Right!' he said loudly. He seemed animated. 'Right!' He took another turn up and down. 'You had all this worked out, and then didn't mention it. You concealed all this from the police, that's what it amounts to!'

'Don't bully me or I'll complain and they'll chase you out!' said Gibbon mischievously.

'Right!' bellowed Mummery, even louder. 'And when you were concealing all this – and I must say it's all very clever – far from sitting on our backsides being totally ignorant as you no doubt think we were, we had recovered the bullet from Luxford's body and sent it to ballistics who came back immediately with the information that the bullet had been deflected off a surface before entering the body. Clutching this valuable piece of information we were about to conduct a thorough and scientific examination of the church ourselves, in the daytime, with proper equipment, without being pushed off ladders and inciting murderers to creep about in the dark by waving torches around . . .'

'I'm sorry!' interrupted the nurse firmly, 'You're making a terrible noise. We can hear you right down the corridor and in the wards. You'll have to go now in any case. How are we, Mr Gibbon, all right?'

She smiled at him encouragingly. Mummery gasped for air.

'Please give me one more minute with Sherlock here. Just one minute?'

She looked at Gibbon. Gibbon made a small nod. She made a sympathetic face at him, wagged an admonitory finger in Mummery's face and left.

'Right!' hissed Mummery, enraged, 'So instead of letting our man lie low, you stir him up. You go about brandishing your extra strong super-power torch in there as though carrying the fiery cross, and if Mrs Tomlinson hadn't seen it and called Constable Mann I think you would have been number three. Of course the one thing we had was a clue. Or rather, *you* had a clue. The footprints. Unfortunately you didn't tell us about them and at the time we should have been busy finding them for ourselves, guess what? Our entire tiny police force is called out to the church because some silly ass has tried to get himself killed there. And by the time we have you picked up and patched up, guess what? "Like the snow falls in the river – a moment white – then melts forever." Burns.'

'They were medium sized feet,' volunteered Gibbon, feeling very subdued.

'Oh God!' Mummery invoked.

'Right!' said the nurse in unconscious imitation of Mummery. 'That's enough. Time's up. Leave Mr Gibbon in peace now.'

Mummery left snarling.

The conference he had called the next day was a sombre and intense affair. The murder of Luxford had attracted a great deal of the worst sort of publicity, as he had expected. The murder of Tom Harris and the circumstances of it had led to an invasion of reporters despite the season of the year, and had reached the front page of *The Times*. It was a small paragraph, but quite enough to make Mummery's superiors summon him to London to ask if he could cope. He had managed to survive and had been drafted more men. It had not been said, positively *not* been said in the heaviest possible silences that another murder would see the removal of him from the scene like grease in a furnace.

Murder Headquarters, as they now had to call it, was a large mobile unit in Mann's drive. His quiet life was ruined. His wife's quiet life was ruined. The daffodils were ruined, squashed at that stage of infinite tenderness when the shoots had just emerged from the thawed earth as pale green snouts. Reporters hung around like crows.

The room in the mobile unit was panelled with oak veneered plywood and was too small and ill-ventilated. Mummery had banned smoking in it, and that had not improved the attention of some. A map hung behind him, showing the layout of the village and the immediate area. In front of it hung a clear plastic film on which Mummery could draw and make notes.

'Now that you have all seen the places marked on the map and

114

have an over-all picture,' he was saying, 'I am going to try to make a summing up of the possibilities. The first two things to consider are the major and obvious ones. One, that there was a connection between the two deaths and that the murders were carried out by the same person or persons, two that they were unconnected and therefore weren't.

'We know now that the bullet that killed Luxford was deflected off the stonework of a column. John Gibbon – more of him later – believed that the bullet was intended for Tom Harris and that it killed Luxford by accident. That may or may not be the case. It could still have been intended for Luxford and the gun may have moved more than we are able to establish. The gun is being traced separately and as soon as we know more about its history and where it was bought by whom, we may make a big step forward. If it has been stolen we will still have made a step forward because we will know we're dealing with a professional who may have form, or with a really inspired amateur. Remember we haven't told anyone how it was fired.

'If the target was Luxford, then the motives for killing him are numerous and probably female. He could however have been killed by a man or a woman.

'If the target was young Harris, the motives remain unclear, but the theory that his murder was the second attempt must mean that the boy knew something important enough to someone that he *had* to die. We have to consider that Harris knew that the first murder was a mistake and was intended for him. In which case he must have been a very scared boy. Unfortunately he was also a very secretive boy and his parents know very little about what he got up to. From them we have a picture of a lonely boy, wild, who certainly got about the countryside. He knew everyone and everything for miles around. If something was going on, there is a good chance he found out. That's obviously important. There is a list of people he didn't like for one reason or another. Some are obvious, like people who chased him out of their orchard or reported him to Constable Mann for the things boys get up to. He's stolen sweets from the village shops, broken street lamps, the usual sort of things. Jeffrys the homosexual is worth careful thought, but I don't want any tactless, stupid bullying there. If you have any hang-ups, don't go near him, and I'll have anyone off the case who doesn't play it that way. We need the man for information and I don't want any conclusions drawn. Harris didn't like him, and I want to know why. Gently. No bigotry.

'Now the other chief characters. The Frys. I don't trust him, and Mrs Cynthia Fry was altogether too close to Luxford. George Fry would have a motive for the first killing but we can't find any for the second. Yet.

'The Walkers. Henry Walker is in all sorts of financial trouble and his wife seems to have all the sympathy of Lady Macbeth. She's black and she's a stunner and will no doubt have you all eating out of her hands, so watch it! She runs a boutique which Henry seems to have given her to keep her anchored down a bit, but it must be losing money hand over fist and he can't afford it. I don't know if that has anything to do with all this, but she certainly has a liberated sex life, so I'm told, and our Henry is a man under pressure. I have the feeling he is much tougher than he looks.

'William Luxford. Thoroughly disliked for barging in to this village, turfing the ancient out of the village stores, using the influence of his brother the vicar, and turning it into an antique shop. We will obviously have a look at *his* business affairs. Apart from that, he is generally held to have a poisonous personality, and has recently had a fight with Wilkinson.

'Wilkinson is the local butcher, and we don't know of any particular hate between him and Luxford except that they shared an interest and quarrelled about it, quite violently. They are or were both amateur archaeologists, and although all you knowing people may raise a smile about it, don't underestimate that sort of rivalry. Keep your ears open, and your minds. Who's been poaching on someone else's patch, that sort of thing. That might account for Luxford.

'Mrs Crabbe. She is very proper, attractive, and I can't make out a thing about her. She won't talk much and seems to be withdrawn. I would guess she is another Luxford lovely. Avoid that aspect at all costs when questioning. I think she could be a good witness if she will only unwind and talk. She is *not* excluded from the list of suspects.

'Hazlitt, Meadows, Edwardes, minor characters if you like, but I have learned to be very careful about minor characters. Hazlitt has a rifle and knows how to use it. He's the local poacher and sage and good for information. Write in your notebooks, "Do not upset on any account". You'll get more out of him than Old Moore's Almanack. Mrs Tomlinson seems unlikely but she ran the village store before William Luxford turned her out. Needless to say she didn't like either of the Luxfords.

'Having said all that, I don't exclude others. These are the obvious ones so far, and I may have missed my man – or woman – entirely.

'Now Mr Gibbon. I have explained his involvement and that he is supposed to have been helping us. I don't seriously think he is the murderer of either Luxford or the boy, but be careful. He was on the scene at the church very quickly, and he was the last person to see the boy alive. I know he says he was pushed off the ladder in the church, but we only have his word for it. For all we know he might have been trying to remove the lead smear from the column and may have fallen. He says he traced the murderer's tracks across the fields to where the boy was killed, but he didn't come to me to point them out when I was standing on the road a few yards away. It could all be

116

genuine, it may not be.'

Mummery paused, took a sip of water from a glass. He wondered how much of this they were all really taking in. There was plenty of diligent scribbling in notebooks, but he wished they would listen, absorb, think.

'If he was attacked in the church, we enter the third realm. A murder attempt that failed. A victim that has survived. Let's quickly think about that before I let you all loose to create havoc. If everything Gibbon says is gospel truth then we have to consider several nasties.

'One, the murderer hasn't finished yet and may try again. On Gibbon or on someone else.

'Two, he must believe Gibbon knows something. Gibbon himself doesn't believe he knows anything particularly startling, so perhaps the obvious thing to conclude is that he wasn't to find the bullet mark on the column and draw the conclusion from it that he *has* drawn. If that's the case, then Luxford was killed by accident, and it's Harris that was to be murdered all along.

'Three, something Gibbon knows or has seen without drawing any conclusions is actually dangerous to the killer.

'Four, Gibbon hadn't got there yet, but was about to put two and two together and this was obvious to the killer so he intervened.

'Now we have to keep an open mind on all of these. But if you think back a few minutes and look at your notes, I gave you a whole list of suspects and a lot of reasons. Nearly all those reasons were why they should want to kill Luxford. There were no reasons why anyone should want to kill Tom Harris, yet he seems to have been the real target.'

He paused, satisfied with the dramatic climax. Let them cough and shuffle a bit. He had only one further aspect to consider.

'That will give you all food for thought and should keep you out of the pub. And here's the last thing to consider before you get moving. If Gibbon is telling the truth, and if therefore all we have said about Harris being the real victim is true, then we can also believe everything he has told us about following footsteps across the snow. We therefore know certain things about the killer, and because he or she has made two attempts it's probably fair to assume it was the same person in both cases.

'What do we know? They were able to get access to the church unseen, were able to obtain a rifle and set it up with a reasonable amount of skill, using the bell mechanism to fire it. That doesn't mean we're dealing with a genius, but it shows imagination and careful planning.

'Having failed first time, and having lost the gun, the killer uses a lump of wood or some similar object as yet not recovered. He or she has medium sized feet – which must eliminate someone, I suppose –

and is quite capable of walking across the fields fairly fast, accosting young Harris and killing him before he can get away. They must have moved fast, because the lad was cycling up and down the village and if you look at the map, you will see that the killer must have seen him setting off in that direction, guessed he would turn left to explore the snow in Hundred Row at some stage and at that stage grabbed a weapon and headed off to intercept him. A bike is faster than walking but the killer took a shorter route. He also crossed the river at the right place where he knew it would be frozen and I think we can assume he knew there were cattle in the field and that it would be churned up and the cattle would be noisy. This killer is alert, inventive and knows the terrain. He knows how to set up a rifle. We have got to be able to make something out of all that. It could be a man or a woman. Nothing so far indicates one sex rather than the other. If the lad met a woman, he might not be suspicious. If he met a man, he might not have had a chance. The ice was frozen where he was discovered so we can't tell if there was any struggle.

'Now one last thing which we have all almost forgotten. The letter and the pair of gloves in the church. The deliberate clues? Were both – or either of them – planted? Have they anything to do with the killing at all? I believe the letter was stuffed behind a cushion after Luxford was shot, out of spite, to implicate Cynthia Fry, but of course we don't know who by. It wasn't the killer though, was it, because we believe the killer expected Tom Harris to die, so there was no point in it. Find out who did that, and we've eliminated someone. As for the gloves, I'm not sure. They may be much more relevant. I don't know how or why, but they may be. Equally they may be a red herring, a plant by the killer to put us off the scent. Above all, we still don't know if the killer was in the church or out of it. The gloves may have been pushed there to make us believe the killer was part of the congregation. Everything was set up that way. It is my belief that the killer intended to come back and get that gun and that somehow we prevented him by crawling all over the church and finding it. He miscalculated. The man Hazlitt knew right away it was a rifle shot. But for him and the presence of mind of Constable Mann – and Gibbon, I must say – the whole congregation could have gone home unsearched and we would have believed for a day that it could have been a hand weapon and we had missed it. Who wanted most to leave the church? Fry? Meadows? Walker?

'If the gun had been removed, we would have remained convinced that Luxford, or Harris, had been shot by a member of the congregation. Is that the bluff, or is it a double bluff? A fascinating question. Are we being made to look outside the congregation on the grounds that no killer would deliberately narrow the odds to include himself? In that case the gun was meant to be found.'

He sipped from the glass of water again, wishing fervently it was

118

something stronger. Quarter to twelve. He vowed daily not to drink until midday. Today at least he had been forced to keep to it.

'Now, coming to the burning question of where we go from here, I have to prise you lot off your backsides and out to meet the good citizens. I also need a number to co-ordinate the search for the weapon used on Tom Harris. According to Forensic we are looking for a substantial cubic shape. Perhaps a brick, but they say it is much more likely to be wood, as they would expect fragments from a brick. This blow left no traces of the weapon, so if it is wood, it is smooth and regularly shaped, so don't go making piles of branches. We are *not* gathering firewood.

'The uniformed boys will be here by ten o'clock – fifty of them – so if there's anything to be found I expect to have it soon. We also want a very careful look for anything else. Strands of fibre for example. This murderer had to cross fences, go through a hedge. Of course our Mr Gibbon has worked the same route and has no doubt left lumps of his garments everywhere to confuse us, but that can all be sorted out.

'Now interviews. Mann, you can start with Jeffrys. As the local man you may get more out of him. I'll take William Luxford to start with as he seems to be a truculent individual. I want to know more about his quarrel at this party. Then we'll work through Mrs Crabbe, Meadows, Wilkinson *et cetera*. Let's get on with it.'

Jeffrys was angry and defensive. He had summoned up a cold and magisterial tone which impressed Mann, and which he had obviously used to good effect in his acting days. Mann told himself not to be flustered by it.

'Explain to me, Constable, why you are paying me this visit at all? Do you seriously believe I would have had anything to do with the death of that boy? Am I the sort of man you can see committing a brutal murder?'

'No one has said anything of the sort,' said Mann. 'What I said to you was that we had to interview everyone about the events of that night. Everyone. That's what we're doing. We want to know what people were doing, what they saw, who was moving about. You must know enough about police procedure from the papers, sir, to know we do a lot of work by elimination.'

Jeffrys sighed.

'That's all very glib, but I still take offence. Of course I wouldn't murder him! How pathetically ridiculous!'

'Can we go back to Christmas Day?' said Mann. 'You didn't go out with any of the search parties?'

He knew this perfectly well, but had to start somewhere.

'I wasn't asked, was I? I'm an old man anyway. I couldn't go tramping about everywhere on a night like that . . .'

'Look, Mr Jeffrys, you mustn't assume there's any angle in what

I'm saying, I just want to check the facts . . .'

'I don't believe that at all! I know what some people think! That bastard Harris is putting all sorts of rumours around. He hates me. I don't mean to speak ill of the boy's father, for the boy's sake of course, but I have to defend myself!'

Jeffrys moved over to the window of his living room and stared out onto the rear garden. It was a pleasant, beamed room. A fire burned in a cast-iron grate within a small ingle-nook. The pictures on the walls were numerous and a large number consisted of costume designs for the theatre. Interspersed with these were photographs, signed, of what Mann took to be 'Theatricals' who stared intensely or winsomely at the camera, sometimes through a mist, sometimes with head on hand. Outside, birds were singing noisily, pretending that because the sun was out the year had turned. Blackbirds were pursuing each other vigorously, in love or war. As a gardening man, the constable stared past Jeffrys and saw the well kept lawn and shrubs, the vegetable garden, ancient trees covered with lichen but left in place.

'I see the daffodils are already well up, sir. A bit previous if you ask me. Mine are the same. There's more to come. If we have a hard frost, it'll mark the buds. The snowdrops are already formed.'

Jeffrys turned to him as though he had made a decision.

'Look here, Constable, I know what you're driving at, and we may as well get it over and done with. You know what they say about me here. It's a small place and they're narrow-minded. Yes, I'm a homosexual. No, I've never had anything to do with boys. Is that absolutely clear?'

Mann knew he was staring at Jeffrys with as much expression as a dead cod, but he was a village man himself and unaccustomed to such explicit references to this sort of thing. His police training was thin on preparation in this sphere.

'I'm perfectly well aware that Tom Harris thinks I'm the murderer. He would like that. He hates me, and in my view he's an evil and unpleasant man. He treated that boy badly, and if it hadn't been for his mother I believe young Tom would have taken off years ago, young as he is. It's a sad irony isn't it that it was his mother who got that bike. His father wouldn't have let him have it. He didn't believe in boys enjoying themselves. He's narrow-minded and repressive.'

'But people say that you were friendly with the boy, sir.'

'Yes I was friendly with the boy.' Jeffrys turned to face Mann. His thin rather over-cultivated face was drawn and there was the suspicion of tears in his eyes. 'I was very fond of Tom Harris in a totally fatherly way. I tried to help him. I took an interest in him since his father took none. That's what the village sees as a crime. I feel his death almost as if he was my son, can you understand that,

120

Constable, or are you as desensitised as the rest of them?'

Mann found it difficult to move this conversation along.

'I think I understand how you feel,' he ventured. 'Can you tell us the sort of thing the boy was interested in? It may be very relevant.'

'He was the same as any boy, except for being a bit lonely. He got up to things I suppose, but why anyone should want to kill him I've no idea! Could it have been a maniac? I know that sounds stupid, but I can't think why anyone would do that to him.'

'We know he got around a lot, Mr Jeffrys. His mother says he was out a lot. He used to go fishing and prowl the countryside. He was the sort of boy that might have seen something or someone and he might have told you . . . ?'

Jeffrys considered this carefully. He seemed to be in control of himself again and he waved Mann towards a chair with a sweep of his arm. Mann shook his head silently, not wishing to break the train of Jeffrys's thoughts.

'He was certainly keen on fishing, and would take himself off to the river for hours. He was always after birds' nests, but he didn't take the eggs, he just knew where everything was. He used to do rounds when they were going. He did the papers for a while, then the milk, then delivered for Wilkinson. He delivered for Mrs Tomlinson too before that barbarian William Luxford came along.'

'He didn't keep any of the jobs for long?'

'Not really. I can't say I paid much attention. Delivery boys come and go. It's a tradition.'

'There was no particular reason why he did them for a short time?'

'If you mean was he dishonest, certainly not! He was cheeky and that may have upset some people.'

'He seemed upset by the death of the vicar.'

'I should think he was!'

Mann paused, and then pressed on.

'So did you see Tom Harris with his bike last night?'

'No.'

'Did you see anyone else about? Particularly anyone acting suspiciously.'

'That's one of those phrases policemen love, isn't it!' said Jeffrys quickly regaining his composure. 'What on earth does it mean? I saw people about in the High Street and Church Row, but how on earth would I be able to tell if they were acting suspiciously? There was no one creeping about wearing a black mask and carrying a lantern. I mean I saw ordinary people walking about. I should think I saw almost everyone at some stage, then there was all the commotion of the search for young Tom.'

'So to come back to Luxford, you don't think Tom Harris was afraid of him in any way?'

'I don't think he was afraid. I think he irritated the vicar.'

'How?'

'I'm not sure. Perhaps he was late for church.'

'No. His mother saw to that.'

'He took an interest in the vicar's archaeology nonsense.'

'Oh?' Mann was interested.

'Your Mr Gibbon was asking about that side of things I noticed. At Mrs Walker's party.'

'He's not *our* Mr Gibbon!'

He didn't tell us about that, thought Mann. What other things is he keeping to himself?

'Anyway, what is all this archaeology? All I gather is that Luxford went around with his metal detector and had a lot of fancy theories that he sent off to magazines.'

'They say he found buried treasure.'

'They what!' Mann laughed so loudly that Jeffrys shot him an irritated look. Mann controlled himself.

'Tom Harris used to say that was what the boys in the village said. They reckoned that Luxford and Wilkinson had found a hollow hill full of gold and that was why they quarrelled and hardly spoke to each other.'

'Where was this hollow hill?' asked Mann, trying not to grin too broadly.

'Oh, it's Stone Ford Mount, behind the farm. If you jump up and down on it, it drums. It must be the chalk up there and the thin turf cover.'

'You don't believe any of this I take it?'

'Of course not. It's just the sort of thing all village boys say. But Luxford was genuinely concerned with something, that I do believe. Much as I disliked him, I think he knew something about his subject and was serious. I think the magazines he wrote to were reputable. Wilkinson's the amateur around here, and Luxford really disliked him. Wilkinson is reputed to be one of the real metal detector brigade, that thing in one hand and a spade in the other. They're all vandals around here, I tell you. You should know that, Constable.'

'As a matter of fact sir, I think people here are neither better nor worse than they are anywhere.' said Mann stiffly.

'What, with two murders?' Jeffrys gave an ironic snort.

'That sort of thing can happen in any village,' said Mann coldly, wishing immediately he hadn't said such a crass thing. 'In any case I must move on now sir. I suppose you won't mind if I come back again. It's early days yet and we're just getting the feel of it really.'

'Feel free, Constable. But I hope you find this maniac. I hope there's more going on than just a few enquiries.'

'There is a massive search for the weapon and clues, sir,' said Mann, affronted. 'Our door-to-door enquiries will take in every member of the village. You'd be surprised what we can discover by putting together all the little bits and pieces.'

'And have you discovered something from me?'

'Maybe I have sir.'

Mummery's encounter with William Luxford was a turgid, wrestling affair. Mummery had arrived at the antique shop in good heart, whistling to himself through his teeth and enjoying the sunlight which was so exciting the birdlife. There was real warmth in it, growing warmth, a scent of spring. It made the contents of Luxford's windows look even more shoddy than usual, picking out the chips on porcelain and glass and highlighting peeling veneer. The labels on objects were yellow. Self-adhesive tags were peeling or in some cases had dropped off. Business was obviously slack.

Luxford emerged from an office at the rear which was partially obscured by a Victorian bookcase. Mummery considered that the carving on it could have been done with a hammer and bolster. The books themselves were the sort of job lot that are sold in a tea chest with cricket pads and lidless teapots.

'I don't suppose you've come to buy anything?' Luxford demanded.

Mummery forebore to remark that he couldn't see anything worth selling.

'Afraid not, Mr Luxford. The usual boring round I'm afraid, and more questions.'

'You're not going to ask me about that Harris boy are you? Not after what happened to Peter? If you've got me on your list of suspects, don't you think it's all a waste of time?'

'Nothing's a waste of time if it helps clear things up,' said Mummery, eyeing Luxford with what he hoped was a baleful eye. 'And I think you can help.'

Luxford's round fleshy face would have looked correct on Billy Bunter. His eyes blazed behind his bottle-glass lenses, and he seemed to Mummery to clench his fists, but Mummery kept his eyes on Luxford's, stern (he hoped) and masterful.

'So you do, do you!' the man snarled.

'Yes I do,' replied Mummery.

'Despite everything, you do?'

'I do.'

'I can't refuse you?'

'You can if you wish.'

Luxford hesitated for a fraction of a second.

'Come in the back to the office then. I won't talk about this sort of thing in the middle of the shop. You understand these are my business hours.' Luxford led the way into the back office. The office space was no more than a clearing in a room full of furniture. There was a telephone on a desk, a comfortable leather chair behind it and

123

an array of wooden chairs in front of it that must belong with a dining table. There was not a lot of paperwork about. In fact there was only a blotter with a business card tucked in the corner, saying 'William Luxford, dealer in Fine Art' and an unopened brown windowed envelope that was obviously the electricity bill. Luxford sat down in the leather chair and waved Mummery to one of the upright spindly things. Mummery selected one that looked more sound than the rest and sat down. Even this one seemed insecure and the joints moved slightly with his weight.

'What we have to try to establish,' Mummery said quickly, as Luxford opened his mouth to draw breath, 'is if there was any connection between these two deaths. On the face of it there has to be. It's against all the rules of chance that two murders should occur in such a small place in such a short time by coincidence. So then we have to ask ourselves what the connection could possibly be.'

Was this whole place a front, he asked himself, or was he letting his imagination run away with him? It looked disgustingly seedy and yet that probably suited Luxford when dealing with the Tax Man. If he bought cheap and sold in Town, there might be quite a lot of money in it. How far was this appearance cultivated?

'How's business anyway, Mr Luxford?' he asked as though this were a natural continuation of his previous drift. Luxford stiffened. It was a curious process in which his limbs and features seemed to cohere and take on hardness. His truculence had given way to straightforward nastiness.

'So that's how it is, is it? Snooping! You come in here on the pretence of investigating this wretched boy who has his head staved in, and want to know about my business! Out! I don't care who you are, out! I make my tax returns the same as the next man, and I pay my bills, so mind your own bloody business, and I'll mind mine!'

Mummery sat immobile and stared at a cobweb on the ceiling. Luxford wrung his hands together and puffed. He had leapt to his feet with his outburst and as Mummery was obviously not going to move, he had either to eject him, pursue a higher authority or back down. He decided on discretion. Mummery thought that he had seldom met a man who decided on things so late. Luxford was clearly his own worst enemy.

'I'm not snooping,' said Mummery mildly, 'and it was only to pass the time of day. I'm sorry if I seemed to be prying. It was completely without any angle.'

Luxford had the wit to take it at face value.

'I'm sorry. People say I'm quick-tempered, and I suppose they're right. I do fly off the handle. Have a drink. I will.'

Luxford opened a cabinet behind him, displaying a wide range of malt whiskies, gins, vodkas and liqueurs. He pulled out a twelve year old malt of impeccable pedigree, took a tumbler and poured a vast glass which he offered to Mummery. Mummery took it.

'I thought that policemen were supposed to say they didn't drink on duty,' said Luxford, looking slightly affronted.

'That's only on the movies,' said Mummery firmly, taking a substantial swig. 'In real life, we take what we can.'

'Oh.' Luxford poured himself a drink and replaced the bottle firmly. Mummery smiled slightly, tipped his glass.

'Cheers!' Luxford waved his glass in reply but could not utter the word. 'I'll tell you truly what I thought you might be able to throw some light on,' he ventured, 'it's the relationship between young Tom Harris and various people. The poor lad seems to have had a rough time of it at home, particularly from his father, and gone out on the loose a bit as a result. Here there and everywhere. Had lots of friends and it appears he made a few enemies. Is that a fair summary?'

'If that's your way of saying he was a pest, I can do no more than agree with you.' Luxford had downed half of his drink while standing. He sat down again. 'I don't think anyone would murder him just because he was a pest, do you?'

'Then why? Because he knew something. That's all it can be. Perhaps he even knew who killed your brother.'

Luxford looked at him sharply. It appeared that the thought had not occurred to him until that moment. Not a great thinker, William Luxford.

'It makes sense doesn't it?' pursued Mummery. 'He may have seen something or known something that put the murderer at risk. What I'm here to try to understand is what was it he knew or saw?'

He sipped and looked at Luxford, giving the man time. Luxford shrugged, sipped, put the glass down, picked it up again, sipped, rotated it.

'If I tell you this, will you promise it will go no further? I know, you can't promise in case you have to use it. Oh God! You must know by now that my brother had a certain penchant for the ladies. And the ladies round here seem to have a certain penchant for being horizontal. He ministered to them, loosely speaking. To quite a number of them. That young devil Tom Harris was the very essence of Peeping Tom. Peter told me. I won't mention the names of ladies obviously!' Luxford looked sanctimonious and drank deeply. 'However, you have the scene. Idyllic pasture, summer meadow, long grass. Naked bodies. Sounds. Listen. Pounce. Laughter and running. Tom Harris junior. Confusion and clothes and worrying for weeks. I have to tell you this I suppose, although I didn't want to, but Peter was being blackmailed by the boy.'

Mummery said nothing, but turned his glass as Luxford had done.

'He was quite accomplished at it. Peter had to give him a fiver a week to say nothing. Pathetic, isn't it? Peter felt really terrible about

125

it. He was corrupting the boy by submitting, but the boy approached him bold as brass and said that unless he helped out with his pocket money he would tell the husband of this certain lady, and Peter was so shaken, that he agreed. Then he was on the giddy spiral. I tried to tell him to stop paying, but he told me that boy knew everything.'

'You're making out a good case why Peter Luxford might have killed the boy. Unfortunately, Peter Luxford is the one person who obviously didn't. I say that with no disrespect.'

Luxford finished his whisky. He leaned forward in what was obviously supposed to be an encouraging and confidential manner.

'If he was doing that to Peter, perhaps he was doing it to others . . .'

Mummery frowned at his glass, making a show of pondering deeply. This was all astonishing news, if it was true. Why should he doubt it, it made good sense. He doubted it because of the source, and that was hardly a good rational reason. Young Harris the prowler, always out and about. Young Harris the loner, at perpetual odds with his father. An accidental discovery at first, then perhaps deliberate following. But who was the woman?

'Who was the lady?'

Luxford avoided his eyes.

'He never told me.'

'You don't expect me to believe that, do you? It's vital evidence to the case, you have to divulge it.'

'I can't divulge what I don't know!' Luxford protested.

'Your own brother tells you about Tom Harris and that he's being blackmailed and why, but doesn't tell you who was involved? It doesn't seem likely.'

'It's the truth!' Luxford was angry again, almost at the flick of a switch.

'You said just now that you wouldn't mention the names of the ladies. That plainly means that you know them.' Mummery was extremely formal. He put his glass down on the table and searched in his coat pocket. 'I need the names.' As a matter of fact he didn't have a notebook. He remembered leaving it on the dressing table in the hotel. He pretended he had found it in his pocket.

'Ladies, yes. Lots of ladies. I don't know which one sparked off the blackmail. If you want a list of Peter's affairs, you want a list of every female in this town of beddable age! You can't accuse people of lying in this way! You twist things!'

Luxford was slightly frothy at the mouth and he was spitting small droplets onto the desk. Mummery stared at them, as if fascinated to disconcert the man. Luxford wiped them away with his sleeve. Not an unobservant man despite the bombast and the hiding behind the bottle glass lenses.

'You're saying he could have been with any one of many, and

never told you which?'

'That's exactly what I'm saying.'

'Give me the list then. I may as well know that.'

'I think you know that perfectly well. You just want to drag me through the humiliation of repeating it!'

'I simply want to hear the list from you.'

Luxford shrugged.

'All right. For what it's worth.'

He gave Mummery a comprehensive list that contained familiar names and included those he had never heard of before. Peter Luxford had been a rover.

John Gibbon was feeling a good deal better. He was propped up now, and his arm was just a dull ache encased in plaster that made it as remote as distant thunder. He could no more move it than he could levitate his bottle of orange squash. He had tried to do both.

Contemplating the end of his bed through his one open eye, he used the vertical metal rails as counters as he worked through the possibilities of the events that had led up to his literal downfall. He had gone through it from one to five, when he had a sudden thought. And it was one he hadn't expressed to Mummery. It was all a question of Christmas dinner. He smiled to himself. That was what it boiled down to!

Had he accepted any one of the invitations he had been offered, he would have been with those individuals when young Harris was killed, in the way he had been with the Walkers. Surely Tom Harris's murderer could be excluded from that list?

He thought back to the party and reviewed the invitations. There had been Mann, of course, and the Walkers, Philippa Crabbe, Wilkinson, Jeffrys, the Frys. He wondered why he had not thought of it before. It was miraculously simple. You don't invite someone round when you're intending to go out for a little murder by moonlight.

That left the Harrises themselves, who were obviously out of it, Hazlitt, Meadows, William Luxford and the Hodges from the principals from the church. And of these? As a personal matter, he would choose Luxford and Meadows any time, but this was no time for sloppy thinking. There had been enough of that already.

He watched a nurse rustle through his field of vision, starched as a nun. What weight was he to put on that line of argument? Wouldn't a clever murderer like this one ask him to dinner anyway to establish an alibi, if he was sure he would refuse? But he hadn't refused everyone, he had accepted the Walkers' invitation. But he had done that at the last moment and on the telephone. The others wouldn't know about it. As far as they were concerned, he was safely at home alone. There was just as logical an argument that said that the murderer would invite him to dinner, knowing he would refuse and in so doing establish precisely what he was doing. A case of pinning down the stray, the stranger who might do something unpredictable and disturb the murderer. The stranger who seemed to be helping the police. In which case Philippa Crabbe, Wilkinson, Jeffrys and the Frys were all prime suspects. And then instead of staying at home, he had done exactly what they had feared and had prowled about. So he had got what he deserved.

Gibbon sighed. Either argument was equally persuasive. It also required a cerebral effort that he was finding difficult, yet he felt there must be a way to think his way through it without the visible clues that are supposed to be part of detection.

He made the effort to remove his thoughts to the search at the bridge. It felt rather like the laborious rotation of big guns on a Dreadnought, but he finally got there. Why, when at the bridge, had they decided to go upstream, a direction which he had subsequently discovered to be the wrong way? They had all plunged into the water meadow like hounds following a scent, and found nothing. Had that been an innocent mistake? Who had set them off in that direction? He couldn't remember now. If they had set off downstream, they would certainly have found the footsteps and followed them.

If they were there at the time.

He was excited now, and thinking was becoming easier. Supposing the murder had not yet been committed, and that young Tom was still at that moment cycling about on the ice in Hundred Row? Supposing that while they searched, one of their number had slipped off in the other direction, killed Tom and returned?

But it was Mummery himself who had intervened to stop them searching downstream. It was just an accident he had turned up at that moment. He had wanted to search the roads and had been quite right as it turned out.

Who had he managed to keep in sight at the river? People had come and gone in the dark. Torches had flashed, illuminating and blinding. Voices were more recognisable than shapes. Anyone could have slipped away at some stage.

He remembered then that it was Wilkinson who had suggested that a boy with a bike would take the flat side. Did that make him the killer? Or Hazlitt, who had urged them on? Surely the flat side *was* where a boy on a bike would go. His brain was beginning to jam, seize up, coagulate like porridge. Oh God! Tumbling images.

'You have a visitor,' said the nurse with reddish hair and freckles. John woke with a start, not realising that he had dropped off. The nurse smiled sympathetically. 'You must expect to feel tired from time to time. It's perfectly normal.'

He was looking at Philippa Crabbe. It took him moments to grasp what to say or do. This was not the decisive detective John Gibbon, the man who listened to confidences.

'Please sit down . . .' he said, trying to struggle into a more upright position. The nurse assisted, plumping up his pillows, tucking them under his back. Philippa looked at him appraisingly. Her eyes showed concern, shock. He supposed it was the bandages. They hadn't spared them.

'You *did* take a tumble!' she said. 'Your face is all sorts of colours. And they told me your left arm is broken.'

'I haven't seen my face yet. Maybe they're keeping it from me!'

'It's a very nice face,' said the nurse smiling at her handiwork, 'Matches the curtains!'

Philippa sat down as the nurse left, and put a bag down on his bedside table.

'Fruit,' she said. 'I know that's not original. In fact it's very boring. However I took the opportunity to slip a small bottle of brandy in with it. I hope they don't mind.'

Gibbon looked at her as carefully as she had just looked at him. She returned his gaze steadily. As usual she was carefully dressed, this time in soft tan tweed suit and peach silk shirt. Expensive clothes again. He tried not to look at her good legs. She smiled at him, the same dazzling smile he well remembered, then her face resumed its naturally serious expression.

'You're staring at me as though you were studying a map!'

'I'm trying to read a book.'

'Are you indeed! I don't think you're entitled to do that.' She had coloured very slightly. There was a slight trace of annoyance, or perhaps unease.

'Thank you very much for the brandy anyway. It was a very unkind thought and I'm very ungracious.'

'I've noticed.'

John laughed.

'As bad as that?'

'Yes, I think so. I come to visit an ill man and he examines me like a specimen. I hope you like what you found. Anyway, enough of that, how are you?'

'I'm feeling quite well really.'

'It looks a lot worse.'

'Well the arm aches and the head is tender but apart from that and bruised ribs, I'm well. I shall be out of here in a day or two. Thanks for paying me a visit. Apart from the police you're the only visitor I've had.'

'Why were the police here?' She asked the question too sharply. There was alarm now.

'About my fall. I didn't jump, you know, I was pushed!'

'What!' Philippa looked ashen. The word was delivered as a cry of protest. Gibbon looked at her hard, demanding by his look that she should explain her reaction. She avoided his eyes, forcing him to bludgeon her with words.

'Come on then! Why are you so shocked? What's this all about?'

Three blows. She took a small ivory handkerchief from her pocket and wound it round the index finger of her right hand, using her left. She unwound it again, holding it pinched between index finger and thumb. She re-wound it. Backwards and forwards. It was the only sign of agitation, but in someone so studiously calm it was like turmoil.

'You mustn't think I didn't come to see how you were,' she began in a controlled voice,' but I do have an ulterior motive. I had to talk to you again. There are certain things I think someone else ought to know, but I don't want to tell them to that man Mummery. He's as hard-nosed as some sort of shark. Hammer-headed. I have personal things that I wouldn't normally discuss but that are really *troubling* me, and I can only turn to you.'

'I think I understand,' said John encouragingly. 'As long as these aren't things that would help to solve these murders.'

'I don't know, you see. Maybe they are, maybe they aren't.'

There was a pause while they both considered this.

'You'd better sit closer,' said John. 'There is a very ordinary looking young man out there in the corridor reading a paperback who has a professional interest in me.'

'I saw him and thought as much. Why?'

'I think they call it protection. Maybe it's to prevent me running away. There is a school of thought that I threw myself off the ladder deliberately.'

'Did you?' asked Philippa, very seriously.

'You don't seriously think so, do you?'

'I've considered it.'

'Good God! Why?'

'You were the last person to see Tom Harris. You might have killed him. This might all be an elaborate red herring.'

'You believe that?'

'Not now, after giving it some thought.'

'Allow me to assure you I didn't.'

'I said I had come to that conclusion. But I want to tell you about certain things that you must promise not to repeat. Not now. I want someone else to know them though, and the only person I can think of is you. I can only tell you part of it now, while I see if I can trust you.'

'And you won't tell this, whatever it is, to the police?'

'No, John. This is a personal matter. It may or may not be relevant to anything.'

'Then why tell me?'

'In case anything happens to me.'

'You don't believe it will, do you?' John was worried. She sat so

130

solemnly and almost fatalistically uttered her lines. She had to be taken seriously. Quite apart from her beautiful legs and dazzling smile.

'You have to face the fact, that there is a murderer in our midst. It all sounds ridiculous and melodramatic when you put it in words, but there *is*. There have been two killings and an attempt on you. I don't know why there was an attempt on you. Maybe it was a warning for helping the police, and not intended to kill. Maybe it was just to put you out of the way here for a few days. The fact of the matter is that if you get near to these murders, you're obviously in danger. Young Tom was in danger, and he was just a boy, a nosy, unhappy, lonely boy. But he was killed. It must be because of something he knew. He may not even have known the significance of it, but someone cares so little about human life that they crushed his head in. I don't believe it was anyone who has lived in this place all their lives. That was why I thought hard about you. You've only just arrived, and all this happens. But it wasn't you.'

'What made you so sure?'

'I can't tell you that. I just know.'

'Well what is it you want to tell me?'

'Remember what I told you at Lucinda's party? That my secrets aren't earth-shattering but are very personal. This falls into the same category, I think, although there are more sinister overtones. I told you about Peter Luxford, and the gifts he showered me with. Well that was only part of the story.'

'As this is just another instalment?'

'If you like. It's certainly all I will tell you now. He dug up those things. He spent the money on me, and I said nothing, did nothing about it. Do you see where that puts me? It's beyond mere foolishness. I knew where he got it from and that it was theft, but I said nothing. It's no excuse to say I was besotted. He was a very charming man, but he also had the bite of the viper.'

'What was it he had?'

'Not yet, John. I can't tell you that.'

'Was it something to do with his archaeology?'

'I'm not telling you.'

'You have to! It sounds as though it has a lot to do with his death.'

'I can't trust you yet. I can't trust anyone. I don't know if it had anything to do with his death. If I knew for certain I *would* tell you. Please be content with what I've said. I have it all written down safely. I have everything tucked away just in case.'

'Just in case of what?'

'Eventualities.'

'Are you in trouble Philippa? You make these very worrying remarks, but when I try to find out more you slide sideways like a bar of soap. What is it you know? Two people have been killed already.'

131

'I've told you that what I know is safely recorded. It won't be lost for anyone clever enough to find it. Luxford was so inquisitive, it had to be that way. He pried into everything I did, when he knew that I knew about him.'

'But for God's sake, *what about him*!'

'Just dishonest. A weak, attractive man, who spotted a weak, attractive woman.'

John tried to pull himself more upright. He was in a quandary about what to do. He didn't like the sound of things at all, but on the other hand if Philippa was an accessory after the fact in theft or whatever it was that Luxford had done, he had no wish to set the police on her. He made a last attempt to unscramble things.

'Philippa. Tell me and answer me honestly, do you believe that Luxford's death had anything to do with this money he stole or found or whatever?'

'I do.'

'Then aren't you in the same sort of danger? If you know what you do about it, shouldn't you tell the police?'

'I'm not in danger. Why should I be? No one knows that I know what I know except Peter Luxford, and he's dead. Perhaps Tom Harris knew something.'

'And he's dead.'

Philippa looked at him, white and wide-eyed. Perfectly turned out at Luxford's expense, he thought, but where had the money come from? Was her moist-eyed innocence all that it seemed?

'If there was a connection,' she said.

'Come on, Philippa. There hasn't been a murder in this place in recorded history and then we get two in the space of two days. It's reasonable to assume they're connected.'

'I don't think this is the time for heavy irony.'

'It isn't the time for evasion either.'

Philippa stood up.

'I had better go. I've told you too much anyway and you may just tell that hard-nosed Mummery. I think you had better promise me not to repeat anything I've said.'

'I can't promise that.'

'You must.'

'You know perfectly well that I can only promise I won't tell them unless it becomes impossible not to, and by that I mean that if it becomes obvious that it is relevant to either of the murders. I don't know what this all means yet. Frankly you confuse me Philippa. What is this money that Luxford found? You haven't told me. Has he been pillaging some sort of buried treasure? Is this what all the archaeology is about? Gold? Sutton Hoo all over again? Apart from the niceties of legal ownership, what's he been destroying?'

'That's enough! He hasn't destroyed anything, and if I stay here you'll only ask more questions which I won't answer.'

'Do you know who the killer is?'

'Of course I don't!' Philippa was furious. 'You must believe that. It may not even be anyone from the village.'

'I hope you know what you're doing, Philippa. I'm worried about you. This is all against my better judgement.'

'Don't be worried!' She stooped suddenly and kissed him full on the lips. John responded in kind. The freckle-faced nurse found them like that when she entered to chase Philippa out. She smiled and winked at him. Gibbon felt a terrible desperation as she left without looking back. He must get out of hospital. What the police weren't to be allowed to do, he must do himself. The young man in the corridor noted it all.

Mummery opened the door, setting an old-fashioned bell jangling. On the shop façade the nineteenth century air had been carefully preserved. The lettering in sign-writers' Victorian read 'J. Wilkinson. Butcher, Game Dealer, Purveyor of Fine Meat.'

He could hardly say he was the purveyor of bad meat, thought Mummery sourly. It falls into the same category as tied pubs and their eternal signs saying they purvey fine wines, and a fine selection of spirits. Whatever that means.

'Morning,' said Wilkinson in an unfriendly tone. 'I wondered when you would get round to me. These are my business hours you know.'

'They're mine too,' said Mummery evenly.

'Is that so?' Wilkinson's face clouded further. 'Do the police pay compensation for loss of profit? My backside they do! You'd better come in the back room and I'll turn the sign over.'

He walked round from behind the counter, turned over the 'Open' sign, and hung below it a second sign saying 'Back in five minutes.'

'That's what you've got,' he said, displaying it briefly to Mummery.

Mummery heartily disliked the smell of meat and vowed it would be as close to that as possible. Wilkinson led the way into a back room that was both an office and a store for plastic bags, wrapping paper, hooks, knives and saws. It was also a corridor to his huge freezer. The floor, like the floor of the shop, was dusted with sawdust. Mummery saw with distaste that small scraps of meat had already collected here and there. He poked at one with his boot.

'You can't help that!' said Wilkinson contemptuously. 'That's what the sawdust's for. I have to get the mince from out the back.'

Mummery took out his notebook and opened it in an attempt to impose his control on the situation. It would be so easy if someone had been dissected into small pieces, he thought, eyeing the array of evil steel on the wall.

'Murderous, aren't they?' said Wilkinson with what could only be described as a pantomime leer.

'Look here,' said Mummery, 'this is a serious business. Two people have died. I am here to conduct a formal police interview and I am asking for your co-operation. If necessary I shall ask for that formally too.'

'Getting shirty!' said Wilkinson, but he appeared to settle down. 'Go ahead then. Mrs Tomlinson always gets here in about ten minutes time and I've got to bone a leg for her.'

Mummery ignored this.

'I want to know what you can tell me about your movements at the time of the murders,' he said firmly. Wilkinson stared at him. Mummery felt that it was like the pause between lighting the touchpaper on a Roman Candle and waiting for results.

'You what!' he finally croaked. He sounded as though he was being garotted. Mummery laid down his notebook with what he hoped was a general air of insouciance. He felt even more conscious of the armoury of sharp weapons at Wilkinson's command.

'It is a standard question we have to ask. We compile a picture of where everyone was at the appropriate time . . .'

'Listen, Inspector Mummery, you know perfectly well where I was, so don't try the old "where were you at the time of the murder" with me! Ask Charlie Brooks. Me and half the right-minded population of this place were in the "Feathers" as you know perfectly well, minding our own business, as opposed to the other half who were storing up riches for themselves in heaven or whatever it is they do in church. Doubtless there were one or two citizens who were already afflicted by the known poisoning effect of drink who had retired to bed early, but most of us were having a good time!'

Mummery coloured a deep shade of red. It was not at all in his nature to take impertinence gracefully. The highlights of his nose, chin and brows shone with an ominous glow.

'We don't need any clever remarks, Mr Wilkinson,' he said with chilling calm. 'You say you were in the "Feathers" at the time of the murder.' He picked up his notebook and wrote in it laboriously 'Jacob Wilkinson. At time of murder of Peter Luxford, states was in the "Feathers".'

'Can you produce witnesses to confirm this?'

Wilkinson snorted.

'Of course I can! Half a pub full.'

'Will you name them please sir, so that I can corroborate this statement.'

'Don't be a pain, Inspector.'

'I must advise you, Mr Wilkinson, that it is an offence to be obstructive to a police officer doing his duty.' Mummery felt good

134

about that. It seemed to stop Wilkinson too. There was a pause for reassessment.

'All right, I was in the pub and you can check it with Charlie Brooks, Harry Thomas, David Rose and any of the others. I don't even understand what the point is. We all know who was in the pub and who was in the church, and how could anyone in the pub do the killing?'

'Patient investigation is what solves cases sir,' said Mummery pedantically. 'The piecing together of all facts that may not at first seem related. Where were you when young Tom Harris was murdered?'

The sudden change of tack shook Wilkinson. He shrugged, seemed at a loss and shook his head, but there was alarm on his face. A very fit man, Mummery thought, a man who could run fast, perhaps? Certainly a strong man, weathered, accustomed to being out and about in all seasons. A man who disliked Luxford and made no bones about it. A man who shared the same interests, or more to the point, who was separated by these same interests. It was quite possible for two grown men to contemplate murder over some ancient site, over some ridiculous disagreement over methods or metal detectors or articles written to journals. But Tom Harris?

'I was at home. I suppose. How do I know when he was murdered? I only know when Alf Hazlitt knocked on my door saying you were organising a search party, and you know best when that was. I can't say I looked.'

'So you were alone before that?'

'Yes I was. I asked Gibbon to dinner, but he said he had his own. It might have been better for him if he'd joined me. You don't know when Harris was killed do you? You're only trying it on.'

Mummery ignored this accurate barb.

'So you have no witnesses to confirm your whereabouts at or about the time Harris must have been murdered?'

'Look, where do you get this jargon from? All this whereabouts rubbish and ats and abouts! I was at home from the time I left the Walkers' place until Hazlitt knocked me up. That's all I can tell you. I haven't got an alibi, and by God I don't need one either!'

'Thank you, Mr Wilkinson,' said Mummery suddenly shutting his notebook in which he had written virtually nothing. 'That's all.'

'What do you mean that's all?' Wilkinson reacted as he had expected. 'You come in here, virtually making accusations that I'm a murderer then announce that's all and just walk out! What's that all about?'

'It means I have nothing else to ask for the moment.'

'Oh is that so? I'm very glad to hear it!'

Wilkinson strode before him to the door, reversed the sign again so that it read 'closed' on the inside, removed the 'Back in five

135

minutes' and opened the door with a ping!

'I suppose you don't want to see what I put in my sausages?' hurled Wilkinson as a parting shot. Mummery smiled mechanically, showing no humour, and left. 'Have a look for fingernails . . . ?'

He was not at all sure how he should assess this interview with Jacob Wilkinson. Or that he had done particularly well.

Mummery's end-of-the-day meeting was not characterised by jollity and humour. The men were tired and restless and wanted to get home. The crowded temporary room smelled strongly of wet coats and wet boots. Some boots had a strong agricultural reek to them. It had been a messy and unrewarding search. At least it would make some of the fat beggars fit, he thought unkindly. Most of them looked out of place. Podgy town coppers who didn't even dig the garden. If necessary he would have them ploughing up fields, and he would let the podgy ones have the first shift.

'So what have we got after a hard day's labour?' he asked rhetorically. The meagre haul was behind him on a table. 'What you might call your average rural knicker collection, which in the present case is particularly unedifying, half-a-dozen snares, a lot of spent shotgun cartridges – I don't know what clown bothered with these – and no weapon. For your information, gentlemen, I have now had the report from forensic and fingerprints in London on the gun. It was as clean as a whistle. There are indications of glove marks, so whoever set that up knew what they were doing. As for the rest of the bell tower, the prints lads report that anyone who left prints up there must be six feet under. "The dust is thick as a pile carpet" – I quote, and there's nothing on any uprights. Which makes us all that much more interested in the pair of gloves we originally found in the church. They're looking at these now to see if they can get any points of similarity, but they've already said it'll be difficult. However, the glove marks on the gun are from pigskin, and the gloves in the church were pigskin, so we have a good start.'

He paused. The men were trying to look interested, but had a distant air. One or two were staring at the ceiling.

'Now I know you've had a hard day's slog, and it's all been unrewarding so far, but you aren't off yet, so don't go to sleep on me. The boy's bike is being examined as well. The only prints on that are the boy's. If you pause to consider that, what does it add up to? A clever devil, that's what it adds up to and in my view it adds up to confirmation that both murders were carried out by the same person or persons. I haven't ruled out the plural. We have one murder, committed by remote control with no prints on the weapon, and another murder carried out with a weapon we can't find, and which we may never find, as it was probably a wooden mallet or something similar. You can be sure it was used as a jolly winter Yule log some

136

time ago. So this particular beggar is calm enough to take it home, light a fire and warm his hands in front of the murder weapon. Calm, cold-blooded, well-considered. Those are the characteristics. Those are the things we should be looking for on the house-to-house enquiries. Remembering always that the ones who have all those characteristics are the ones who can put on an excellent act. Someone here is cunning. Dead cunning.'

He saw a regeneration of interest. The distant air, born of weariness, was dispelling as morning mists dispel in the sun. It was essential to keep them alive to everything. Mummery was an experienced and wily organiser of men. He had to be.

'Now I think we can assume that our friend isn't finished yet. He or she or they intended to murder Gibbon. I'm certain of that, although I had my doubts about Mr Gibbon at first. There's only one question to apply, and that's what for? The answer is as blindingly obvious as it always is – because he knows something or has seen something or has formed some view or has sufficient facts to form some view that will put the murderer in danger. We've got a man sitting outside his hospital room at all times. But he's discharged tomorrow. We'll follow him. Discreetly. The gentleman in question has developed a severe case of the Sherlock Holmes.'

He paused for the snorts and laughter he expected. They were alert now, attentive to every word.

'Now as they seem to accept him, that's good news for us in some ways. The problem is that chummy the murderer will be the one who is keenest of all to be friendly and if Gibbon has already put two and two together he isn't telling us. I think he would if he had, therefore it follows that he's got about two and one-and-a-half, and is going to go poking about and lifting stones and peering underneath, which is a very dangerous occupation for an amateur. Now Mr Gibbon has a theory, about which I won't at the moment comment, that the original shot was meant for young Harris and that the killing of Luxford was a mistake.'

This produced an interested murmur from the tired men.

'Considering how popular Luxford was with almost everyone, you can give that theory what weight you like. Now I think you can all go home and we'll start another sweep tomorrow. And while we're about it, we'll be keeping our eyes open for digging. Newly turned or recently turned. It will have to have been before the frost. I have a whiff of something fishy about this archaeology business. Both Luxford and Wilkinson were keen on it, and maybe – no more than that – it has some bearing on things. Perhaps someone found something valuable and disposed of it quietly. Just keep your eyes open for anything odd.'

He stopped and moved aside towards Mann to indicate he had finished. He beckoned to Sergeant Frewin as well to join them.

137

There was much scraping of chairs and clumping of boots as the men left.

'I don't want to over-emphasise this archaeological strand,' Mummery said to the two men, 'but after talking to Wilkinson I think there may be something in it.' Mann pulled a dubious face. 'Well, what do you think, Mann?'

'Talking to Jeffrys, I don't think so, sir, he thinks it was all a bit of nonsense. He told me he was a homosexual, sir. If that has anything to do with anything. Not boys, he emphasised.'

'Is this all in your report?'

'Yes sir.' Mummery nodded. He would read it later.

'Well, I'm bearing in mind that William Luxford is a so-called antiques dealer, and feels dishonest. I can't put my finger on anything yet, but he was very keen to tell me his brother was being blackmailed by young Tom.'

Mann scratched his yellow thatch.

'Well?' prompted Mummery, 'Reactions? Luxford says young Tom spied on his brother with women and blackmailed him to the tune of a fiver a week.'

'In that case,' said the sergeant, 'I can understand Tom Harris being killed, but not *after* Luxford.'

'Exactly. Unless young Tom was making a business of it. Perhaps Luxford was only one of his victims. Perhaps the story's a lie to put us off the scent of something else. At this stage I just don't know.'

Mann had been pondering. His face was corrugated accordingly.

'It isn't very nice to think about it, but it *is* possible young Tom was blackmailing people. He had money from time to time, and I don't think you could describe his parents as generous.'

Mummery was slightly surprised by this analysis.

'He did have one or more jobs. He earned money. Who did he work for?'

'Meadows. And Wilkinson. Both of them.'

'This place is sealed like a Kilner jar. Wilkinson again, eh? I don't know what to make of that gentleman. He has no alibi at all for the time of either crime. Or at least he says he was in the pub when Luxford was shot and was at home alone when Harris was killed, if he was there at the right time. He's a fit man and could move about quite fast if he wanted to. And he doesn't have too much respect for the police. Asked me if I wanted to look in his sausages for fingernails . . .!'

Mummery smiled to himself slightly at the memory.

'Perhaps I should take him seriously and we should do just that.'

'I shouldn't mind it, I must say.' said Constable Mann, a satisfied expression on his face. There would be no prizes for guessing who would volunteer.

'Don't worry, Constable, I expect we shall find a way of bringing him to heel. In the meantime there is still Molly Luxford to go and see. She seems almost to have been neglected. You will be interested to know that Scotland Yard is flinging a wider net for us. They are investigating our two archaeological friends, finding out if they published anything and when and about what. I know you may think it's a waste of time, Mann, but we must do it. This case and this place have hit the headlines now as you've seen. The place is crawling with reporters. I couldn't get near the bar last night. You'll be delighted to know that what they're saying is that where there's two murders, there's always three. There had better not be!'

'Wasn't Gibbon supposed to be three?' said Frewin. Mummery looked at him sharply. Perhaps he had been favouring Mann rather at Frewin's expense. After all it had been Frewin of the lugubrious face who had found the letter and gloves in church. He had been keeping him out in the fields and not putting him on house-to-house.

'I was trying not to put that into words,' he said, 'but yes, you're right. We have to find a new lead on this soon. We can't trace the gun yet.'

'Perhaps that is a lead,' said Frewin. 'It's very difficult to buy an untraceable weapon. Someone in this village obviously knows how you go about it, so someone's a clever lad with some expert knowledge.'

Mummery looked at the Detective Sergeant with interest. It was not a new thought to Mummery, who had got there some time ago, but he liked to encourage.

'You know, that's an astute remark, Frewin. I had that in mind, but it got relegated in all this mish-mash of information. For that bright thought, how would you like to interview Mrs Molly Luxford?'

'I'd be delighted, sir.' The long face looked grateful. 'I don't fancy another day in wellies. You're not suggesting that she might be the clever one we're looking for?'

'Don't you rule out anything, and don't rule out the women either.' He paused. 'I suppose I'd better take Cynthia Fry.'

He saw relief flit across Mann's face. He couldn't blame him.

'You had better have a day off, Mann. Blend with the background, having a drink or two, listen a lot.'

'Yes sir!' said Mann delighted.

Frewin, who had hoped Mann was being put out to grass while his career improved, risked a peeved scowl at Mummery. Mummery exposed his teeth at him in rude apology for a grin.

'Don't forget to ask Molly Luxford about all her husband's digging and delving!' he said coarsely. 'In the ground of course!'

The two men left. He pondered the events of the day. So Mann thought young Tom might have been up to blackmail, and he was the village man? He certainly didn't put much weight on this rather far-fetched archaeological business. Interesting.

139

Chapter Seven

Gibbon was feeling very restless. His arm was a nuisance and an encumbrance and undeniably hurt, but they were going to let him out. One more X-ray they said, that afternoon, to make sure everything was in place, then he could go home. Three more hours. One more hospital meal. He wondered what the police would do about him then. A succession of patient policemen had appeared and sat in the corridor for the five days he had now been in hospital. He had spoken to each, got to know his name, only to discover he had been replaced and a new face was put to the familiar uniform. He couldn't blame them. It must be the most boring job in the world.

Would they try to guard him at home? Did he want them to guard him at home? He stared down the bed at the door. A nurse clopped past. He certainly did not. He had thought a lot about the possibility of another attempt being made on him, but decided it was unlikely. First of all he would make sure he wasn't caught so stupidly exposed again, secondly he would take care at night. He wondered if whoever had pushed the ladder knew that the police knew about the bullet hitting the column. Would they keep it to themselves or leak it? It was why someone had tried to kill him, he was certain. If they had leaked that they knew about it, he was safe. He must ask Mummery. If Mummery would tell him. The man was devious.

But then there was the problem of the footsteps. He was the only one who had seen them. Except the killer. There was no doubt that was who they belonged to. Did that still mean that he knew too much for someone's good? He supposed it did. One of his first ambitions was to stare at everyone's feet. He could fit them pretty accurately to what he had seen, or at least exclude those that were obviously too large or too small.

Most of all he felt he had a personal stake in this now, and wasn't going to be put off by having a policeman dog his steps. He supposed this was recovery from shock. He wanted to get his would-be murderer face to face. And what then? Do something very uncharitable? And what if it was a woman? A lovely woman?

'You have a visitor, Mr Gibbon,' said his friend the freckle-faced

140

nurse, who was called Sue. 'She's a she.' Sue grinned broadly. 'You won't do too badly when you get out of here!'

Sue went through her routine of smoothing out the bedclothes.

'Who is it?' demanded John.

'Aha! Wouldn't you like to know!'

She left, and immediately returned. She showed in Clara, shutting the door behind her with a knowing smile.

'Hello Clara,' said John, impressed by the inadequacy of this as a remark. 'I had no idea you were here . . .'

'Why should you? I hear you're well and they're about to discharge you. Your face is a bit multi-coloured! Are you all right, if that's what you ask someone with a broken arm? What on earth happened?'

Clara had picked up the upright chair the hospital provided and moved it to the bedside, where she sat down. She was being very cool and efficient and looked very beautiful, he decided. She also looked concerned. He liked her to look concerned about him. She had dressed very nicely too, and he liked that as well. He felt sick at heart, a lurch, a familiar feeling.

'I'm all right,' he said with studied bravery. All's fair in love or war or separation. She wasn't wearing his moonstone brooch, but that would have been too much to ask.

He would have given a lot to turn the clock back twelve months, before the real friction between them had started. She was wearing a slightly sour perfume that he remembered but couldn't name.

'I fell off a ladder,' he said, 'or rather, I was pushed!'

'The police told me you had had an accident.'

'How did they trace you?'

'They didn't trace me. You gave them my address. When you filled in the forms. You probably don't remember.'

'I don't.'

'What really happened?'

'Are you prepared for a long story?'

'You came here for peace and quiet. That was the idea.' There was sober reproach in her tone. A hint that if it was sympathy he was seeking, it would be difficult to obtain.

'Have you been reading the papers? Have you seen about our murders?'

Clara looked shocked.

'No. I don't know anything about this!'

'I'll try to explain. I'm the innocent in it all!'

He explained and Clara listened. From time to time she asked questions quietly. She looked pale and concerned and was critical of the way he had acted on his own.

'Do you understand how frightening this has all been to me?' she asked. 'Why let yourself in for this danger? There's a uniformed policeman outside the ward. That's obviously how serious it is. I'm

141

angry too. We agreed on separation! What you've done looks like a deliberate attempt to embroil me. I know that sounds unkind to you, but what else is it?'

John coloured and was angry.

'So you think I did all this as attention seeking?'

'In a way, yes. Not consciously perhaps, but why else should you get mixed up in it!'

There was an angry silence.

'Only to occupy myself,' said John.

'Oh John! Don't delude yourself!'

He stared at the mound made by his feet at the end of the bed. She was right again, she was always right. He had taken a risk and was quite pleased with himself in a way that he was helpless in bed and that she had had to come.

'You've put me in a position where you can't look after yourself. Where I can't walk away. What am I going to do? How do I get away?'

She was looking at him with clear, clear eyes. He knew he had always been too possessive about her, had stifled her. That was where the trouble had started. Pressures, sexual rejection, sulking. They had paid each other in measure. Clara was a post-graduate chemist, he stamped library books and was jealous. He had started the hate he supposed, for she had always loved him. 'I'm fully mobile,' he said, 'apart from having to go through doors sideways!'

She smiled despite herself.

'Don't make me laugh, John, you'll only make me sad, and then we'll both be unhappy. I wondered if I could help you until you're better. If you don't want that, say so, and I'll go away immediately. I'll help on the strict understanding that we keep ourselves to ourselves. I could stay in the pub and come in in the day-time to cook. You can do your own cleaning. I don't see why I should spoil you.'

'Thank you very much. I'd like that. But you can't stay at the pub.'

'Why not?' Clara's voice was suspicious. 'This is not an excuse for us to get together again, John. This is two friends helping out.'

'Of course. I understand that.'

Liar.

'I meant about the pub that it's full of journalists. This place is notorious. Apart from that, you can imagine the gossip it would start.'

'Which do you really care about? My comfort or the gossip?'

'Both.'

'I wish I could believe you!' she said. 'But if I accept the situation I want to find out who did this to you. Don't expect a nurse and bottle-washer. I was never made for that. I want to *know*. I shall be frightened until I find out. Not knowing is the worst thing on earth.'

John stared at her, astonished at her firmness and strength. Clara laughed, fully and spontaneously.

'Your face is a picture, John Gibbon. You can't do much and this has to be resolved. *I* don't have any ambitions as an amateur detective, and I don't see this as an excuse for us to be thrown together. It's no use sitting there trying to look reformed, because nothing has changed. Just now the old John Gibbon shone out like the Eddystone light.'

John was confused, disconcerted. She was obviously not prepared to heal old wounds, and with her usual knack she had laid him open with the skill of a surgeon. He felt pain that was much more real than the ache in his arm. It showed on his face and Clara saw it and was ashamed.

'I'm sorry,' she said. 'That was unkind, and I suppose I'm feeling malicious. Can we agree with the arrangement I've just suggested?'

Her honesty always left him breathless. He loved that honesty and it also terrified him. One day he might get accustomed to it.

'Of course. I'd like that very much.'

'Then take Philippa Crabbe for example, who better to pay a visit? She may tell me what she won't tell you for shame. We have to know for example what Luxford dug up that puts her on the wrong side of the law. It may be the key to everything, or it may be nothing. Maybe Tom Harris knew what Luxford had found or stolen or whatever. Maybe Philippa Crabbe is the murderer and also a very good actress.'

'You know, I'd never thought of that,' John conceded, 'I'd always seen her as a victim.'

'But then you're a man, aren't you?' said Clara.

The vicarage was Georgian with a Victorian conservatory tastelessly glued to the side. It was set back by the depth of a formal garden from the road. The garden was splendidly neglected, the terraces showing like geological layers. Patches of lawn had been mown between them like cultivated paddies.

Frewin opened the garden gate that was twinned with a five-bar gate to the drive and walked up the mossy gravel path that led to the front door. Great bunches of daffodil and snowdrop leaves clustered on each side, but it was too early in the year for more than a green show. Behind these, fine bushes had so intermingled as to make the species of any one indistinct. Luxford had been no gardener. Too busy plucking other blooms, thought Frewin with a flash of sour Puritan morality.

He pulled a fine original bell-pull, oblivious to its period authenticity. The woman who answered the bell was quite tall, which for some reason he had not expected, in her middle forties, and also elegant. She regarded him without curiosity. Perhaps she was always distant, perhaps the death of her husband had exhausted her. They were the eyes of a listener or a counsellor, Frewin decided, accustomed to giving help. Right for a vicar's wife.

'Yes?' she asked, holding the door ajar.

'I'm Detective-Sergeant Frewin, Mrs Luxford. Can I have a word with you?'

'Of course.' Resignation in her voice. She held the door open and he walked into a hall decorated with a dark blue paper of Chinese influence, covered with pale blue chrysanthemums in blossom. He had a glimpse of gilt picture frames, Victorian oils of brooding mountains, and then was led into a reception room. There was no other word for it. It had the air of a combined best room and waiting room and smelled of wax polish and fireplace. He found himself looking for the pile of magazines, but instead was waved to a fragile mahogany dining chair covered with brocade. Four of these stood round a glossy mahogany table. Molly Luxford took another and settled down opposite him. The stretch of wood between them was like a chestnut fresh from its shell. He felt at a disadvantage. That was a bad start to an interview. Rule one, control the subject.

'I'm sorry to disturb you, but I have to ask a few questions.'

'I expect you do. You're not disturbing me.'

This disconcerted him too.

'Can we start by you telling me what you were doing and what happened on the night in question?'

'What night in question? You mean the night when my husband was killed, I suppose. You needn't be afraid to put it bluntly. There's no point in mincing words.'

'Yes. Thank you Mrs Luxford.'

If Frewin had been able to see into the dim, blind, distant future, he would have found that he was forever destined to remain a sergeant. He had lost control again.

'I was in the house here watching television. There's always good things on on Christmas Eve. I had things to do in the kitchen too, and I read a book after that.'

'You didn't see any reason to go to church?'

Frewin was fighting back now. He injected a slight critical edge to his voice.

'No. I didn't want to go. Why should I? I married the man, not the Ministry.'

'I just thought, as it was Christmas Eve . . . an important day in the . . .'

'Church calendar?' she supplied. She looked at him icily and Frewin shifted his position to sit up straighter. The chair groaned and he prayed it wouldn't collapse. 'Christmas is a time for celebration and unity and happiness and families. There were no such feelings between me and my husband. It would have been a sham.'

'You didn't get on, obviously?'

'You have a knack of stating the obvious, Sergeant Frewin. You don't have to treat me delicately or like a simpleton. My husband, as the world now knows, was an inveterate lecher. They used to call people like him a disgrace to their cloth. I was really sorry for the women involved. He was a worthless man, and I used to love him. Nevertheless when all the grieving's over, I think the world's better off without him.'

There was a considerable pause. Frewin removed a nervous hand from the mahogany and watched the imprint of his fingers slowly evaporate.

'Can you tell me more about his interest in archaeology?' he asked.

'Why are you interested in that?'

'We think there might just be some connection between that interest and his death. We have to explore everything.'

'And what about that poor lad Tom Harris? I liked Tom a lot. Has it anything to do with his death?'

'We don't know.'

'Are they connected? Surely they must be in some way. This is a tiny place. Chance is impossible.'

'You really think so, Mrs Luxford?'

Molly Luxford looked annoyed. What she thought of Frewin was plain on her face.

'Can we stop this third-rate banter? We're talking about my husband, whatever I thought about him, and about a young boy that I knew. It's all very well for you callow policemen to come wandering in asking juvenile questions, you do it all the time I've no doubt, but you might at least try not to be flippant.'

Frewin blushed, a thing he had not done for many years.

'There was no intention to upset . . .'

'Intention! I don't think you were doing it with intention!'

Frewin puzzled over this one, and decided rightly that it was insulting.

'I am a police officer,' he intoned, 'and I ask you to answer my questions.'

'And that remark is probably the second last refuge of scoundrels!' said Molly Luxford triumphantly. Frewin wondered if Luxford had committed suicide, poor sod.

'I still want to know more about his archaeology.'

Molly Luxford bit down her next reply. There was no advantage to be had by baiting the man further, and everything to be gained by getting rid of him.

'What can I tell you?'

'What he did. What his interests were. It's a subject I know nothing about. Why he had some sort of feud going with Wilkinson the butcher. Whether he ever found anything valuable. All that sort of thing.'

'I suppose you're one of those people that thinks archaeology is about digging for buried gold? No, don't answer. My late husband was an amateur dabbler, but one who knew quite a lot. His particular interests were the Bronze Age and early Saxon periods. This area is littered with Bronze Age earthworks and mounds. Of course a lot of the evidence is under the plough now, but much of it is also in the woods that cover the hills round here. It is relatively recent woodland, two to three hundred years old, and things were never ploughed. He spent a lot of his time drawing and plotting and mapping. Things that might seem entirely boring to you. Occasionally he went digging, but not for buried treasure! He had an auger for taking soil samples and sometimes used a spade, and yes, he had a metal detector, just for a bit of fun.'

'And did he find anything?'

'He found many things, but I doubt if they were the type of things you are referring to. He has discovered at least two round barrows, and rediscovered perhaps three others that the Victorians seem to have got to. He wrote two papers about his discoveries that were published, so he wasn't such a rank amateur as all that. All about the round heads and the long heads and their grave artefacts. The round heads never reached Ireland you see, and their forms of artefacts seem to come from Spain while those in England seem to resemble those from France and Italy. Brachycephalic, they call it, Mr Frewin. Can you spell that, or aren't you taking this bit down? He found a skull to prove it, in a burial. Properly reported of course. There was a full scale dig and some temporary excitement. When he wasn't out digging he used it as an excuse to be out philandering. You know what that means I'm sure. That's the polite way of putting it.'

Frewin was blushing again.

'Can you tell me the journal he published these things in?' he asked.

'I'll show you the articles,' said Molly Luxford, getting up and crossing to a bookshelf with a glass front. She took out a magazine and leafed through it, showing Frewin an article with sketches illustrating pieces of incised pottery. The article had been written by the Reverend Peter Luxford, M.A.

'All good stuff,' he said fatuously. She gave him a dry glance. 'What was his quarrel with Wilkinson?'

'What's this supposed to be relevant to?'

'At this stage, I suppose we don't know. We're just picking at any ends.'

'Do you know, Mr Frewin, that's probably the only candid thing you've said since you came into this house. I like you much better for it.'

146

'Thank you,' said Frewin, greatly discomfitted. 'But forgive me if I point out that I'm supposed to be asking questions and taking down answers.' Molly Luxford gave him an encouraging smile. It was the sort you might bestow on a two-year-old who won't eat his prunes.

'Can we get back to this Wilkinson business? What was the rivalry about?'

Molly Luxford shrugged.

'I don't know if I really know. Peter used to say that Wilkinson was as much a butcher about his archaeology as he was at the block in his shop. He claimed Wilkinson was a total ignoramus. Now he *was* one of the hack and blast brigade, and yet he always accused Peter of the same thing. They have had terrible rows. Wilkinson always accused — — that word again — always accused Peter of following him about, spying on him and then stealing his discoveries. I know it doesn't sound like grown-up behaviour, but then it wasn't.'

'Is it possible that one of them found something valuable?'

She looked at him with a face of scorn again.

'What Peter found *was* valuable. It may not have been earth-shattering, but anything that adds to the general weight of knowledge and is original is a pearl. You ought to know that as a policeman.'

'I meant valuable in the vulgar way the world looks at it!' said Frewin with studied weariness. This female was a pain. 'Gold, coins, that sort of thing. Did your husband find anything like that?'

'No. And if he had, it would have been sent off immediately to the British Museum.'

'I have to stress this point.' Although it won't make me popular, he thought wearily. 'Can you be absolutely sure? Could he have found something and not told you?'

Molly Luxford did not flare up. She gave it perfectly serious consideration.

'All right, I said no in the first place. That was a defensive reaction. It would be much more truthful if I said "of course he could". I must say I sometimes wondered where he got all his money from, and that's a candid remark for you. He had a certain amount of money in investments that he'd been left and didn't tell me about or share. I would have thought he needed all that for his womanising. I used to say to him that above all I hoped he wasn't treating them cheaply.'

Frewin stared at her in a bovine way.

'You discussed his . . .'

'Affairs, as they call sexual adventures. Not in any detail. You can't imagine I would want to know? I told him he could keep the sordid details to himself, but he must behave properly to the women. There wasn't to be any illegitimate births, broken marriages, suicidal teenagers, that sort of thing. Nothing medieval or squirearchical about it. He was after all just a weak vessel.'

Frewin stared at her open-mouthed. So far he had failed to write anything in his note-book.

Cynthia Fry had let Mummery in without demur. He had been circumspect about the time of his visit, but it had all been very basic. George was safely in the Foresters. Mummery had seen him cross the door at five o'clock as he did every evening and knew that he wouldn't be seen again until nine, when he presumably rolled home and bellowed for food.

The first of the Tudor cottages had been christened 'Peartrees' – presumably by Cynthia Fry. Mummery felt cramped inside its low-beamed rooms. He was an elbows-and-legs person and felt very much that the place had been built for the stockier artisans of a harsher age. Even the door handles seemed to be at low level. A large cat overflowed from the window ledge, not deigning to notice him except for a twitch of one ear. Pieces of china stood on available ledges – the mantelpiece, a plate shelf, a walnut escritoire. Two wing-backed chairs upholstered respectively in chintz and leather formed a dam in the centre of the room. Cynthia was struggling through this obstruction, indicating that he ought to do the same. These objects were positioned in front of a fire that might have been stoked up for a martyr. Mummery made the mistake of trying to take off his coat in the limited space available and dealt a brass chandelier a ringing blow that skinned a knuckle.

'Woops, be careful.' said Cynthia. Mummery muttered under his breath about stupid bloody light fittings, and silly bloody remarks. He looked round hopelessly for somewhere to deposit the heavy garment, then put it on the floor hoping it would serve as a reproach, but Cynthia appeared not to notice. She still seemed preoccupied with shoe-horning him into the leather roasting-seat. He clambered into it and spread his jacket out wide.

'Would you like a cup of tea?' she asked.

As Mummery still felt bitter at having to see George into the Foresters without having a drink himself, this made him forget to pretend to be polite.

'Good God no! An iced beer would be nice though!' When Cynthia stared at him nonplussed, he modified his snarl to what he hoped was a coy and encouraging smile. 'I know everyone has this stupid idea about policemen on duty . . . Just pretend I'm not on duty . . .'

'I'll join you then,' she said. 'George will be on his third pint by now.'

She opened the escritoire, to reveal that it was serving another function. It was well stocked with bottles. None of them appeared to be more than half-exhausted. Mummery caught himself making the

148

hypocritical observation that this woman was obviously fond of her drink.

'Whisky?' she asked with unerring accuracy.

'How did you know?' leered Mummery.

'I guessed.' She had poured herself a large gin and bitter lemon. His whisky was impressive.

'You've obviously come to ask questions.' Cynthia arranged herself in the chintz-covered chair. Nice legs, thought Mummery who was not given much to such musings. An attractive woman. He could understand Luxford's interest. She looked very much like a shop-bought doll, the way she presented herself. Too much hair lacquer, too much make-up. An effective disguise.

'Is there anything I can help with? I've given it a lot of thought, of course. This killing of Tom Harris is horrible. I'm afraid at night now, I must say. Why kill a *boy*?'

'You sound as if you understand why Luxford was killed.'

Cynthia gave him an innocent twitch of a smile and clammed up.

'Do you?' he pursued. Her sky-blue eyes widened. It was not a metaphor, after all, Mummery thought. Perhaps she had exceptional optic nerves, or perhaps she practised it in the mirror. 'We know that you and Luxford were . . . close. I think you had better be honest with us.'

Cynthia sat more upright. The nice legs had disappeared. The blue eyes were hard and angry.

'Who's been talking to you? Has John Gibbon been saying things?'

'Now I find that interesting. What does John Gibbon know that we don't know?'

'Nothing that you can't guess at, I imagine. I confided in him.'

'Well he hasn't broken any confidences. He told us nothing. Perhaps you had better confide in us. The first thing we can clear up is this letter you wrote to Peter Luxford.'

As he spoke, he produced the letter from inside his jacket. Cynthia stared at it, appalled. He held the envelope out to her, for her to read. She glanced at it, and then back at him.

'Where did you get it from?'

'From the church. It was tucked under a cushion.'

'What!' She wasn't acting now. She looked utterly flattened. 'That's completely impossible. There's no way it could have got there.'

'But there it was.'

He wiped his forehead. It was hellish hot. She made no attempt to take the letter from him so he balanced it on the arm of his chair and sipped his whisky. She stared at it.

'I assume you didn't put it there,' he said.

'I certainly didn't.'

'Then the only other person who could have put it there was Luxford. Unless he gave it to someone else, or it was taken from him.'

'Why should he do that? And even if he had, why should someone leave it in the church?'

'You tell us.'

'For you to find. For you to suspect me.'

'That would seem to be the idea.'

'And do you? Suspect me?'

'Until we catch someone, I suspect everyone.'

'Have you read that letter?'

'Yes.'

'Then you know all about me. And all about Peter Luxford and me. It was a letter I should never have written.'

'Every letter is when things go wrong. If we all proceeded on that basis we would never put anything in writing.'

'It makes me feel ashamed just to think about it. There's no reason why my husband should know anything about it, is there? He would go berserk. I said a lot of sexy things in there.'

'You did.' Mummery nodded his head soberly. Privately he thought it was fairly average of its sort. 'We have no reason to let your husband know about it unless it turns out you did murder Luxford.'

'Of course I didn't! And if I had, would I have been so stupid as to leave that in church? Good God, Inspector!'

'No, I think we are supposed to believe it accidentally fell from your pocket or your handbag. Or maybe we are supposed to believe you were carrying it on you and when Luxford fell shot, you realised it was incriminating evidence and hid it. How about that as a theory?'

'But you said "fell shot", which implies it was done by someone else. I wouldn't be likely to be carrying the evidence on me if I intended to do the shooting myself!'

'Unless you are very clever and this is an elaborate double bluff. And I do think you're clever, Mrs Fry. You have adopted an outwards personality that entirely conceals your inner self. I think you would have done something just like that.'

'Would have. So you don't really think I did any of this.'

'I wouldn't go so far as to say that. Let's say I think it's more likely someone lifted that letter and left it under the cushion deliberately so that it would be found, knowing we would search the church. Someone wasn't well disposed to you, Mrs Fry, and that someone had access to that letter, which must have been in Luxford's possession. I think we can guess that someone was jealous of you, in that case. How's that as a theory? Another woman. One who wouldn't have been too amused to find a letter like that from you to Luxford.'

'He must have left it lying about.'

'Maybe he showed it to her deliberately. I gather our Peter

Luxford would have been quite capable of doing something like that.'

She stared at her shoes.

'Yes he was.'

'Then who was most likely to take it from him and do that?'

'Lucinda Walker.'

Mummery finally struggled to his feet and shoved his chair back from the fire. The letter on the arm fell to the floor. Before he could react, Cynthia Fry had snatched it up and thrown it into the heart of the fire. He had an instant's thought that he ought to plunge his hand into the flames and snatch it out, but as quickly realised he wasn't going to risk that.

'That was very stupid, and a very serious offence! You've destroyed evidence!'

'That wasn't evidence, and that was my own property. I can destroy that if I want.'

Mummery glared at her. If it had nothing to do with the murder, she was right.

'We have a copy of it, anyway,' he said spitefully. To his horror, Cynthia Fry began to cry. Time to go. And she was probably right about Lucinda Walker. 'I think I had better go,' he said. 'I'm sorry this has been distressing . . . ' He held out his hand, and she automatically extended hers to shake it limply. She avoided his eyes. Her hands were small. The gloves would not have fitted her. But then, she could have got them inside. It didn't prove they weren't hers.

Clara believed in getting things done. She had driven to John's house, off-loaded him and his belongings, settled herself in to the small spare room, and was ready to go.

'If Philippa Crabbe is in the state you say she is, the sooner I pay her a visit the better,' she said. She had to admit to herself she liked the house. She lit a fire from the small amount of coal and wood she could find, and put on the fan heater to try to warm the place up. The frozen turkey in its bag in the freezer gave her heart a wrench. She must fight hard not to feel sorry for him. She knew she was over-compensating by being brisk and jolly – things she normally hated – but it was a pain-killer that worked. She sat John in a chair to keep him out of the way. He rested his plaster cast and wasn't disposed to argue. He was finding he was more tired than he had thought he would be.

'I'll shop properly tomorrow,' she said, 'and I'll get a bottle of wine from the pub when I come back from Philippa Crabbe's.'

'But what are you going to say to her?'

'I don't know yet, and won't until I get started. We must find out more about the money, and what she knows about all that. I believe it is the key to the whole thing. Quite apart from the fact I want to see the lady who so obviously fancies you.'

'It's you I fancy, Clara.'

He was looking at her with a doggy, lost look. What she feared.

'Nonsense. And we're having none of that. We must agree on it, or I'll leave immediately. Say you agree.'

'I can't make myself do it.'

'You'll have to, or I go this moment.'

'I don't have any option, do I? I agree to keep my thoughts to myself, but I can't agree to not thinking them.'

'I'll settle for that.'

He had all the old power to confuse her. She fled the house. The evening was sunny, and the air smelled sweet with presentiments of spring. It should have lifted up her heart and soul, not moistened her eyes. It would still be dark early, she told herself. Punishment for nostalgia.

Her walk took her through the village, as Philippa lived in the last house in the High Street before Hundred Row. The house faced the west end of the church and the street-facing rooms had a reasonable aspect because it was set well back with a fine cottage garden before it. Trees stood in the grass of an orchard. The grass was pale yellow with the small flowers of early crocus, and snowdrops formed green tufts towards the far hedge. Coltsfoot, that candle for the death of winter and the conception of spring, showed uncoiling stems amongst other weeds. Clara noted it all with approval. A garden that promoted the humble and beautiful flowers of the hedgerow as much as it promoted flowers for the vase. A considerable section was given over to herbs. Wild chives were forming green spearlets like hundreds of coloured matchsticks. Rosemary bushes glowed with the earliest of blue flowers. There was a whiff from the leaves of wild garlic. Behind this area, wild blackthorn was already green and trembling with impatience. A true delight.

Clara had hardly noticed the house as a result and was now conscious that it was stone-and-brick, and must be late seventeenth or early eighteenth century. Wisteria climbed the left gable, but had stopped short of the north face. Japonica had been trained over the stonework on wires. Like the garden, it had been maintained but left alone. The bell pull was still worked by wire and Clara could hear it jangling somewhere inside. She had her first feelings of panic about her intrusion. Philippa might take it very much amiss, and she could hardly blame her if she did.

She pulled the bell again. The jangling was vigorous enough, but there was only silence.

An empty house, she thought. It had that quality of vacancy that cannot be explained by the heard noises of the ear, but are heard through other senses, or are perhaps perceived rather than heard.

152

Approach the door of an occupied house and you know it is occupied.

Was Philippa in the garden? There must be another one round the back. A flagged path led off to the left beside the gable. She walked along it, looking first into a comfortable sitting room that was empty, then into a bathroom with window ajar. She felt very ashamed peering into that. Walking past the gable she saw that she had been right and that another garden stretched out behind. It was even bigger than the front and had outbuildings towards the rear and a greenhouse. The ground had been very recently turned in one long strip of it. A fork stood thrust into the ground. Surely someone had been working that day?

The kitchen must be at the rear. In a house of this age it would be, with access direct to the kitchen garden. She continued round and saw that she had been right again. The kitchen door was ajar.

'Hello?' she called politely, outside the door. She knocked on it with her knuckles. The same vacant noise. She called out again, and eased the door open, to call louder. As there was no reply she stepped inside, leaving the door wide behind her so that it did not seem such an intrusion. Her eyes became accustomed to the darker interior. Philippa had not done her washing-up. It was after five and yet her lunch plates were still on the table. More signs of vacancy. Clara opened the door leading from the kitchen. Beyond was a hall with stairs leading up. She called again, her voice sounding nervous to her own ears. No reply, no sound. She stepped through into the hall. It had a brick floor with an Afghan rug. Off it to the left was an open door. The room to the right of the front door, she thought. Still calling 'Hello' as though it was a talisman, she pulled it further open and peered in. A study or library. The walls were shelved out and filled with books. What spaces were left were occupied with prints of flowers or dried plants. A Victorian cast-iron fireplace brimmed with branches of exotic plants complete with seed pods and cones. In the centre of the room was a vast mahogany table with a reading lamp, typewriter and papers spread on it. On the floor behind a chair was Philippa Crabbe.

She could not have been asleep and was contorted, knees drawn up, head twisted to one side. Her shoes were both off and one hand was gripping the leg of the chair. The room smelled, and there was a mess of vomit on the floor.

'Oh God!' Clara called loudly, to hear the sound of her own voice. With horror and fear of the inevitable she steeled herself and walked forward. She took Philippa's shoulder and pushed it to and fro. It was unyielding.

'Oh God! You're dead aren't you!' she said loudly to herself. 'I ought to lift your head to make sure. I can't do it! But I have to check . . .'

153

She took a deep breath and lifted up Philippa's head. Her teeth were bared so that she appeared to snarl, and half of her face was soiled. Philippa's features were blurred, the skin slumped and relaxed in death. It was a very unpleasant sight to Clara, who felt her stomach heaving. She replaced Philippa's head where it had been. She straightened up and began to tremble violently. Her legs were actually shaking. It was a sensation she had never experienced and she had to sit down quickly. She withdrew the chair from under the table and forgot Philippa's grip. Her hand released its hold and Clara stared at it on the carpet as it relaxed, moving slightly. She sat down on the solid leather seat and shut her eyes for a few moments, squeezing them together hard, collecting herself. What was she to do? Police. That was obvious. She had no idea if there was a phone in the house and hadn't seen one. Check again and make sure the victim *is* dead. That was what you were supposed to do, even when you are sure. Disturb things as little as possible. Keep your eyes peeled for anything unusual. Clues.

She rose shakily from the seat and stooped again beside the glaring face. She reached out trembling fingers and despite her aversion to the feel of cold flesh put a finger on Philippa's eyelid. There was nothing. She reached down and felt for the pulse in the outstretched arm. The weight of the inanimate limb surprised her, and she had to grasp the arm with her left hand to lift it enough. If there was a pulse she couldn't feel it and the wrist was clammy and cold. She put the arm back again and looked around her.

Philippa had been sick around the room. She had been writing before she had been overcome. Sitting where she was at the table, Clara was surrounded by cellophane envelopes in which dried, pressed specimens were preserved. Some of these had been removed from their packets and were on the table loose. There was gum, coloured inks, steel nibbed pens and several boxes of gold-plated artist's nibs. Above all there was a Morocco bound gold embossed book, the size of a ledger, in which she had been drawing and making entries in a very upright script. Clara flipped quickly through the book. It was thick, and full of entries in the same dense upright hand. Some of the pages were illustrated with clear, very precise and beautiful drawings in inks of varying colours which had then been coloured in with the same medium or with a mixture of gouache, watercolour, pastel and ink.

She had just been colouring a drawing which Clara recognised as a native orchid, and a bottle of sepia ink and a pen lay on the table. Beside them was a sheet of blotting paper and a palette with three compartments for water-colour. There was a glass of water and an empty coffee cup, saucer and spoon.

'Make it natural causes!' said Clara aloud, knowing in her heart that it wasn't and that John had been right.

It suddenly occurred to her that the murderer, if this was murder, might still be there. She left in panic, heart pounding, caring nothing about telephones and ran towards the police station, towards John, not caring who saw her.

Mann knew he could never blend with the background and had long ago given up trying. A policeman is a policeman, even after four pints. It didn't stop people being convivial, but there was always that constraint. But tonight it was interesting. They were trying to pump him for information, which was natural enough. He had had three pints and was trying to concentrate.

'Why should anyone want to kill a *boy*?' Meadows was demanding for the group of them. It included George Fry – already well inebriated – Jeffrys, Wilkinson, Charlie Brooks the publican, Hazlitt and Edwardes. They were all looking at Mann for the answer to this key question. He couldn't blame them and they had taken a reasonable time to get round to the subject.

'If we knew that, we'd know everything,' he replied with impressive stupidity. Meadows made a face at Charlie Brooks.

'Which means you aren't going to say anything,' said Meadows. Mann merely shrugged slightly, sipped his pint and looked pleasantly attentive.

'He obviously knew something he shouldn't have,' said Hazlitt, very much to the point. 'Boys generally do. He was always a lad for getting out and about. I don't think this was the work of a maniac and all that claptrap we've been getting from them reporter fellows in the "Feathers." They reckons they turn up after a murder. I reckons that since some of them seem to make a good living out of it, they'd be quite capable of doing it!'

Hazlitt's sally didn't produce any of the levity he had expected.

'Well we can still have a joke now and then can't we?' he protested. 'I reckon someone knew what they were about, anyway.'

'Someone in the village,' said Wilkinson.

'Has to be,' said Hazlitt. 'The police must reckon that. Someone with local knowledge. I know it ain't a pretty thought. It could be one o' us.'

This produced such a chorus of angry protest that Hazlitt was finally abashed.

'All right, all right. I shall be very happy to be proved wrong! I think we shall all be happy when someone is put away. I liked young Tom and I reckon that whoever done that wants putting away. And I'm only saying that because of Eric there. Myself I'd put the beggar out of his misery and save everyone a lot o' trouble!'

They were standing or seated in a half circle around the open fire that was the glory of the place on a winter's night. The reporters had made an attempt to invade the place when they found the beer was

155

better than at the 'Feathers' and that the bar was more cosy. They had been successfully frozen out.

'Do the police believe the same person is responsible for both deaths?' asked Jeffrys sombrely. His mannered delivery and careful enunciation were effective in restoring calm and concentration. The half circle of men sipped their beer in the firelight and watched Mann's face. Mann enjoyed a long pause, sipping from his own glass before replying.

'I'm not at liberty to discuss what the police do or don't believe,' he said pedantically.

'Look, we quite understand it puts you in a difficult spot, Eric,' said Charlie Brooks, trying to pull rank, 'but you've known us all for a long time and we can't all be murderers, and you must see it isn't very nice for any of us. We're grasping at straws, Eric. The thing is, there must be some things you can tell us that would make everyone feel a little less hunted. It's all right for you, no one suspects *you* of murder. In fact you're the only one here who isn't a suspect. And while we stand here having a friendly pint, you may for all we know be about to arrest someone!'

'No comment,' said Mann.

'Oh come on, Eric. There must be something you can tell?'

'Oh come on yourself, Charlie! You're putting unfair pressure on me. I'll be forced to go to the "Feathers" if you keep it up.'

'I shall be glad to see you go, if you can't be more friendly!' said Charlie, a man noted for his skyrocket temper. 'That's the truth!'

'But what no one has explained,' interrupted Edwardes in slow rustic vowels that drowned out further conflict, 'What no one has explained is how anybody managed to fire the gun from the tower and hide there and then get out unseen.' He examined his pint against the light as though the truth lay there somewhere at the bottom of his glass.

'It proves it wasn't any of us in the church, don't you see that!' bellowed George Fry. George was slumped in a Windsor chair, too near the fire.

'It was rigged up,' said Wilkinson. The others stared at him. 'It must have been if no one came down the stairs. Ask Eric.'

'That's an interesting idea,' said Mann non-committally.

'Maybe it was Charlie after all,' said Hazlitt with a sudden evil grin. 'He wasn't in the church.'

'I was here, you old devil, that's why I wasn't in the church! And you know it!' Charlie had lost his temper again. His face was flushed and angry.

'Well, I only said that seeing as how I wouldn't want you to be left off the list of suspects,' said Hazlitt slyly. 'We may as well all be on it . . .'

'You don't want to say things like that, not even as a joke.

156

Policemen have to take notice!' shouted Brooks, waving at Mann, hoping for denials. But Mann wasn't taking notice. His expression was remote, as if he was miles away. It was in this attitude that Sergeant Wakefield caught him as he crashed through the stiff outer door.

'Come on, Constable. We're wanted.'

There was no mistaking the urgency in his voice. Mann put down his glass and walked swiftly out.

'Oh God, not more!' said Jeffrys.

All the lights were on in the house and the curtains were pulled. Upstairs there was the sound of people moving about, doors and drawers being opened and shut, voices. The noises of search.

In the study the only light on was the desk reading lamp, a construction like a brass scallop that could be bent this way and that on a flexible stalk. It made a clearing in the gloom and shone back off the mahogany. Philippa Crabbe's body lay on the floorboards, covered with an incongruous fluffy yellow blanket. The rug on which she had died had been removed earlier so that the vomit could be analysed. The unpleasant smell remained.

Mummery stood back watching a medium-sized man in a grey flannel suit with a blue shirt and button down collar who was working at the table close to the light. The medium-sized man wore steel rimmed spectacles that flashed from time to time as he moved about. He had a large case in front of him and an assortment of small jars, slides and polythene bags. The doctor. He had been driven post haste from London at Mummery's request. Mummery held his chin in his right hand, while propping up the elbow with his left in a study in contemplation. Clara sat in the large chair she had earlier occupied, but this was pushed against the wall out of the circle of light. Beside her stood John. Wakefield and Mann stood easy by the door.

The doctor moved away from the table, felt in his pocket and produced a pencil torch.

'Excuse me,' he murmured and stooped to lift the blanket. They could see him shining it at the head of the body, then he stooped, folded the blanket quickly back, examined the eyes, pulling back a lid. Next he opened the inert mouth, produced a swab from his hand, wiped it across the tongue, replaced the blanket and returned to the table. There he wiped the swab across a slide. He then stood it in a box that already contained many slides. Saliva and blood. The cup and saucers were carefully encapsulated in sealed bags on the table, together with the palette, ink bottles, pens. The table itself was silvered with white powder from the fingerprint men.

'Definitely poisoned,' said the doctor. He was in his mid thirties and was much younger than the conventional idea of a police expert.

157

'Certain?' asked Mummery.

'Certain. Everything points to an alkaloid. Convulsions, vomiting, rictus and of course death.' He looked grim.

'Would it be quick?' Mummery voiced all their thoughts.

'Quick enough to debilitate once the stomach had absorbed it, but it might take three hours to get in to the system, especially if the stomach was full. From the onset of symptoms it would be very rapid if the dose was high, and overpowering. The person would feel nausea, start to vomit, faint, lose control of themselves rapidly. There would be nothing they could do at that stage. It would be impossible to get help for example. Impossible to move in fact.'

'Whoever gave her that is an animal!'

It was John Gibbon, his face white with rage, and his voice shaking.

'All murder is horrible, Mr Gibbon,' said Mummery gently. 'Perhaps we just get more accustomed to the sight of it in the force, but it never ceases to shock. I won't keep Mrs Gibbon here any longer than we absolutely have to, it must be very unpleasant for you both. Of course,' he paused and looked at Gibbon, 'it could have been suicide you know. We can't be sure it was murder. Maybe she had a reason for removing herself.'

Gibbon looked blankly at Clara. It had never occurred to him after what Clara had told them about the open doors.

'That must be impossible! I don't believe it! She wouldn't leave everything open like that.'

'Really? Even with convulsions and sickness?' Mummery removed his hand from his chin and folded his arms across his chest. The dim light gave his face sinister shadows, high-lighted his hook nose. 'Why do you say that?'

'When she came to see me she was frightened. At least I think so. She was certainly very worried, and I think she must have anticipated something like this. She must have known someone was after her.'

'When she came to see you in hospital?'

'Yes.'

'You haven't told me about this,' said Mummery ominously.

'You knew she'd been to see me. Your man in the corridor was making notes of all that.'

'As far as he was concerned it was just another fruit-bowl-and-flowers job. He was there to protect you, Mr Gibbon, in case you hadn't noticed, not to listen to your private conversations. We try to give people a few rights to privacy you know, despite what the Press says. By God, if you've been withholding information, I'll have you put inside!'

His anger at the death of Philippa was very obvious. He had been showing a studied calm up to now that had simmered visibly. John resisted the temptation to hurl back an angry response in justification. He laid a restraining hand on Clara's arm before she could leap to his defence and they sat in silence, looking at Mummery. The doctor coughed gently, felt in his left pocket and produced a handful of rubber bands. He began to wind these tightly around the necks of the clear polythene bags containing the inks, cup and saucers. Mann and Wakefield looked briefly at each other, kept still.

'Well it is a very serious matter,' said Mummery at last in tones that were much modified from his previous rage. 'What did she say, Mr Gibbon? You'd better tell me all of it.'

'She *did* come on a fruit-bowl job or whatever it was you called it. But she was alarmed and distressed. You would expect her to be, wouldn't you? We talked about Luxford and about Tom Harris's death. Philippa didn't want to come to the police you see because of her own involvement with Luxford. She wanted to tell me as an insurance policy I suppose.'

'Well, it didn't work, did it?' said Mummery unkindly. Gibbon ignored the remark.

'She told me she was involved inadvertently in what she saw as criminal activity.'

'And you didn't tell me this!'

'It was only yesterday, for heaven's sake! What's more she swore me to secrecy. You were talking about privacy, well I was respecting her privacy. She thought she was in no danger because no one knew what she knew except Luxford, and he was dead. I told her I thought she might be in danger, but she wouldn't listen.'

'So what was it she knew?' Mummery sounded strangled.

'She knew that Luxford was digging up something precious and selling it. That was the money he was spending on her. They were lovers as you know.'

'No I didn't know. That must be something else you forgot to tell me!' Gibbon pondered.

'I suppose I never had time to. She told me about it at Lucinda Walker's party, then before I had time really to tell you anything, Harris was killed and I was in hospital. You must have guessed.'

'Guessing is one thing, knowing another. So she might have had a motive for killing Luxford and even Tom Harris.'

'That *is* ridiculous.'

'Look here, Mr Gibbon, I can see you had a soft spot for Mrs Crabbe, but that doesn't remove her from the list of suspects for one or other or both the killings. Why didn't you tell me about this digging up of things?'

'I've already told you that she swore me to secrecy. I was going to tell you if it became obvious it was relevant. She made me promise not to repeat anything she said. Again, remember this was only yesterday.'

There was a vast sigh from Mummery.

'I'm afraid you've been very stupid, Mr Gibbon. I suppose it's my fault for letting you help us in the first place. If you'd told me this yesterday she might still be alive.'

'How do you know that!' protested John hotly. 'If I had told you this yesterday you would have come crashing round questioning her and she would have denied everything anyway.'

'We might have scared the killer off.'

John was silent. It was all true. Put in an impossible situation, he had been partly responsible for her death, he felt sure. He had been trying to conceal this from himself ever since Clara had come running into the house and poured out the news.

'I'm sorry. I'm terribly sorry. I expect you're right. I can only say that I didn't have time to think.'

Mummery's head nodded up and down. He had understood all along, but just wished these amateurs would leave it to the professionals.

'Look, I understand, Mr Gibbon. Things have happened very fast. We must stop anything else happening, that's vital. You've been out of circulation, but we've been busy. Is there anything else she said? We will want a statement from you with all this written down.'

'*She* said that she had all *this* written down. Safely recorded. Whatever it is.'

'You are a strong advertisement for the return of the rack, Mr Gibbon. What has she written down? Where? Give us the information!'

'That's all I know. This is what she told me – she said Luxford had spent money on her and that she knew it was from something to do with his amateur diggings and that she didn't want anyone to know about her and Luxford and stolen money being used in that way. Then she said that this was written down. She didn't explain what "this" was and I didn't pursue it because it didn't seem important at the time. She had no idea who the killer was of either Luxford or Harris, so presumably that isn't what she wrote down.'

'Have you *anything* more precise?

John considered carefully, trying to remember her exact words.

'I got the impression that it was a record of whatever was being dug up or perhaps where it was. She had to keep it from Luxford himself, she said. Somewhere he wouldn't find it either, and that he was very inquisitive.'

Mummery snorted.

'If I hadn't been a sympathetic listener and encouraged her, I'd have learned nothing!' John protested at the snort. 'It's very easy to criticize when you weren't there. You wouldn't have got anywhere with bullying.'

'You didn't get so far yourself, did you, Mr Gibbon?' growled

160

Mummery as though he had his jaws clamped round a bone. The doctor, who obviously had a habit of it, cleared his throat and coughed again.

'May I suggest that while you continue this, ah, debate, I remove my material for analysis? I have to get back to London you know, and it's a two hour drive.'

'Yes of course,' said Mummery crossly, 'but before you go, can you give us some indication as to the type of poison? It'll be at least two days before I get anything verbal from your chaps, knowing the speed at which they work. At the present alarming rate of mortality we could have another two bodies on our hands by then.'

'I hope that's an exaggeration,' said the doctor drily. 'Without committing myself I think it was a vegetable alkaloid. I've had a good look through the drawers over there and they're full of material that could either be used medicinally or as a poison. Everything she collected seems to be native, so working on that basis we have a limited choice. Wolfsbane, hemlock, henbane, perhaps agaric. All of them would certainly do, and they're all fairly common.'

'How would it be done?'

'I should think it would be put in the coffee. Coffee is bitter enough and from the remains in that cup, it looks as though she had it black and strong.'

'Would it be difficult to prepare the stuff?' pursued Mummery.

'Good heavens, no. Strictly kitchen cookery.'

'It would keep as a liquid extract,' said Clara. 'If it was kept as a powder, a vegetable alkaloid would lose its potency.'

'That's right!' said the doctor turning to her. 'Absolutely right. You know about this sort of thing?'

'A bit. I'm a chemist of the postgraduate variety, so it's incidental to my work.'

'Then you know all about it.' He flashed her a quick smile, as one professional to another and began to place the polythene bags in compartments inside his capacious case.

'She was a fine draftsman too. Or rather, draftswoman.' He gestured to the leather bound book. 'This is an excellent drawing of an orchid. He read from the page. "The Dark Winged Orchis, found May, woodland predominantly beech, north of village". She had a pressed specimen. Look, here it is.'

He held up a cellophane bag that had been lying on the table. In it was the pale pressed ghost of a flower.

There was a knock on the door of the study. Mann turned and opened it. A man in plain clothes addressed Mummery.

'Ambulance is here, sir.'

'All right, ask them to come in.'

The doctor snapped the catches of his bag noisily.

'I get the message, doctor,' said Mummery. 'I don't think there is

161

anything else you can usefully do here. Will you go back with the ambulance?'

'No, I'll drive back myself. I'll examine the body again as soon as I get back. I presume we shall have to perform an autopsy?'

'Yes.'

'In the meantime then, I'll test for the poison. Wrap this place up carefully. Tell your men we could be looking for any bottle or phial. Keep absolutely anything. You'll need a whole forensic team I think?'

Mummery sighed. He was sighing a lot this evening.

'Yes, I think I shall. We'll carry on through the night and should have fingerprinted everything. What about all these samples of flowers? She's got a whole collection of them.'

'There's only about a dozen that could possibly be of interest, and your experts will know which.'

Mummery nodded. Two men in uniform entered with a stretcher. Mummery indicated the body.

'I'm afraid she's there, gentlemen. We've taken our photographs . . .'

The ambulance men put the stretcher down beside the blanket-shrouded figure, removed the blanket, picked the body up and transferred it. Covering it again with the blanket, they lifted the stretcher and left, the doctor following them. John and Clara had watched the proceedings with a feeling of remoteness, as though this were all happening on a screen, to others.

'Now then,' said Mummery when the door had closed behind the stretcher-party, 'what do we do with you two? Are you all right, Mrs Gibbon?'

'As well as can be expected,' said Clara forcefully. 'I'm not at all accustomed to this sort of thing, but will survive.'

'We will have to complete the thorough search of the house. I don't want to leave that for a moment. If there's anything of importance here we intend to get it first time. Sergeant, will you and Constable Mann see if you can help?'

When the other two men had left the room, Mummery began to prowl around the room, looking at the books on the walls, peering at prints. He blew his nose noisily while staring at a hectic coloured print of a dianthus. It was the signal for a new phase in the discussion.

'Look, I know I was annoyed just now,' he began, 'but you can see my reasons. You were asked to help in a general way by listening and asking a few questions, but before we can get any answers or even a report from you, you get shoved off a ladder because you are already doing your own amateur detecting. We *hate* amateurs. They mean trouble, and you're no exception, Mr Gibbon. I will grant you that you seem to have got it right so far. You were even ahead of us on the footsteps. Now we have another death on our hands, and quite apart

162

from the human tragedy of it all, the Press will crucify us, and when my pay comes up for review in three months time I am very unlikely to receive the increment I believe I deserve unless I have this particular homicidal individual under lock and key. All these things considered, this is not one of the happiest days of my life.'

He addressed the whole speech to the dianthus before turning to look at John and Clara. He tucked the handkerchief into his jacket pocket and tried to look severe. The effect was merely mournful.

'I'm sorry,' said John. 'I'll sit down tomorrow and give you a verbatim account of everything everyone said. Most of it was totally trivial, I really can assure you.'

'But was there any *pattern* to it? We look for patterns, for recurrences, for symmetry. We may be able to see something that you can't.'

'I have no idea so far who committed these murders, if that's what you're asking. But I do think that this death is because of the same thing, and I think that same thing is a thing of value. I don't believe that people have been murdered because of Peter Luxford's sex life. You know, since we're being candid, I object to the way you're treating us. Clara is very upset at finding Philippa's body like that, and I'm very upset too. I liked her very much. Now she's dead, and I was nearly killed, and you talk to me as though I'm responsible for this in some way. Whatever is going on here, it was certainly going to happen whether I lived in this place or not. Don't you agree?'

'I suppose that's true.'

'Of course it is. You're using the situation to put pressure on us, to see if there's something that can be squeezed out of us. Apart from what you now know, there is nothing else to tell. Can we please go home?'

'Very shortly. I'd be obliged if you would wait around for ten minutes or so in case we want to ask anything.'

John looked at Clara questioningly. Clara nodded.

'All right,' she said, 'But I would like to get out of here. It doesn't smell very nice and I've had enough of the horrors.'

'Would you like a drink? I'll leave you my flask.'

'No thank you, Inspector.' said John. 'Just let us out of here as quickly as possible.'

'We will.' He moved back to the door. 'Please don't disturb anything. Although we've printed practically everything, I would really appreciate it if you would just sit. Just stay put. Please?'

'All right!' said John crossly.

'Thank you,' said Mummery with mock humility, and left the room. Outside he quickly found Mann.

'All right, Mann, several things while I remember them. The gloves have been traced to London, and were bought by a man as far as the sales girl can remember. The gun was bought in London.

163

Whoever we are looking for travels there from time to time, and knows how to get their hands on a gun. Or knows someone who does. Next, there is something very obvious about these three crimes, that up to this moment I hadn't noticed.'

Mann stared at him expectantly.

'Haven't you noticed something that is identical in every case?'

'No sir,' said Mann with transparent honesty. 'Not a thing.'

'They all have two things in common. I don't know why I didn't see it immediately. The first thing in common is that they have nothing in common. That is very unusual. The second thing they have in common is a total lack of fingerprints. That may not be so uncommon, but it's very interesting.'

Mann pondered, running fingers through his lank hair.

'What do you make of the first point, sir? I see what you mean. It never occurred to me either.'

'I don't blame you for not seeing it, but it's part of what I've just been complaining to the Gibbons about. Pattern. This killer's pattern is to use a different method every time. One shooting, one clubbing with a blunt instrument, one poisoning. The consistency is the determination to be inconsistent. This killer is thinking up a different way to create the maximum confusion and make us think there may be more than one killer at work. I don't think there is. I also think that all the crimes are related. As for the absence of fingerprints, I've never seen anyone so careful. I've been slow about that too. If we'd found a print, any print, we'd have been through the whole village. Because we found none, we haven't, and our murderer will know he's safer every day that goes by and we don't print every man woman and child. So tomorrow we do just that. We print everyone over the age of twelve. That'll scare the hell out of them!'

In the study John and Clara were finding it difficult to take their eyes off the spot where the body had been. They sat in silence for a while.

'I wish I hadn't refused his bloody whisky,' said John. 'I only did it out of pique.'

'I know.'

'Are you still very shaky?'

'No, I'm much better now. It sounds a cruel thing to say, but I felt better as soon as they took her away. It wasn't a nice way to die. Why choose that way? There's a particularly nasty mind at work that poisons a botanist with a vegetable poison. Why?'

'Perhaps she had it on the premises and the murderer knew.'

'But why would Philippa Crabbe make vegetable poisons?'

'Then perhaps it is suicide?'

'Or we are supposed to think it is.' Clara shook her head. 'I don't know any of the people involved, I never met her. What do you think?'

164

'I don't think she would commit suicide, but having said that, how can you ever be sure?'

'She wasn't a very good botanist, so I'd be surprised if she managed to make a fatal dose of poison.'

John looked at her sharply, surprised.

'Why do you say that?'

'That pressed flower isn't a Dark Winged Orchis, or she got the habitat wrong. It doesn't grow in woodland, it grows on chalk downs.'

'Are you sure?'

'Yes. I know a bit about flowers, and particularly about orchids. We studied the fungus mycelium in the cortical cells because they produce carbonaceous material . . .'

'Look at the drawing again, and at the sample,' said John urgently. 'I don't believe she'd make a mistake. Just look at the place. It's a small museum.'

Clara got up, impressed by the excitement in his voice. She examined the illustration carefully.

'That's a Dark Winged Orchis,' she said. 'Do you think it's all right to pick up the specimen?'

'I don't care. Just check it.' He was beside her, picked it up, gave it to her. Clara held it under the brass-yellow light of the scalloped lamp.

'That's a Dark Winged Orchis too. I don't understand. She's got the habitat wrong, everything else is all right.'

'Maybe,' said John, 'and maybe not. Let's go back a page.'

He felt in his pocket and found nothing useful, then patted his jacket, found and took out his wallet. He extracted a credit card from its window.

'No prints,' he said as he turned the left hand page over and to the right revealing the drawing beneath. They saw revealed a pen drawing in pale green ink of a bunch of pearled mistletoe. It had been delicately coloured with accurate insubstantial hues. The caption on the facing page was in the same dense upright writing.

'"Mistletoe. Viscum Album. Flowers March to May. Taken from oak, north of village."' read Clara.

'What do you make of that?'

'Very little. Mistletoe is not my strong point.'

John sighed.

'So much for that. I thought she might have left us a clue. She said it was written down, and I wondered if this was it. It might be something that most people wouldn't identify. She was a very clever person and I can just see her disguising whatever it was in some way. Especially if she thought she was in danger.'

'Well let's look at it again.'

They examined the drawing, looking for hidden meanings in its

165

shape. After a few minutes they had to agree there was nothing apparent.

'Why don't we look up mistletoe in one of her books?' asked Clara. 'After all I don't even know if it's called Viscum Album.'

They returned to the book-lined wall beside the fireplace and John was the first to find an encyclopaedia of flora.

'It *is* Viscum Album, but it doesn't grow on oak! At least there don't seem to be any authentic records despite popular myth about Druids. It grows on poplar in particular and on apple. The particular species that does grow on oak doesn't seem to occur in Britain.'

'Another wrong habitat or wrong species.'

'Next page,' said John turning back again. They were now looking at a sepia ink drawing of a plant with scarlet flowers that had a purple-black base. The leaves were a curled froth like cow-parsley but more succulent. The note on the opposite page read 'Common red poppy. Papaver rhoeas. June to September. Cornfields, north of village.'

'That's no poppy,' he said. 'Do you know what it is?'

'No.'

'But this time the habitat is right, unless we know nothing at all about wildflowers.'

They began a search through the books. It necessarily meant that they had to thumb through every page, stopping every time an illustration showed a flash of red. Clara found it. She pointed to a coloured plate.

'That's it,' John agreed. 'Pheasant's-eye. Adonis annua. What's the relevance of that?'

'Let's turn the pages back,' said Clara. 'What's next?'

John turned back again with the edge of the card. The next pages were blank. And the next and the next. Then there was a drawing of Bladder Campion that seemed to be properly defined and described. They checked it carefully and it was. So was the Bush Vetch before that. The previous pages were all filled with similar drawings, all beautifully coloured, back to the beginning of the book.

'We'd better turn it to where it was left open,' said John, and did so. 'What do we make of that?'

'It looks as though all the information, if that's what it is, is in the last three drawings. I can't think of any other good reason why she should leave three blank sheets except to isolate and draw attention to those three.'

'Ideas?'

'Let's sit down for a moment and think.'

Clara returned to her chair and John perched by the table. They both clutched botanical guides. They had always been able to think in this concentrated way in the old days. It was perhaps their scholastic training. Certainly John liked library quiet, and the scene

166

now was very reminiscent of that. The yellow light was sufficient to illumine her blonde hair. Her face was studied and serious and her mouth puckered as it always did when she was thinking. It was a strange situation to be put in to try to win back your wife. He certainly wanted to win her back, and it had brought them close. He studied her face and thought of other times in other places when calm like this had been as intimate as skin on skin, as breast on chest, the calm before or after love-making in those days before criticism became an ogre that consumed.

'Have you thought of anything?' she suddenly asked, looking at him.

'Not yet,' said John guiltily. How could he tell her what he had been thinking?

'You looked very contemplative.'

'I was watching you.'

He decided he had nothing to lose by the gamble. The very oddness and tension of the scene might work to his advantage.

'I know. I was watching you do it.'

'I didn't know I was observed.'

'John, you will always be so obvious!'

'But is there hope?'

She looked at him. He was afraid. He awaited a wound.

'There may be. But we must take everything very slowly. You must resist the impulse to force me at every available moment. Do you understand? I don't think you do, you know. You don't have to push yourself at me for me to love you, you simply have to allow me to be a spectator. Men seldom understand that, it's the failing of the sex.'

John must have looked hurt and penitent at the same time, because she suddenly made a deprecating gesture, pursing her lips and slightly tilting her head.

'I'm sorry. This is no time for a lecture. We must try to get to grips with these flowers. This is no game going on here, and for all I know, you could be next. Just because you escaped doesn't mean you're safe.'

From overhead they could hear the sounds of men moving furniture about. Doors opening and slamming, scrapings and creaks. The reality of methodical search. The reality of a death and the seriousness of the crime. Clara was right. He thought of the captions to the three entries.

'If there is a clue here, then it's pointing to the north of the village.'

'I don't know this place from Brighton Beach. You have to help me.'

'Well, I've run over almost every yard of it. I should know it by now.'

'Run?' Clara looked puzzled. With a shock John realised that she knew nothing about his mortification of the flesh by muscular pain. He was embarrassed.

'I've been keeping fit.'

She looked at him with amusement, despite her earlier solemnity.

'Jogging,' he said defensively.

'I can't imagine it,' she said, 'but I believe you if you say so.' There was an impish smile on her face.

'To the north of the village,' said John with as much dignity as possible, 'is downland and there is indeed a wood. If you care to wipe that silly smile off your face, I can tell you all about it. There is a considerable copse, not on the top of the hill but just below.'

'Oak trees?'

'I don't know. Thinking about it, I suppose there are. You tend not to pay much attention to the species.'

'So the two wrong habitats could point to oak trees in a wood to the north of the village.'

'It's in private land,' said Gibbon in a voice that was suddenly a croak. 'There's a pheasantry on it, and it's in the wood.'

Clara was the first to break the silence that fell.

'This can't all be a mistake can it? We aren't deluding ourselves?'

'We may be, but there are too many things unanswered to ignore it.'

'What shall we do? Tell Mummery? That's the first thing we have to decide. What do you say?'

'He's not very pleased with me at the moment. However I don't think we say anything until we've had a look. It may be a nonsense. Do you agree?'

'Yes. I think it's the right way.'

Mann entered. He came in too abruptly for good manners, as though he had been instructed to see what they were up to. He stared at the books in their hands.

'Reading material,' said John cheerfully, but unconvincingly.

'Flowers,' said Mann, for want of anything else to say.

'There's nothing else in this room. We promise we haven't been making prints all over the place.'

'Chief-Inspector says you can go now. He doesn't think there's anything useful to be served by you staying on.'

'Thank you.' John took both books and walked over to the shelves where he put them back in the gaps left. Mann watched him carefully. John felt irritated by the appraising stare, but said nothing. 'I suppose this means another late night for you?'

'I'll be here all night I should think,' said Mann. There was an uncontrolled note of satisfaction in his voice that Mummery had made it plain he was to stay. 'Is Mrs Gibbon all right now?'

'Yes I'm quite well. I expect I shall have the horrors later on, but John will look after me.'

168

Mann nodded. He was wondering what sort of a relationship these strange people had. He held the door ajar for them to leave.

'Right, Constable Mann, what's this word you want with me in private?' Mummery asked. They were in the bathroom because it was the only place where they could escape the attentions of the band of eager seekers. Mummery was sitting on the lavatory without a shadow of self-consciousness. Mann chose to stand. Every surface glistened with the same silvery dust. The fingerprint men had been and gone.

'With all this happening and the rush over here, I've only just been able to put it together and make a connection, sir. It was something that was said in the pub earlier this evening that started it off. You told me to listen, and I did. Something fitted.'

Mann was eager. Mummery patted his pocket for his flask, remembered where he was, pretended he was looking for his handkerchief instead and made a great play of blowing his nose.

'I may be all wrong of course, you understand that, sir. Of course it may mean nothing at all . . .'

'Look here Mann, spare me the protestations and embarrassment. To err is human, to forgive, divine and all that sort of thing. Get on with it!'

'I think I may know who the murderer is, or at least who killed Luxford.'

'Yes . . . ?' It was almost a scream.

'Wilkinson.'

Mummery looked at him sharply.

'Go on.'

Mann told him what Wilkinson had said in the pub.

'No one knew that the gun was strapped up there, sir. We kept that secret. He tried to cover himself and did it well. It was just a small slip. I don't think anyone else would even notice.'

They went through it again and again. When Mann had finished Mummery wiped his nose. He looked very thoughtful.

'It all fits,' he said 'Everything I was saying earlier, the connections, they could all be true.'

'I feel I could have got here sooner. I wasn't quick enough.' Mann seemed upset. The lank slab of hair kept dropping over his forehead and no amount of smoothing would keep it back.

'What would it have prevented?' asked Mummery reasonably. 'You couldn't have stopped what happened tonight. While you were in the pub, this had already been done.'

'By that man!'

'We don't know that.' Mummery did produce his half bottle of whisky. He offered it to Mann who shook his head. 'Don't insist on blaming yourself, Constable. You're being unfair to yourself. I

169

would much rather congratulate you on getting there before we all did, because I believe you may well be right. And whatever you may think about what has happened, it's my report that goes in, and that will say what a smart piece of work you've turned in. Understand?'

'Yes sir, I understand.'

'Good. Now one last thing. As it isn't closing time yet, you make your way back to that pub and say just a little. Tell them they're all going to be fingerprinted tomorrow, hint we've found something, say nothing about the cause of death. You know what to do. Let this all get back, get around the village. This will put our bird up, and we'll watch every move!'

'Yes sir.' Mann left, still looking mournful rather than comforted.

'Oh sod!' said Mummery loudly to himself and drank a good deal more. 'We have to have the fingerprints! If we had had them earlier, we might have saved this life at least. Mummery, you're a failure.' He blew his nose. 'So now the great Detective Inspector Mummery thinks he knows who the murderer is, and knows what a fool he's been and feels sick with his own stupidity, and still doesn't know why. We have to be led to that. Very dangerous.'

'I'm going to the pub,' he announced to his men in the house. 'Don't grin like that, I'll be back in ten minutes.'

Chapter Eight

Mummery's day started with a telephone call in his hotel bedroom that woke him. He was bad-tempered with the receptionist, demanding to know who it was. He had only got to bed at four in the morning, he complained. The receptionist gave as good as she got, telling him in no uncertain terms that it was hardly her fault. She was middle-aged and formidable and Mummery knew he had lost the exchange. There was a click and a pause. The receptionist was obviously enquiring.

'It's a Mrs Walker,' she announced frostily. Mummery reflected that she must know perfectly well who Mrs Walker was.

'I'll speak to her.' Mummery's voice, he thought, was like ice to her frost. He had a fair inkling of what Lucinda wanted to talk about.

'I would like to come and see you,' said the attractive voice

170

urgently. 'I've just heard the terrible news about Philippa Crabbe. It's terrifying. Who will be next? Why her?'

'What do you want to see me about?' Mummery cut in brusquely. He was not going to give her an easy time.

'I'll tell you when we meet. I don't want to talk over the telephone.'

'All right, but you will have to give me an hour. As you will appreciate, I've had a long night and you've woken me up. I would like to go through the usual civilised procedures of shaving, having a shower and some breakfast. Are you sure you want to come here?'

'Why?'

'The place is full of reporters. You'll be hounded.'

'I hadn't thought about that. You're right. Could you possibly come to me? My husband is out. He's already left for London.'

'Yes, I think it would be a better idea.'

'Thank you so much. You're very kind.'

Despite himself and despite the cynical snort he gave as he replaced the receiver Mummery felt flattered. He had to admit that he looked forward to meeting lovely Lucinda.

She had dressed for him too. He had given the reporters the slip by the simple expedient of walking out of the rear door to the car park, and then walking through the village. It was a sunny morning, and that and her tremendous smile were exhilirating. She also wore a deep cut dress that Mummery could not fail to appreciate. I feel less tired, he told himself. These things are good for a man of my age. He was surprised that Lucinda was black. He had known she was, but never thought about it. He was shown into the hall where she tried to take his coat from him by extending her arms to him. Mummery declined. The gesture was charming though.

She led him into the sitting room.

'Please sit down.'

'Why?' asked Mummery unreasonably. It was his rude reaction to a general feeling that she would wind him round her little finger if he wasn't careful. He was immediately ashamed of his gaucheness. 'I'd rather stand if I may. Can't sit while a lady stands, and I prefer to listen on my feet.'

The room was quite cold and was too bare for his taste. The sunlight was falling in a slab on the floor, and it would soon warm up. Nevertheless it felt unloved, as though it was a hired room rather than part of a house. Mummery sniffed the scent of an unhappy marriage.

Lucinda was momentarily nonplussed by his refusal, then laughed nervously.

'I don't know what to do next. I don't like you just standing there.'

'Then tell me what you want to tell me. That's the best way.'

'I'm completely shattered by the news about Philippa. Was it suicide? What happened? I can't find out anything. No one seems to know. It's very alarming, and I don't mean just me. I think everyone in the village is terrified that this maniac or whatever will kill again. How did she die?'

'I understand your concern, but I'm afraid that for the moment I can't talk about it.'

'I don't believe you can't tell me something. I knew her so well, it doesn't seem possible . . .'

'I know. We knew you knew her well.'

Lucinda sat down herself. She was no longer trying to keep up the dazzling façade and the strain was showing.

'At least tell me if she was murdered. Are any of us safe?'

'I'm sorry. In due course we will make a statement. Probably later this morning. I hope you didn't bring me here to quiz me about Mrs Crabbe's death? I think there was something else, so why not tell me what it is?'

Lucinda fiddled with a bracelet.

'I know you found a letter in the church from Cynthia Fry to Luxford. It's been worrying me a lot. In case it confused everything and you wondered what it meant.'

'Yes, we did wonder what it meant,' said Mummery gravely.

'I'm afraid I put it there.' Lucinda looked at him appealingly. Mummery nodded several times, said nothing, waited.

'I was jealous. I'm sure you know all about Luxford and how silly certain women have been . . . ? I found it in his house. In circumstances where I had every right to be upset, do you understand? I believe he left it for me to find deliberately. I found out he was that sort of man. I didn't like Cynthia Fry, still don't, but with all this I feel a bit more sympathy. Anyway I took it.'

'I suppose you carried it around with you?'

She looked at him in some surprise.

'Yes.'

'Why did you hide it under the cushions?'

'Because I wanted it to be found.'

'Well of course!' snapped Mummery suddenly. He conveyed very clearly that he had not hurried a cooked breakfast and his shower just to be told the obvious. In addition the bacon was beginning to give him acid indigestion.

'Let's try it again. When did you hide it?'

Lucinda looked as if she might cry. Mummery scowled to show he would not be impressed.

'It was after Luxford was shot, wasn't it?' he pursued. 'You might as well tell everything. You saw your opportunity to drop Cynthia Fry in it, and took it. If there was going to be trouble, you thought, this should fix her up nicely.'

172

'Yes.' Lucinda spoke in a very small voice. 'Don't lecture me about it. I've regretted it ever since. It was on the spur of the moment. I've been desperately worried in case it set you off in the wrong direction.'

'It could very well have done,' he said severely. 'It was a very stupid and malicious thing to do. Luckily for you, we had some idea it might have got there in this way.' He paused. 'But why did you put your gloves there as well?'

'What gloves?'

She stared at him blankly. Mummery was watching her very closely and was convinced her reply was genuine.

'I didn't put my gloves anywhere. What's this about?'

'Just testing,' said Mummery.

John woke up in the spare bedroom on a mattress on the floor boards. In those waking moments, suspended on a see-saw that gently rocked between waking and sleeping and waking again, he considered the ironies of his present situation. There was Clara, his wife still, alone in his comfortable bed, in his house, in his pyjamas while he, complete with plastered limb was rolling about on a striped horsehair mattress with buttons like walnuts.

But Clara wasn't in bed. He heard a kettle being filled, cups rattling, kitchen cupboards opening and shutting. He had not noticed how silent and lonely the house had been until then. It is a rare pleasure to lie and listen to the domestic bustle of others. Then he remembered Philippa and woke. The realities instantly crowded in like spectators at an accident. He gave himself one more minute to savour the sounds and associations of what had once been marriage then forced himself up, struggling with his plastered arm.

Clara was flopping around in the kitchen in his dressing gown and his over-sized slippers. She looked very much a creature of the morning and very much as he remembered and loved her. He kissed her on the back of the neck and she didn't bother to move away. He sternly resisted the temptation to do anything further, and awarded himself ten merit marks.

'I have a large scale Ordnance map of the area, Clara,' he said as though the kiss had been a mere aside, or as natural as breath, 'let's look at that before we leave.'

'Good morning John, that would be a good idea.'

She asked if he had slept well, he said yes but his arm was stiff, had she slept well, she said yes, his bed was comfortable, and they settled down side by side with the map and coffee.

It was a six inches to the mile sheet, rather yellow from age and inclined to roll itself up into a scroll if let go. The whole area was shown in exact detail. To the north of the village was the cluster of trees they were looking for, shown as mixed deciduous and coniferous woodland, and marked Neme Copse. Inside its larger defined area was an inscription in the dense Gothic script used for antiquities which read 'Earthworks'.

'So that's what we're looking for.' said John. 'It's very obvious really. I've never looked at the map for antiquities before. There's hut circles and stones all over the place, look.'

'There always are at this scale,' said the practical Clara. 'And that's where the pheasantry is?'

'Yes. It's only a collection of enclosures and sheds like a rather sub-standard zoo. I had no idea that the mounds and things weren't natural. There is a deep ditch and quite a slope all round.'

'We'd better get our things together. We need a spade, a bag in case we want to bring anything away, and I suppose it's boots and old clothes. You'll have to lend me what you can. I didn't come prepared for anything like this.'

'We've got a good day for it.'

'Poor Philippa Crabbe. I woke once, thinking of her. I thought of you too. And that there may be danger. Have you considered that?'

John looked at her thoughtfully.

'Yes. It's probably just as well there are two of us.'

She gave him a fond smile.

They set off almost immediately, trying to look like casual walkers rather than workers, an effect spoiled by the spade which John had put blade first inside a canvas bag and carried under his arm. They walked in a wide arc from Gibbon's back garden across the water meadows, crossing the river at the ford.

Once over the river, with feet already wet, they kept to the bank, distancing themselves as far as possible from the village and hoping not to be seen. This brought them out onto the road leaving the village which started as Hundred Row. They crossed the road and set off up the hill towards the copse above them.

'What a glorious day,' said Clara, 'under any other circumstances. Do you think we've been seen?'

They paused at the foot of the long green slope leading up to the copse. Crossing that they would be most visible. They looked around but could see no one. A car passed along the road, and from the village they could hear sounds of other traffic. Birds, delighted by the sunlight, were in full voice from trees where buds began to swell. Rooks made a racket and scattered untidily about in the sky. The sun had warmth in it, and they were hot from the walk.

'I don't think so,' said John. 'Anyone who can see us would be visible themselves. Who would be out and about up here anyway?'

They walked on upwards.

Tucked down at the hedge with six men, Mummery made a small gesture for everyone to be still.

'Innocent as babes,' he muttered to himself.

174

'They're heading for the wood,' said Mann.

Mummery had split his men. A small team was busy in the village taking fingerprints. Mann, Wakefield, the other two plain clothes men and two uniformed officers were with him in pursuit. He had left a plain clothes man all night outside Gibbon's house in expectation of something of this sort. The detective had been shrewd enough to keep an eye on the back way out and immediately reported by radio.

'Across the open bit then,' said John and he and Clara set off at a very brisk walk that was almost a trot. The slope was quite steep here, and their legs soon ached. They were glad to halt at the edge of the copse and regain breath before crossing the wire fence that surrounded it. John held up the top strand of barbed wire so that Clara could ease herself through, and then she did the same for him. On the large trees at the edge of the wood there were at intervals small white enamelled signs saying 'This wood is private property. Keep Out!'

'I hate signs like that,' said Clara. 'They make me feel angry with the people who put them there, and guilty for being here at the same time.'

'Let's get out of sight.'

They walked on into the copse. The earth underfoot was covered with a thick layer of leaf mould, and here and there where the light blazed through there were broad areas of green leaf, blades of incipient bluebells and the fragile leaves of wood anemone. They walked down a steep dip into what appeared to be a broad ditch and scrambled up the other side. The side was riddled with burrows, rabbit or fox or even badger. In their excavations the animals had turned out the white chalk that underlay the surface soil. It looked like the spillings of a careless baker.

'This is a man-made ditch, isn't it?' said Clara.

'Yes. We're going up the ramparts of the earthworks obviously. The pheasantry is on the far side.'

It would have been idyllic with the birds singing and the sun glittering through the branches, but they felt nervous and Clara could not dispel the feeling of a cold chill. The sheds of the pheasantry were mundane enough when they came upon them – a series of runs backed by coops. The only notable thing was that they were well wired with a square mesh and that the coops were built off a brick and concrete base. They were positioned up against another bank of earth so that they were in the sheltered lee, and were surrounded by trees.

'Where are the pheasants?' asked Clara, 'or am I being stupid?'

'They won't be put in until later in the year,' said John. 'I think they call this place a mew if they have domesticated pheasants, or else they hatch eggs under hens and raise them here.'

'There's our oak,' said Clara in a sharp, excited voice. She pointed

175

to a huge old tree abutting a coop and half-way up the bank. Beneath it was a considerable hole like a badger's set which had apparently been filled in again. A tell-tale spill of white chalk spread over a considerable area around it. They stood under the canopy of branches and looked carefully around.

'There are no other oaks just here,' said John. 'The rest are beech.'

They were silent, listening, intruders who were about to confirm their intentions. Blue tits flicked from branch to branch, chittering noisily and scattering the husks of buds they were destroying. A blackbird turned leaves noisily. There was song everywhere, but there seemed to be a heavy hush.

'I don't like it here very much,' said Clara. 'Let's hurry up. We shall look such fools if we're caught digging by the owner. What shall we say?'

'Truffles,' said John firmly. 'After all it is an oak tree.' He unwrapped the spade and they advanced to the loosely filled depression at the base of the tree. It had been started by erosion apparently, with rainfall washing loose material away from beneath mighty arched roots. Then some one or something had burrowed in beneath so that the space was like a small cave, about five feet high, reducing abruptly and then stopping, filled in with white chalk. It reminded John of Arthur Rackham drawings, with gnarled and twisted roots arching around them into a woodland cathedral full of writhing shapes and sinister forms. He stuck the spade into the chalk material. It was as soft as sand.

'You can both come out of there!' commanded a loud voice. They jumped violently, jerking round full of apprehension. Wilkinson was standing four square behind them with a levelled shotgun. 'Put that spade down,' he commanded. John did so. His heart was pounding. He looked at Clara. She had gone white as a sheet. 'Now walk out and do everything slowly and carefully.'

John's mind was racing. What should he do? Throw himself at the man? Could he just shoot them and get away with it? He remembered Tom Harris. Would he shoot them anyway? Why had he not guessed earlier? The stranger, the incomer, the man who hated Luxford, the amateur archaeologist. It was all so very obvious. Whatever it was was hidden here.

'How did you follow us?' John asked. His voice came out as a trembling, feeble sort of noise, not the dignified tone he intended.

'I didn't in fact follow you. I was here first and heard you coming. I could hardly avoid that. You've been a great nuisance, Mr Gibbon. It's a pity you should have found this place. How did you know where to look?'

Wilkinson looked genuinely puzzled. The gun was held very steady at waist level. Wilkinson the butcher, John kept thinking. His brain seemed to have gone limp and stupid on him, he could think of

176

nothing to say, and thought it better not to tell him anyway, in case someone else found the clues. If he told this man, he would certainly destroy them when he had finished with them.

'What are you going to do with us?' he croaked.

Before Wilkinson had time to say anything in return, there was a tremendous rustle of leaves. Wilkinson swung round with the gun, which was caught by the barrel by Mann, who had sprung out from somewhere. Both men were rolling about on the ground in an instant. There was a shattering explosion, and a smoking hole appeared in the ground a few feet from both men. Wilkinson appeared to freeze and let go the gun which Mann snatched. In that moment the whole area filled with men who swooped with one accord upon Wilkinson, pulling him to his feet, forcing one arm up behind his back, clutching him round the neck. Mann got up and stood panting. John and Clara recognised Mummery and the plain clothes men. Clara began to tremble, and John put his arm quickly around her feeling her body shaking.

'You murdering bastard!' said Mann in a savage voice. It was unlike the casual Mann that John recognised. Wilkinson's red face was contorted, half strangled by the man gripping him round the neck. Mummery indicated to the man holding him by a nod of his head that he should ease off a bit.

'I never killed anyone!' snarled Wilkinson. 'I never did!'

'You are under arrest, Jacob Wilkinson,' said Mummery. His voice was grim and dead and without any expression. 'You are warned that anything you may say may be taken down and used in evidence. Is that understood?'

Wilkinson contrived to nod despite the head-lock he was gripped in.

'Take him away,' said Mummery in the same flat tone. He did not even look at the man as the two uniformed constables took an arm each and Wilkinson was led back into the wood.

'I never killed anyone!' he yelled. The rooks answered. They were swirling in uproar, raised by the shot. Blackbirds were screaming their warnings. It seemed as though the whole wood was in fear of this murderer and took flight.

'Are you both all right?' Mummery asked John and Clara. He stood close to them, looking into their eyes. His face was quite blank. John had never seen it as grim as this. There was a terrifying withdrawn quality, as though he himself had been mortally wounded and was going through the correct motions before facing imminent death.

'We're both all right,' he replied woodenly.

'Good,' Mummery nodded, apparently to himself. He turned about as though to watch the retreating figure of Wilkinson and the two uniformed men, trailed a little way after them. He paused beside

177

Mann, who was staring thoughtfully in the same direction. In the silence they heard his flat voice quite clearly.

'Constable Eric Mann, you are under arrest for the murders of Peter Luxford, Thomas Harris and Philippa Crabbe. Anything you say . . .'

Mann started to run. It was completely futile, because he was not fit and the plain clothes men were. They soon caught up with him. Mann picked up a rotten piece of wood and flailed around with it. The end flew off the piece of wood. He threw it at his pursuers and tried to run again. They tackled him and the heap of men thudded down hard in the bottom of the ditch.

Mummery had not moved from the spot. Neither had John and Clara. They were stunned by events, particularly John. Mummery was grey with apparent pain.

'It's always a terrible thing. It's even worse when you have begun to like someone.'

'It can't be true!' John Gibbon managed to say.

'But you can see it is. It took some time, but it all became very clear. That was a very close thing. He was fast, and if Wilkinson hadn't been as strong, he might have managed to kill him too. It would have been the perfect touch. What is it that's in there, that's the thing we all want to know? Wakefield, use Mr Gibbon's spade.'

Mann was brought back by the other two men. They held him facing the rooted cavern. He glared around him, the yellow hair lank over his face, a slight snarl on his lips. Eric Mann as a violent creature, Eric Mann as a killer. Sergeant Wakefield drove in the spade again and again, throwing out loose chalky earth and flints. He stopped abruptly and bent down, scrabbling with his hands, wiping. He stood up and showed them what he had retrieved. Despite its coating of grey-white clay it was unmistakably a bar of gold.

'It's full of them in there!' he said.

An official press release had been given to the reporters, who had rushed around, making up the last bits of local colour and had disappeared to file copy. They knew the next excitement would be the trial. The village was noticeably quiet by evening and the 'Feathers' had returned to its accustomed bucolic charm. Mummery sat in the residents' lounge with a very large whisky beside him. He still looked grey and shaken, and seemed to have shrunk into the leather armchair. John and Clara faced him in similar chairs, but were perched on the frame of theirs', watching him, listening. The room was flooded with evening sun. Outside, the birds who had never stopped singing all day as if in mockery of the whole proceedings, were trilling away in ecstasy, unthinking, unable to stop, responses triggered by the sun.

'It's his wife I'm sorry for,' said Clara. 'Do you think she knew

178

anything about it?'

'No. I think she was totally ignorant of everything. She's in deep shock and has been taken to hospital.'

Mummery held his glass of whisky up to the sunlight and watched the deep amber sparkle.

'Please take us through it all,' said John. 'How and when did you realise? It makes me feel so stupid, so unobservant. It never occurred to me for a second, yet it should. And at the very last I was certain it was Wilkinson. Totally convinced. When he appeared with that gun and Mann dived at him, I thought Mann was a hero.'

'Wilkinson never intended to use it. He wanted you out of there long enough to get that gold and leave. Mann saw his opportunity and tried to kill him, pretending he was rescuing you but Wilkinson was too strong. He had a lucky escape. There's no doubt Mann meant to kill him, and it would have been ideal, wouldn't it? Wilkinson the murderer caught red-handed, hero policeman dives to rescue, killer killed in struggle. Mann's crimes would have died with Wilkinson. I expect he has a considerable amount of that gold secreted away somewhere. He could afford to lose the rest, and it was the only way out.'

'Can you start at the beginning?' said Clara. 'I'm the new girl in all this, and I'm lost. What was the gold, what was Wilkinson's part in this, why was it necessary to kill three people? In short, what was it all about?'

'Well, your husband was coming close to finding out a lot of the answers and you certainly supplied your bit by unravelling the message in that book. Let's start right at the beginning.'

'Yes please,' said Clara.

'Your husband was right. Luxford was not the intended victim of the first shot, it was Tom Harris. The bullet struck the column in the church as he discovered and it was deflected. We have the bullet and it is partially flattened. The tape holding the gun had slightly stretched and it was just enough with the recoil to allow the barrel to move about three or four degrees of arc. That was sufficient. Mann had set the whole thing up, and had gone home to await results. It was the obvious place to be. Someone was bound to come for him, so he made a good act of having had a few drinks, or probably had had a few drinks, then you, Mr Gibbon, come pounding up to the door as he expected. The real shock must have been when you announced that someone had shot the vicar. It wasn't at all what he had planned, and it meant that Tom Harris would have to be finished off very quickly in case he put two and two together. In the meantime, Mann exploited Luxford's death very successfully. The man was a thorough lecher. There must be plenty of people who hated him. It was ideal.'

'Why the business with the gun in the first place?' asked John. He

179

and Clara were sharing a bottle of wine. He poured her some more and ate an olive from a dish on the table. He offered them to Mummery who made a face at them.

'Why the whole business of the church and the snow? Mann was determined to make the motive as obscure as possible, and to make as many people as possible suspect. By not having to rely upon any human agency to pull the trigger he achieved just that. There was no way it could be narrowed down to anyone inside or outside the church, it could have been any individual in or outside the village. The snow would confuse things beautifully at first, because it must seem as if the killer had been inside the church until the gun was found. I think if he had had the opportunity, Mann intended to remove that gun and dispose of it, leaving the thing as just another unsolved and insoluble crime. And it would have been, except for your presence and then my men. I believe he had returned to obliterate the lead smear on the column when he saw you, Mr Gibbon, inspecting the thing. That must have been a nasty surprise so you were nearly removed.'

'But the gold,' said Clara. 'And Wilkinson.'

Mummery sighed.

'Yes, that's where we could have started if we'd really known. Because we had no fingerprints there seemed to be no point in taking elimination prints from the start. Wilkinson was put here as a 'sleeper'. He was part of the gang who carried out the bullion raid eight years ago on a security van and got away with two million. The money was never recovered, the others are inside. Wilkinson, what ever part he played, was never even brought to trial. His job was to move in somewhere quiet like this, conceal the bullion and lie low with it until they all served their time. We shall find out all about his background in due course. His pretence of being interested in amateur archaeology gave him the perfect excuse for prowling the countryside and being seen doing it. I don't know how many times he may have moved the stuff about even. Certainly he made a perfect excuse for himself for being seen with his metal detector and spade. You can imagine his horror when Peter Luxford takes up the same game, but for real. He must have lived in perpetual anxiety that Luxford would find it. He obviously tried to see him off his territory and his particular period of interest as he had buried the stuff in an Iron Age fort. As far as we can gather at the moment, Luxford *did* find it. It was the source for the money that he needed to pay for the presents he gave to his female friends. He looted it periodically and I will bet his unpleasant brother William has enough contacts to fence it very efficiently. He's under arrest as well for theft, although we have to call it suspected theft at the moment. What seems to be emerging is that Peter Luxford never mentions his find to anyone, and doesn't know it "belongs" to Wilkinson. You can imagine he thinks he's stumbled on the proceeds of a theft, and intends to keep it all to himself. He feels about Wilkinson in just the same way as Wilkinson feels about him. A nice irony, you'll agree. The trouble was that young Tom Harris followed Peter Luxford about the place. Yes, he was a Peeping Tom, but just a boy, curious.'

'Not so innocent though,' said John Gibbon.

'He may have been a bit worldly wise in some respects but I suspect he was a total innocent in others. William Luxford made a great point of telling me that young Tom was blackmailing Peter Luxford for a fiver a week to keep quiet about his sexual activities. Said Tom had been spying on him. I daresay he had. A solitary boy, out and about a lot, follows the vicar with another man's wife. No doubt they think they've found a discreet spot, no doubt Tom knows exactly where it is. It's probably been used for the same illicit things for centuries. So Tom watches. Boys of his age do. It's part of their education in a country district, the same as taking the cows to the bull. I don't mean to be vulgar, Mrs Gibbon . . .'

'I don't mind,' said Clara, 'What's vulgar in that?'

'Nothing, but some people might think so.'

Talking was helping Mummery to recover from the shock of finding that a policeman was the killer. Talking and whisky. He seemed to be gradually wriggling himself more upright, to be emerging from the womb of the chair. He even produced a handkerchief and buffed-up the end of his nose. A good sign.

'Anyway,' he continued, 'there's no proof that Tom Harris was doing anything of the sort and for the sake of his parents I prefer to keep it that way. It seems to me highly likely that that nasty specimen William Luxford was just trying to provide a motive for someone killing Tom Harris that had nothing to do with the bullion. After all, William knew about the gold but I doubt if brother Peter told him where it was, since they were such nice people. From William's point of view, Peter's death was a disaster. He would have to try to find the stuff himself. Then Tom was killed and it might begin to look as if there was a connection. William had to dispel that if he could and gave me a picture of a juvenile blackmailer who might be on the list of almost anyone. He also gave me a formidable list of his brother's lady friends to assist me in the wrong direction. Our obsession with Luxford's sex life has led us astray throughout.'

'So what was poor Tom's downfall?' asked Clara gently. She had threaded her arm through John's now and they were clutching hands like youngsters.

'He saw what he shouldn't,' said John. 'That was what poor Philippa thought, and she was right.'

'And he made the mistake of doing what a good boy would. He went to the police,' said Mummery. 'That's the bitter part of it all. He told Mann he had seen Luxford removing bullion. We don't know the details yet of course, but obviously Mann decided he would have the lot and swore Tom to secrecy. Tom would respect that, being a country boy, being innocent in that way. So then Mann decided to kill Tom. Killing Luxford was an added bonus if you like, but was no good to him, so he went back and killed Tom anyway. Clubbed him with a mallet or something similar, well you know all that, Mr Gibbon . . . No weapon, no fingerprints, a very simple but clever crime. It had to be someone with local knowledge, but that didn't matter any more. The only clue to the thing was the footsteps that you saw. We may be inefficient on the broader things, but by God we've got the foot measurements of everyone in this village. Except Constable Mann. Of course!'

'What do you think did happen?' asked John. 'I wondered if Tom Harris was really dead when we were busy looking for him, or if it was all a wild goose chase. Mann was so convincing, organising the search party and all that sort of thing.'

'I think Tom was already dead. Didn't Mann make sure you went the wrong way at the bridge?'

'I don't know if he made sure, we just seemed to go by instinct.'

'Humph.' Mummery considered this. 'Then he was there to make sure you all trampled the tracks if you went the right way. He didn't reckon with you returning to do your Indian stalker bit. You were beginning to be a nuisance to him, Mr Gibbon. He may have seen you returning from that expedition and followed you to the church , in which case he had two good reasons for killing you. As it was he managed to put you out of circulation long enough for the snow to melt and you to be the only person to have seen the footprints. Then of course I briefed everyone about what you thought and at least I suppose that removed you from the danger of another attempt. Just think about it. Mann was there, and in on everything, privy to all sorts of confidences. I really took to him. I even thought that he was wasted as a village bobby and that when we had finished on the case I would put in a word for his promotion. I've already filed a very good report on him for reacting so fast to young Harris going missing. I shall have to cancel that!'

Mummery shook his head sadly. He was becoming lugubrious again. He reached out for the whisky bottle.

'Do you think you should?' asked Clara. Mummery caught her eye.

'No, I don't think I should, but I shall anyway. We'll have dinner soon and I'll be all right.'

'You mustn't turn this into a personal issue,' said Clara sternly. 'It isn't a question of fault that you liked him. John liked him too, didn't you?'

'I was completely fooled. Young local bobby, salt of the earth, efficient, always there, that sort of thing. Perhaps I should have

182

thought a bit more about the "always there" bit. I suppose I still like him in a way despite the terrible nature of his killings. He had a charm and candour . . .'

'They often do, Mr Gibbon.'

'And what about poor Philippa Crabbe?' asked Clara. 'How did she get involved in all this? She seems to have been a real victim.'

It was getting dark now. The sun had dropped suddenly, as it does in the early part of the year. A young man in a grey linen jacket tapped at the door then came in and stooped before the imitation log fire that occupied the ancient fireplace. He lit it and long pale butane flames flickered up the chimney.

'Excuse me,' he said rather belatedly. 'It will be getting cold tonight. Do you want the light on?'

'No.' said Mummery without any grace. 'Just leave it as it is.'

The young man made a tight grimace at the ceiling and left. 'Hate those bloody fires,' said Mummery. 'Worse than the electric ones with flickering flames.'

'We had just got round to Philippa,' John reminded him. 'What about her part in all this?'

'If anyone was really a victim of Peter Luxford, she was. He was fifty per cent responsible for it. She was always out and about on her botanising and must have followed Luxford or accidentally seen what he was up to. She didn't appear to know though, did she?'

'From what she said to me,' said John, 'I can't really be sure. She referred to "things" so vaguely. It was deliberate. She didn't want me to know, and now I suppose we may never know. She did know however that it was theft to take whatever it was, and that in allowing herself to become a party to it all she was in trouble. But how did Mann know anything about it? How did he know she even visited me?'

Mummery sighed copiously.

'That's all part of our wonderful system. The constable at your door made a note of your visitors, so we all knew she had been to see you. We even discussed it at our briefing. Or at least I did. I blurted it all out, made sure everyone knew everything. As Mann knew that Luxford was spending part of the proceeds on Philippa, she was dangerous. For all he knew she knew everything. When you didn't run straight to us with a full story after her visit, Mann must have been in a spot. Either *she* was holding back, or she had told you what she knew and *you* were holding back. He couldn't get at you just then because of Mrs Gibbon, but he couldn't take a chance with Philippa Crabbe either. She might still be alive if she hadn't visited you.'

They ruminated on this for some moments. John re-adjusted his plastered arm which had a tendency to slide off the arm of the chair.

'That's a terrible thing,' he said. 'I thought she was in danger. If I hadn't had this arm because of my bloody curiosity she wouldn't have had to visit me in hospital, and would still be alive.'

'And so on and so on, Mr Gibbon. Don't start to blame yourself. This drama was going to run its course with or without you. We shall never know what would have happened if you had never been here, so what's the point of trying. It's just the same as me saying that I should have known it was Mann at an earlier stage. It's no good and it leads to depression. However it was the death of Philippa Crabbe that made me begin to suspect Mann. The information that she had been to see you could only have come back through you or the nursing staff or us, the police. It was a wild outside contender at first, but I did have the thought. There was no one in the force who could possibly have a motive except the local man. Then when Mann took me aside and gave me a whole tale about how Wilkinson had let slip that he knew about the gun in the belfry and how the murder was committed when we had never released the information, I began to wonder even more. Why hadn't he told me earlier? He made a very sincere and convincing job of it. So I told him we were going to fingerprint everyone in the village and let him loose to spread the word as I expected, because of course it drew attention away from him. I also went down to the "Foresters" and checked his story. Wilkinson had made a remark all right, but it was nothing like as positive as the tale Mann told me. Wilkinson was unfortunate enough to float a theory. Mann was waiting for something like that. Of course by alerting everyone to the fact we were taking prints we flushed Wilkinson out. His prints are on record and he would have been identified. He had to get that bullion fast and get out of the country.'

'I see,' said Clara. 'And we blundered in at that moment.'

'You did. And I had Mann in tow and was watching him.'

'How did he know about poisons?' asked Clara.

'That should have led us to him as well. A country boy who trained in London. We were so obsessed by the rest of the people in this village and who was or wasn't native, that we ignored Mann again. No problems for a policeman to know where you can buy a gun. As for gaining access to the house, it had to be someone Philippa Crabbe trusted and let in without demur. A policeman or her friends. She wouldn't want to refuse to see him, in her guilty state of mind. For all we know, he made the coffee. As for making the poison, he could have done that in the garden shed. We're checking now.'

'And what about the gloves?' asked John. 'You traced them to London and they were purchased by a man.'

'They're the right size for Mann of course. I think we shall get a positive identification from the sales girl. That must have given Mann a nasty moment, because I told him that when we found out and he didn't even blink. Mann used them to set up the gun of course, then decided there was no better place to dispose of them. If he took them home and tried to get rid of them his wife might see him, poor woman. He had a problem. That was one thing about the gloves I saw right away. You can't dispose of anything much at this time of the year unless you burn it, like the mallet no doubt. You can't stuff anything in a dustbin because they won't be emptied for at least a week, and you can't bury it because the ground's too hard and you can't drop it in the river without making a hole. So he left the gloves to compound the general confusion and indicate that someone in the church owned them and had something to do with the gun.'

The three stared at each other, talked out. There were still many questions they could explore but they shared the same shocked weariness. Clara asked the final question.

'Has he confessed to any of it?'

'No. We're going to have to do all the work in this case. Mann is tough.' Mummery looked slyly at John and Clara. 'And what are you two going to do now?'

'I think we'll walk home,' said John. 'We could do with a bath, a fire, just a bit of relaxation.'

'That wasn't what I meant, but it'll do for an answer,' said Mummery managing a smile.

They walked back towards John's house from the 'Feathers'. The clock on the church tower was lit and showed a quarter to six. Around the rim of the western sky a band of light lingered that was pale blue merging with blue-gold and then faint yellow. It showed up the crowns of trees as a sharp black lattice.

'Well, we missed the sunset,' he observed. 'It's clear. It must have been a spectacular one.'

'I don't believe in sunsets,' said Clara, giving him a smile, to take the edge off her observation. They passed Lucinda's sad boutique, Wilkinson's shop, shuttered.

'Don't stop,' said Clara, feeling him slow down.

They passed Mann's house, deserted. His wife had gone away. They passed the Harris house, lit but quiet and paused on the bridge to stare down at the water that flowed as black and silent as oil. Something small rustled in the hedgerow, a wren perhaps or a mouse. A coot in the reeds uttered its cry and splashed.

'Well, are we going to try to make it work?' Clara asked.

'Yes we are.' He looked at her. She was staring downwards. He could only just make out the expression on her face. She was smiling.

'Are you going to give up jogging?' she asked.

'Immediately. It's far too dangerous!'